In the darkness, Rahotep threw himself on a tangle of fighting men. His hands slipped on flesh that had been thickly oiled. Then they met hairy skin, an animal's pointed ear! The Pharaoh was fighting for his life against some monstrosity that mounted a beast's head on a human body.

Rahotep struck out with his fists, blindly. The monster wriggled toward the corner. Rahotep stepped forward in pursuit and came down on one knee as his foot caught under a second body. His fingers closed about metal.

Suddenly the room was filled with light. The Pharaoh was moaning, and in his upper breast was a dagger...a dagger whose hilt was now in Rahotep's hold. Save for those who had just entered, the room was empty. *To these witnesses he was an assassin caught in the act!*

"As exciting an adventure as any in modern science fiction."
—*Fort Worth Star-Telegram*

SHADOW HAWK

Andre Norton

FAWCETT CREST • NEW YORK

Almost two thousand years before the birth of Christ, a conquering army marched out of the heart of Asia Minor. The conquerors overran other lands and peoples unchecked as they moved westward, for their warriors possessed a new and effective weapon—the horse-drawn chariot. Those who tried to defend their countries against these newcomers were swiftly battered to the dust.

Among the defeated nations was Egypt, already very old and once mighty. So bitter were the Egyptians against the alien invaders that when they were finally able to expel them generations later, they attempted—with excellent results—to erase all trace of their occupation in the Nile Valley. To this day, therefore, we do not know who these Hyksos were, where they came from, or how long they ruled—merely that they held Egypt for a time, introduced the horse to that land, and were accounted worse than devils by its inhabitants. This was a time of intrigue, of danger, of dissension within the ranks of the Egyptians themselves, since the more conservative of the Pharaoh's officials favored a token tribute to the Hyksos and no open break. It was also a time when a young man might dare great things. Highborn Egyptians entered officers' training at about ten years of age and became active combatants at fourteen or fifteen. Both of the royal princes who led the first attacks upon the Hyksos were in their teens.

Only in the far south of Egypt and in Nubia (modern Sudan) did the old Egyptian way of life continue feebly during the years of alien occupation. Nubia—the Land of the Bow, ruled by a viceroy of the Pharaoh—furnished archers for the Desert Scouts, a corps famed for over a thousand years in Egyptian records. Their skill was so widely known and respected that in foreign tongues the name for Egyptian was also the word for bowman. And it was in Thebes, the ancient capital of the south, that a successful revolt against the Hyksos took fire in 1590 B.C. Egyptians, once again united, beat back the enemy and established an empire that dominated the southern Mediterranean for centuries to come.

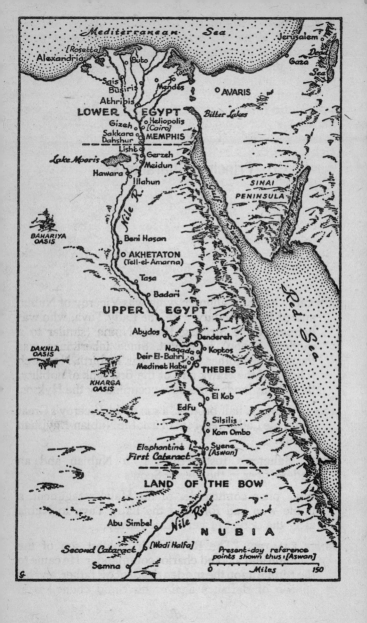

Principal Characters

RAHOTEP: son of Ptahhotep, who was Viceroy of Nubia, and of his secondary wife, the Lady Tuya, who was heiress of the Striking Hawk Nome (similar to a modern duchy) in Egypt. Since inheritance was through the mother, Rahotep was, by birth, Nomarch (Duke) of the Hawk and of the first rank of nobility, though his lands were now occupied by the Hyksos.

UNIS: Rahotep's half brother, a son of the Viceroy's Great Wife, the Lady Meri-Mut of a noble Nubian-Egyptian family.

KHETI: Rahotep's foster brother, a Nubian and an underofficer in the Desert Scouts.

METHEN: once commander of the Hawk's regiment, a noble who had followed the Lady Tuya to Nubia after the defeat of her father's army.

PRINCE KAMOSE: "The Royal Heir," eldest son of the Pharaoh and a noted chariot commander. He came to the throne upon the sudden death of his father, and his speech of defiance against his timid council is in existence today. Under his leadership the Egyptian forces won their first victory.

PRINCE AHMOSE: his younger brother, who became Pharaoh in turn and founded the great Eighteenth Dynasty, which made Egypt an empire. He was a military genius and a well-qualified ruler who established an unbeatable army and united Egypt in new prosperity.

THE ROYAL MOTHER, QUEEN TETI-SHERI: heiress of the Theban line. Grandmother of Kamose and Ahmose.

THE ROYAL WIFE, QUEEN AH-HETPE: daughter of Teti-Sheri. According to Egyptian custom, she was the wife of her brother, Sekenenre III, first of the active fighters against the Hyksos. Mother of the Princes Kamose and Ahmose.

PRINCE TETI: "Teti the Handsome" fanned the fires of revolt in Nubia when the Theban rulers marched against the Hyksos, cutting loose the rich southern province and making it his kingdom. He was successful for only a short period. Ahmose crushed his revolt and re-united Nubia to Egypt.

LORD NEREB: a high-ranking officer in the newly formed royal army, serving under the Royal Heir, Prince Kamose.

KHEPHREN: "Voice of Amon," high priest in the Temple of Amon-Re at Semna. Since Amon-Re was the patron god of Thebes, his priesthood supported the Theban rulers. Though there were numerous gods in Egypt, Amon-Re, symbolizing the power of life inherent in the sun, was widely reverenced.

TOTHOTEP: "Voice of Anubis," high priest of the Temple of Anubis at Thebes. Anubis was the god who watched over the dead, and his priests defended the tombs and offered sacrifices for those who lay in them. They were rumored to have prophetic powers and in the very ancient days of Egypt had the right to slay ritually a Pharaoh too old or ill to rule.

PEN-SETI: priest of Anubis at Semna, uncle of Unis.

VIZIER ZAU: most powerful of all government officials, the Vizier was answerable only to the Pharaoh, and in his hands many of the administrative duties rested. At this time, the Pharaoh could appoint any able man to the post, though formerly it could be held only by his own son.

GENERAL SHESHANG: officer belonging to the conservative party at the Theban court. Though supreme army commanders had to be of royal blood, able men could rise in the ranks of officers and were to be feared by weak Pharaohs for their power.

ICAR: sea captain from the northern Mediterranean enslaved by the Hyksos.

1

Border Patrol

No wind arose over the parched land to drive away the overpowering stench that billowed out in a dirty yellowish smoke from the filthy huts of the squalid Kush village. The Nubian-Egyptian archers of the Desert Scouts went about the business of setting fire to the huts with the competence of long practice. When the roofs of untidy thatch or tenting of badly cured hides had fallen to ash, they would pry apart the stones of the circular walls, and another raider nest would cease to exist as a border menace—for a while.

The Kush were like ants, wearily decided Rahotep, the young captain of Scouts, who stood on a hillock that raised the chieftain's hut above its fellows. You could plant your sandal forcibly on a hill, or even go so far as to dig up the tunneled earth beneath, getting bitten in the process. But within a day or two another city would spring into being in its place.

A curl of smoke wreathed his head, and he coughed. But he did not retreat from his post. He knew—as did every one of the outwardly unconcerned archers under his command—that there were hostile eyes watching—with hate and, he hoped, a little wholesome fear. Though a tangle of dark, barbarian bodies lay among the huts, not all the Kush of this village had ended with the red war arrows of the patrol in them. And Rahotep had not ordered a pursuit for captives—there was too long a sprint across the desert wastes to the fort to be burdened with prisoners.

"They will not hole up here again, Lord!" There was the ring of honest satisfaction in that observation. Kheti, Rahotep's underofficer, swung up the hillock with a hunter's loose-jointed tread. The Nubian towered a good six inches over the slighter, more delicately made Egyptian, for the captain was of the old stock from the north with no mixture of blood. The tall bow, which only Kheti could string, projected above both their heads as a regimental standard. When the smoke caught Kheti, he grimaced and spat.

"They will find another nest soon enough!" Rahotep said.

"So be it!" Kheti had the cheerfulness of one who is ready to accept orders and carry them out, but who is not required to plan any campaigns on his own. "Do men not know that to a cruising Hawk none of such pestilent holes will long lie hidden?"

Rahotep's level black brows knitted under the straight edge of his striped linen headdress. The reminder of his lost heritage in Egypt was irritating. It was folly to claim to be the lord of the Striking Hawk Nome when that holding had been for a generation in the firm grip of the Hyksos invaders. He was only Rahotep, a landless, and almost friendless, officer of Scouts, not the Hawk. Even that title was used against him jeeringly now by his half brother Unis and those who would flatter Unis. "Shadow Hawk" they called him—lord of a shadow land.

A few more roofs fell with puffs of denser smoke, showers of sparks. As the archers worked away at the walls, Rahotep measured the angle of the sun with a frontiersman's knowledge. They must be away before nightfall.

"A short space yet." Kheti caught his glance aloft. "It is a very great pity we were not able to send Haptke to his unsavory fathers. But one cannot always have the full smile of fortune."

"Now!" The captain thrust the baton-flail, which was the symbol of his authority, into the belt of his short kilt and gripped the bronze sistrum-rattle, used to alert men in the field. He swung it with a sharp crack of the wrist, bringing from its wire-strung beads the buzz of an angered viper.

As the archers assembled in a loose line of march, Kheti pushed into his commander's hand a small clay image he had fashioned when the call for this patrol had come to the fort. Rahotep held it out in the sunlight, well aware that hidden eyes saw it and that hidden ears would hear every word he had to say in the tongue of the Kush.

"Haptke." He gave the Kush chieftain the name by which he was known to the Scouts. "Haptke, son of Taji, and all those who follow at his heels, his warriors, his swift runners, his friends, those who eat from his pots and lie in the shadow of his hut, who rebel, who lay waste the land, who kill with ax and knife, spear and arrow, who may think of wasting the land or killing, upon them and their lord Haptke lies now this curse. And as I do this, so will it be done unto Haptke and those I have named—in the sight of Amon-Re, Lord of the High Heavens, and of His son upon earth, Pharaoh, Lord of the Two Lands!"

Though the Kush speech was harsh, Rahotep managed to give it the roll of a temple chant. He raised the clay figure over his head and hurled it against the flame-marked wall of Haptke's late headquarters. The sun-dried clay burst into powdery rubble, and the archers gave cries of approval. Men had done their best against these raiders; now the aid of the gods had been invoked as well.

They left the ruined village with the famous distance-eating trot of their corps, herding with them the spoils they had taken—asses and a brace of fine Sudanese grey-hounds, now snapping and growling but towed along by leashes in the hands of their new masters. The archers were inclined to regard this as a successful foray, but Rahotep would have gladly traded four times the value of their booty for the certainty of Haptke's death. They might have destroyed the den, but the lion had gone free to ravage again.

Sun-browned vegetation of the dry season closed about them as they threaded a path beside a narrow water course where the stream had sunk to a series of scummed pools. Disturbed insects arose in clouds, and Rahotep used his captain's flail for a flywhisk as their pace carried them on steadily. The regular thud of sandaled feet was echoed by the sharp clatter of asses' hoofs on water-smoothed gravel.

They had reached that section of scrub land bordering the true desert where red clay was broken by stone outcrops when a shadow swept across the ground, bringing Rahotep's attention skyward. Over that unclouded bowl glided his own symbol, a hawk. It appeared to hover above the column of men and animals, as if in that dusty company it had found the prey it sought.

Coasting silently, the bird moved ahead of the archers almost like a guide. It was losing altitude, drifting toward the ridges of sandy hills through which their northern road ran. Then—in an instant—it swooped and was out of sight.

"The Messenger of the Great One hunts." Kheti's voice came from behind the captain. "Wish the Servant of Re, Horus-of-the-Keen-Eyes, luck as good as ours has been this day, Lord."

Rahotep slowed to a stop and whirred his sistrum in an imperative jangle, which halted the whole line of men. No, he had not been mistaken! He heard again a thin, yowling cry from beyond, a sound he could not identify.

Dagger in hand, he moved up the slope, picking his way with a stalker's caution. Kheti, belt ax unslung, was at his heels. They went down to their hands and knees as they mounted the rise behind which the hawk had disappeared. Then, lying flat, they edged forward to look down upon a scene so amazing that Kheti uttered a grunt of pure amazement.

There was a cave hollowed in the drop below them, and before it, a ledge of stone, scoured free of earth and sand by the wind. Stiff and contorted, her muzzle a mask of snarling, death-frozen hate, a gaunt female leopard lay there, the matted fur about a chewed arrow shaft in her haunch bearing witness to the long hours of her dying.

A quarter-grown yellow-furred cub, as stiff in death as its mother, huddled against the wall by the cave mouth. And on its back perched the hawk, its sharp-beaked head turning slowly from side to side as it considered intelligently something before it. The bird's attitude was not that of hunting eagerness or of rage, but one of curiosity, as it watched a small bundle of black fur.

The black fur ball opened its kitten mouth and spat, arched its back, and raised a claw-extended paw to menace the feathered intruder. But to Rahotep's amazement the winged hunter did not retaliate with punishing talons or stabbing beak. Its fierce head lifted and it voiced a scream, beating the heat-hazed air with its wings, though it did not fly.

Rahotep topped the rise, but his descent was more rapid than he had planned as clay crumbled under his weight and he coasted down in a miniature avalanche of sun-baked earth. The hawk screamed hoarsely for a second time, and the captain made a propitiating sign with his dusty fingers.

The hawk took to the air, spiraling steadily up into the late afternoon sky. Rahotep watched it go, fearless and free, before he turned to the small, belligerent warrior in black fur.

This was no helpless baby creature, but a growing cub with open eyes and a wide thing's temper. Though it must be starving, its little body showing a rack of bones beneath its fur, it was alert for his every move, as quick with its hissed warning as it had been when facing the hawk.

The rattle of gravel and more clay announced the arrival of Kheti. Granting the cub full room for fear of frightening it into a retreat that would carry it over the ledge, the tall Nubian surveyed the dead leopardess. He prodded the body with his ax and stooped to inspect the chewed shaft protruding from her body.

"Kush. But it is an old wound. She has been dead two days at least."

Rahotep made a swift pounce. His fingers nipped the.

loose skin behind the cub's head, and the cub voiced the same yowling cry that had first drawn his attention from a distance. He picked it up, its four paws sawing wildly at the air.

"Horus pleases to give a gift, Lord," Kheti remarked. "Now I wonder why. Gifts from the Great Ones who rule from beyond the sky often carry mixed luck with them. And a leopard who has a hide akin in color to that of the Kush—though such are rare—is notably vile of temper. However, this is so young a cub, he may yet be brought to follow at the heel and obey on the hunting trail or in war. He is strong to live—aye, and fight, too—when his sister and dam have died. But shield those claws, small as they are, Lord, if you do not wish to bear some smarting battle wounds!" He laughed as the enraged cub wrinkled its small mask in a snarl and continued to beat furiously at the air.

Rahotep shook out the folds of his cloak awkwardly with his left hand. Kheti seized one corner of the stout length of cloth and threw it about the struggling captive, helping to make a heaving bundle that the captain pressed against his chest as he reclimbed the heights and went down to join his waiting men.

He jogged ahead to the ass herd. Yes, he was right. There was a mare with a very small colt running beside her. And with the assistance of several would-be leopard tamers, and some expenditure of effort, he acquired a measure of milk in an earthenware cup. As the party moved on, the captain carried the now limp and exhausted cub in the crook of his arm, lowering a strip of linen first into the cup one of the archers held ready and then putting it into that small, panting mouth. The cub caught the idea quickly enough, sucking avidly, only its black head protruding from the cloak wrappings.

"A strong one indeed, Lord," commented the cup bearer. "Shall I try for more milk now? Hori has the she-ass ready in a leading rope."

Rahotep shook his head. "We cannot delay again this side of the river. Once across that—before Re departs from the sky—"

He saturated the rag with the last few drops of milk and felt the persistent tug of the cub's mouthing. They marched with all the precautions proper in hostile country—with an alert rear guard and flankers out. The Desert Scouts were well seasoned patrolmen. But the captain did not intend to make camp until they reached a site he had earlier marked for that purpose because of its defenses. Haptke and his band of border raiders had a reputation for predawn attacks. Not that the Kush could ever hope to catch any company of Scouts unprepared— as they could the unwary farmers of the northern fields. But Rahotep had long ago learned that, in the border wastes with the Kush nosing about like lean black hounds, no wise man took chances.

Their trail dipped into a cup of faded green about the dwindled river, where the mud of the banks was cut again and again by the hoofs and pads of the animals that came there to drink. The captain took the fording as slowly as his sense of duty allowed, savoring to the full the soft wash of water about his feet and legs. But that welcome moisture dried all too quickly as they breasted the slope beyond and came to the hill, with its crown of ruins, which he had set for their goal.

The defaced statue of a seated king frowned over them toward the lowlands, facing in challenge the border and the lands of the Kush. Clay and sand had silted up about its base, but in the sunset's red glow Rahotep could still read the royal name—Sesostris, the Theban Pharaoh, first of his name, who had added Nubia to the holdings of Egypt almost a thousand years before the captain had been born. A Pharaoh of pharaohs indeed, before whom the Kush had groveled and slunk away like wasteland scavengers. If only such a one ruled today! The leader of Scouts raised his baton in salute as he passed that brooding king of stone.

Time had breached the walls of the ancient fort; its inner courts were half filled with rubble. But those same walls were more protection against a rush attack than the open desert hillocks beyond.

One of the archers who had been on flank duty came in with a gazelle slung over his shoulder, and a fire was made.

The loose animals were turned into the roofless enclosure of the old granary. They would be watered sparingly, but tonight they must go hungry.

Rahotep began his rounds of the encampment, inspecting the picket lines of the burden asses, stationing or checking upon sentries. Then at last he came to stand at the foot of the statue once again, looking south. There was no movement, not even of a dust devil raised by a wind puff, between the fort and the river. But he doubted that they lacked trailers. Haptke's men lurked there, ready to avenge their defeat on any straggler they could cut off, eager to spear-point an attack if the chances of success seemed good.

The captain turned to the west, where the sun was a scarlet fire on the horizon, still almost too brilliant to face. He stripped himself of his emblems of command, the sistrum from his wrist and the baton-flail, and laid them on the sand. Then he kicked off his sandals and stood humbly before the greatest of Overlords, the sun. Rahotep looked straight into that blazing glory of red and gold before he made the salute of a warrior to his commander, his palms earthward at knee level. Having done so, the Egyptian straightened once more, proud in his heritage as a believer in Re, and chanted:

"I give praise when I see Thy beauty,
I hymn Re when He sets."

From the camp came the answering boom of the archers' rich voices:

"Who hearest him that prays,
Who hearest the entreaties of him who calls upon Thee,"

"Who comest at the voice of him who utters Thy name—" the captain intoned, and thought that the words were re-echoed, as if by the stone figure beside him. "Thy name—Thy name!"

Rahotep drew his upper arm wearily across his grimed

18

face, longing for a few comforts—water to wash in, fresh clothing. To such simple luxuries had his world shrunk during the past five years. But tomorrow, if Re favored them, he would have those again when they reached the fort.

He gathered up sistrum and flail and went down into camp, seating himself cross-legged on the mat Kheti had spread for him. There was another cup of milk to be fed to the cub. But when the captain took up his own portion of roast meat, the small furry head turned in his direction, the little mouth opened in shrill complaint, and tiny teeth tore eagerly at the shred he proffered.

"That is good," Kheti commented. "This one was almost weaned. He shall be the easier to raise for that. We have had a profitable foray this time, Lord. It will be long before Haptke can make trouble again—if he ever can. And a Great One has been moved to honor you with a gift—that very Great One who is the totem of your own clan—"

The young officer smiled with a bitterness that made an odd shadow on his youthful face. "Did you yourself not say, Kheti, that gifts from Great Ones are to be suspect, that they sometimes bring with them mixed fortune?"

"True enough, Lord. But it is also true that when a man's fortune has long been dark, then any change may be for the better—"

A jackal barked in the desert. Rahotep tensed, and the leopard cub hissed at the sudden tightening of the captain's grip upon its body.

"You believe that my fortune has been dark?"

"Lord, are we not foster brothers between whom there is little ever to be hidden? Do I not well know why you, the son of the Viceroy, run the desert with the Scouts and do not instead take your ease and hold a measure of power in Semna with your equals? And when your brother, the Lord Unis, comes to be Viceroy in his turn, it shall fare even worse with you. On that day, my brother, it would be well to depart from this land, lest you be made to eat dust, and the eating of dust is not for the Hawk—"

"I am not the Hawk!" Rahotep countered, but his

control was better as he put down the cub and ran his fingers soothingly along the curve of the small feline head. "There is no such nome, there is no longer an Egypt as there was. Have not the Hyksos, those sons of Set—those eaters of offal, followers of the Eternal Darkness—overrun the land? They have broken asunder the dwellings of the Great Ones, defiled the sacred places, slain those who would stand against them for the honor of the Two Lands—"

Kheti shrugged. "To every king his day. These defilers of the north have sat overlong in the high seat, and they do not sit there by the graces of your Amon-Re. Suppose someone arose strong enough to tumble them from that seat; would not those who marched at his back rise with him? And if the Hyksos are driven forth from the lands they have stolen, would not such lands come again into the hands of those with a rightful claim upon them? Do not throw aside your heritage, my brother—but neither can you claim it by standing afar from its boundaries."

"You have been talking with Methen," Rahotep half accused.

"Brother, you have friends as well as enemies in this land. The Commander Methen served your grandfather, the Hawk. He was loyal to your mother, the Lady Tuya, when she came into exile. Is it not reasonable that he wishes to see her son in his rightful place? And there is no future for you in Nubia. Should your father depart to his horizon—may Dedun of the Many Goats forbid that disaster"—Kheti made a warding-off-evil sign with crossed fingers—"then shall the Lord Unis rule this land and you shall be nothing. For *his* mother, the Lady Meri-Mut, has mighty kinsmen to favor her son. Also they are allied with Prince Teti—"

"Teti is close to a traitor! He sees Nubia as a separate kingdom with the crown on *his* head!"

"That is as it may be, brother. But neither he nor the Lady Meri-Mut forgets that one of their ancestors sat on the throne of Egypt itself for a space and held the Crook and the Flail of Pharaoh over north and south together. In troubled times such as these, that might happen again. To be king in Nubia is to be more than halfway to Pharaoh in Egypt, if a man is strong and daring enough! We do not want to see Unis viceroy here—would Egypt profit if Teti sat in her high seat?"

"But my father has set his face against my going north—"

"Aye, the Viceroy has no wish to lose an officer upon whom he can depend."

Rahotep shivered, though as yet the chill wind of nightfall had not found them out. It was true. In the eyes of his father, Ptahhotep, Viceroy of Nubia, he was merely a responsible officer of Scouts. Since his mother's death, he had been cut off from the life of his father's court, a fact that weighed heavily on his spirit. He had been sent from one border fort to another and had grimly centered his existence upon his profession, learning from the archers with whom he coursed the desert all they had to teach.

There was no love between him and his half brother, Unis. Unis was his father's heir, for he was the son of the Great Wife, the Lady Meri-Mut, heiress of an important family of mixed Nubian-Egyptian blood. Rahotep's mother, the Lady Tuya, had been only a secondary wife, though she was indeed heiress of the Striking Hawk Nome in the Egypt her son had never seen. She had been sent south to safety after the invading Hyksos had overrun her father's holding and had killed him in a last battle.

While Rahotep's mother lived, he had been given all she had to grant him, the ancient learning, the training of a nobleman, everything that could be taught by Hentre, her father's administrator-scribe, and Methen, who had once commanded the Hawk force in the field.

After her death, Rahotep had been dispatched to the frontier posts, ostensibly to further his military training. It had been done under the seal of the Viceroy—that remote man who he found it difficult to believe was, in truth, his father.

Ptahhotep had long been under pressure to throw aside the title, Viceroy of the Pharaoh, and rule in his own name in Nubia. But he had never done so. He must know, however, that when he died, Unis would not be content to remain "Royal Son of the South," but would strive to a greater title and fuller power. Yet of late there had been tales drifting south from Thebes that a new Pharaoh had mounted the high seat, one ready to don the blue crown of war against the invaders. Methen had talked restlessly of that. If Theban rulers did rise again—! Rahotep stirred. He had always been moved by Methen's stories of past glories, by the older man's urging for action against the Hyksos. Yet his orders, under the Viceroy's seal, held him to the frontier of the far south.

Now, again, came the bark of a jackal, repeated thrice. Rahotep was on his feet, gazing into the dark. He heard the challenge of a sentry, and then the rattle of someone hurrying through the rubble-choked ways of the old fort.

A runner, his almost naked body coated with dust, pattered into the circle of firelight and stood with heaving chest. He saluted the captain and then stooped to pinch up dust to throw upon his twisted headcloth.

"Grieve, Lord. The beloved of Re has gone to his horizon. The Viceroy Ptahhotep lives now only in the sunset!"

Rahotep froze. Then mechanically he bent in turn to gather up a handful of the gritty clay and smear it across his face in mourning.

"Blessed be Re, Who gathers His children into life everlasting." He made the conventional answer. But somehow he could not believe what he had just heard. Ptahhotep had always been remote, as remote almost as Pharaoh. But in Rahotep's world he had been a secure fixture. The captain could not imagine a Nubia in which his father did not rule.

2

Pharaoh Summons

"When did the Lord Ptahhotep depart his life?" Rahotep did not know what inner suspicion prompted Kheti to ask that question. But the answer was as startling as a Kush arrow between one's shoulder blades.

"He has been beyond the horizon these thirty days and he will be laid in the place prepared"—the runner's lips moved silently as if he were engaged in some calculation—"three days from this sunset."

Rahotep stared, astounded. "But it takes seventy days to properly prepare the body—" he began almost stupidly, and then licked his lips to taste the flatness of the mourning dust. To hurry the burial of a great lord in this manner was unheard of, and he was alerted to danger as he might have been by a sentry's warning.

"It is said that the haste is necessary because the Lord Ptahhotep died of poison from a sand thing he trod upon in the garden," explained the runner delicately.

"Thirty days," repeated Kheti. There was a metallic note in his voice. "And only now are the tidings brought to the Lord Rahotep. Where have you dallied on the road, runner?" His hand shot out, fixing upon the other's bare shoulder. On his face there was a look many a delinquent archer would have recognized and feared.

"I am not out of Semna," the man sputtered. "The Commander Methen is at Kah-hi and I am of his sending. And this also he told me, Lord." He looked beyond Kheti to Rahotep. "That you might know the truth was in my words—to say to you, 'Remember that which you wear on your right thigh and be warned!'"

Rahotep's hand fell to brush across that now faint scar, covered save for a finger's breadth by his short warrior's kilt. And the hidden meaning in that warning was clear in his mind. It was Unis's spear that had made that scar years ago during a lion hunt. Unis had been noisily remorseful for his clumsiness, a clumsiness that had never been explained to the satisfaction of either Methen or Rahotep. If Unis now ruled in Semna—and so in Nubia—that fact alone would explain both the captain's ignorance of his father's death and the hasty burial. Something was badly amiss. Rahotep turned to Kheti with crisp orders.

"This command is now yours. Send me Kakaw with filled waterskins. Runner, take your ease here and come on in the morning with the Scouts."

He thought he might have to argue against Kheti's potests, but the underofficer only nodded and called for the archer Kakaw, a noted tracker who had served as a messenger and knew the desert paths by day or night.

"Be sure, Lord," Kheti said as Rahotep, a waterskin thong cutting into his shoulder, prepared to leave, "we shall make a quick march to Kah-hi. There are those here—and there—who are your men in all ways."

It was midmorning when Rahotep sighted the palm trees marking the fields about the post of Kah-hi. He sketched an answer to the sentries' salute. Within the shadow of the gate another man stood waiting. He stepped forward, catching Rahotep by the shoulders and drawing him into the half embrace of close friends.

"It is well with you, boy?" He studied the drawn young

face under its mask of trail dust, noting with approval the other's assured bearing and his unconscious aura of authority—as worn by a man not only used to giving orders, but also understanding well the reason for giving them.

"It is well with me, Methen. But it is not well—" He stopped in mid-breath, warned by the narrowing of the older officer's eyes. "I have come at your summoning," he ended more formally.

"There should have been an earlier summoning and not from my lips." Methen revealed a flash of anger.

But it was not until they were in Rahotep's private quarters that Methen, leaning against the wall by the bathing slab while the captain ladled the welcome water over his parched skin, spoke crisply and to the point.

"Unis had taken into his hands the gold seal of office. He controls Semna and Nubia for the time being. Now he plays a waiting game—"

"A waiting game?"

"One of Prince Teti's captains came at once. It is rumored that his lord follows him closely. The Lady Meri-Mut has received this captain in the inner courtyard twice. Unis has sent messages to all commandants of border forts. They are to detach ten men here, twenty there, ready for some unknown service when the Viceroy orders—"

"Messengers to the forts! But here at Kah-hi—surely Hamset could not have kept secret such news!" Rahotep drew the towel back and forth about his thin middle, frowning. True, he had been out on two patrols during the past thirty days, once spending ten days away from the fort. But in Kah-hi quarters were atop one another. It was impossible to keep any secrets from eyes or ears. And he knew of old how not only truth, but also the most extravagant rumor, spread from man to man as fire licks across a plain of withered grass.

"It seems that Kah-hi was overlooked in this general diffusion of important news," commented Methen dryly. "Your supply train came in yesterday—that would have brought Hamset some knowledge. But—officially he had heard nothing before my own arrival. It was only when I did not hear from you that I discovered what had been arranged."

Rahotep smiled wryly. "Unis takes the precautions of an elephant hunter to steal upon a flea. Does he believe that I shall gather a host and march upon Semna to wrest Ptahhotep's seal from his finger—?" But his smile faded as he watched Methen's sober face. "He can't!" he protested. "To think that is sheer stupidity, and Unis cannot be accused of that!"

"Unis is not stupid; he is only human. He does, as all of us, judge others' motives by his own. It is what he would do if he stood in Kah-hi and you sat in Semna. Why do you think you have been so long assigned to Kah-hi?"

"I am a captain of Scouts, we patrol the border, and Kah-hi is the first fort to front the Kush—"

But Methen was shaking his head, and his expression suggested that he had expected brighter wits in his protégé.

"Kah-hi is the least of all the border forts, the one most exposed to danger. Should the Kush arise in force and overrun this territory—as they have done in the past and will doubtless do many times in the future until we have a Pharaoh strong enough to teach them wisdom—Kah-hi would speedily cease to be. And among all the Nubian forces the losses are the greatest among the Scouts."

Rahotep put one hand against the water-splashed wall. He felt a little sick and dizzy, as if a mace had crashed against the side of his skull.

"My father sent me here." His voice was hardly above a whisper.

"You have lived five years on the border," Methen replied. "There are venomous creatures hidden in the sands of Semna's gardens—as the Viceroy himself discovered at last. A man can defend himself against the Kush. Against such secret sand creepers and those who may plant them in his path, he has a lesser chance.

26

Ptahhotep may have saved your life by seeming to agree to throw it away—"

The sickness that had been a bitter taste in the captain's mouth ebbed. Methen's tone was measured, his words well chosen. Now Rahotep clung to the hope that he spoke the truth. His father had been aloof, but there had been no dealings between them in the past that had suggested that the Viceroy had a twisted or evil nature. One could better believe that he had deliberately sent his younger son into an open danger to protect him from a more subtle peril at home.

Perhaps that stab of suspicion and the relief that had followed with Methen's words sharpened the captain's wits, for another thought came so quickly that he shared it with the older officer.

"A son who did not come to mourn his father upon the tidings of his death could be rumored a traitor—could be accused of lingering to make mischief—" Rahotep dropped the towel and kicked it away, reaching for a fresh kilt to buckle on. As he slid his dagger home in the belt sheath, he heard Methen laugh softly.

"You have not filled your head with sand after all, boy. But I also do not doubt that Hamset may have received certain orders with his supplies—"

Rahotep had taken up his baton-flail; now he swung around to face the other. His usually well-curved lips were set in a thin line, giving his face some of the remote sternness of the forgotten statue in the ruined fort by the river.

"Hamset's orders are for the officers under his command. But if I turn over to him my baton-flail, he no longer commands me and dares not stand between me and the outer gates of Kah-hi."

Methen folded his arms across his broad chest, and Rahotep braced himself for a hot retort. To Methen, the warrior's life was the best one. He would hardly support the captain's resignation from service.

But instead he was nodding. "I could wish you were

leading a company when you reach Semna. But there are those there who have not forgotten bread eaten in the past, nor where true allegiance lies."

"It is said"—Rahotep pulled the words out of childhood memory—

"'Fight for his name, purify yourselves by his oath, and ye shall be free from trouble. The beloved of the king shall be blessed; but there is no tomb for one hostile to Pharaoh; and his body shall be thrown into the waters.'"

"It is so said," Methen echoed.

"But"—Rahotep pointed out the obvious—"where is there a Pharaoh to serve? I take no oath to Unis!"

Methen smiled. "To that also we may find an answer in Semna. But the road lies open to our feet, and Re anchors His sky boat for no man. We must be on our way before sundown."

The elderly commandant of Kah-hi did not reach for the baton Rahotep extended. His face, seamed by years into a pattern of sun wrinkles and skin-over-bone, showed little expression. His eyes, heavy-lidded, rose neither to his youthful subordinate nor to Methen.

"There comes a time," he spoke meditatingly, "when a man is no longer pulled hither and thither by ambition or desire. Dreams die and take with them some of our fears—so that one is empty of both. I, Hamset, hold this fort of Kah-hi and do what I can also to hold back the Kush. What care I for the problems of greater lords and captains? The Viceroy is dead. I have no order over any seal concerning you. Go as you wish, Captain. It is fitting that a son bid a last farewell to his father. Who am I to interfere in other matters? You are detached from Kah-hi in all honor—here you have served ably and well. And you are also authorized to take with you an archers' guard of your own choosing—" His voice trailed into silence, but when Rahotep would have thanked him, he held up a forbidding hand.

"Go your way but tell me nothing, Captain. I am the commandant of a small and well-nigh-forgotten post, and that position I would keep until I depart to the horizon. I have no official word concerning you—and to strange stories that may have been whispered in a man's ear hinting this and that I am deaf. But you do well to march out of Kah-hi before I am forced to take other action. May the fortune of Re be with you—you have been a good officer, young and foolhardy at times after the fashion of youth, but nevertheless you have earned your bread here."

He did not even raise his eyes when Rahotep gave him a last salute, so perhaps he never knew that Methen granted him the same recognition. And he did not appear later when, after the arrival of Kheti and the rest of Rahotep's company at the fort, the young captain chose his ten men. All of them were young, all were without wives or families in the quarters to tie them to Kah-hi. And they marched from the fort two hours before sundown without seeing Hamset again.

The leopard cub traveled in a bag, the thongs of which were slung over Rahotep's shoulder. None fed or tended him save the captain, so that while he snarled and spat at most of the men, he began to give a grudging respect to the one who carried him, and at last willingly allowed himself to be handled and suitably caressed behind the ears and under the jaw like a tame cat.

They did not reach Semma until the fourth day, though Rahotep pushed the pace. The vast western fort with its thirty-foot walls had been finished some three hundred years before. Then the Pharaoh had ruled from the delta in the north beside the bitter waters to Kerma in the hot lands of the far south. Now there was no king in Egypt save the Hyksos lord in his delta city of Avaris, and in Nubia none paid him tribute.

The gate sentries were brusque. Rahotep guessed that if they had been a little more sure of their ground, he might have been turned away. That they were not sure was a small indication that Unis might still be two-minded concerning his half brother's importance—or else not expecting any bold move on Rahotep's part.

Kheti's hand rested lightly on his belt ax as he looked about him speculatively.

"It is always good to pay respect to the dead," he commented, "but even the Great Ones do not demand that a man lay his unguarded hand within the jaws of a wild lion. It might have been well, brother, to have set yourself a more northern goal than this fort." His nostrils widened as he drew in a deep breath. "There is a smell about this place which alerts the wary."

The fortress troops with their tall shields of red-and-white-spotted cowhide, their spears and slings, were in contrast to the lean, dark desert coursers among whom Rahotep had lived so long, and he found himself estimating how well they might stand up against a determined Kush dawn rush.

Rahoptep's company, rounding a storehouse to come to the Hall of Judgment, stopped short to survey in open wonder a light vehicle being driven slowly back and forth. Two hundred years earlier the Hyksos had broken the Egyptian army with their ruthless chariot charges, riding over demoralized companies who had never faced horses before. Since then, the princes of Thebes and the southern nomarchs had acquired similar horse troops. But in Nubia they were still unknown.

The stallion in the harness of the light two-wheeled cart shook his head and blew impatiently, the plumes on his metal head crest bobbing up and down.

"There is a proper way to give wings to the feet?" Kheti exclaimed. "Plant those along the border and Haptke will be overrun before he has time to think up any naughtiness. Aah, brother, what a deal of sand slogging they would save a man—"

"Save that those wheels need a road of sorts to follow," observed the captain. The chariot—and its horse—was a marvel right enough, and one that at another moment he would have been content to examine carefully. But the identity of the chariot's master was now a question of importance to his own future.

"Teti is here!" Methen's whispered warning answered that question.

With only a second's hesitation, Rahotep marched forward, his men falling in step behind him. They reached the portal of the hall, and the keeper on duty there arose from his stool, his wand of office out as a barrier.

But as Rahotep brought his baton down, bearing the wand earthward, the man stepped aside nimbly with a half grin. It was plain that, like the sentries at the gate, he was not yet ready to stand against Ptahhotep's younger son.

The sound of raised voices reached the small party as they came into the central hall.

"—in the Name of Pharaoh" someone was saying with that clipped accent that Rahotep had heard in his mother's speech, in Hentre's, and in Methen's. Plainly a northerner spoke.

"The Lord Ptahhotep has departed to the west—"

And there was no mistaking that voice either. Rahotep frowned. As a small child, he had been overawed by the Lady Meri-Mut's autocratic brother, Pen-Seti, Chief Priest of Anubis. As a growing lad he had distrusted the lean dark man with his fanatic's eyes, his iron self-control. And, upon his own banishment from Semna, the captain had known his distrust to be well founded.

Unis had shown little liking either for his uncle in those boyhood days, but they might well have joined forces now. Rahotep believed this was true as he studied the group standing before the empty high seat at the other end of the hall.

Unis, Rahotep decided critically and with an inner satisfaction, had not worn well. Accustomed to the fine trained bodies of the Scouts, the captain found the rounded plumpness of his half brother an indication of softness—of body, if not also of will and spirit. His brother's belly bulged over the richly ornamented belt of his sheer outer audience skirt, and his heavy wig was thick with scented oil, making an extra wide frame for his broad, flat-featured face.

He was accompanied by Pen-Seti, the priest's tall frame bending a little forward as if he were some runner set on the mark. The austerity of his white skirt and shawl and the bony outline of his shaven head made a stark contrast to Unis's softness.

Unis, Pen-Seti, and—Teti! The rebel Nubian prince was seated on a stool, leaning back against one of the blue lotus-carved pillars, his handsome face, with its sparkling eyes alert to the slightest move, turned to the scene as if his host had arranged it for his amusement.

Fronting this triumvirate was a stranger. By his dress he was a high-ranking officer. But the insignia heading his baton, the symbol painted on the corselet of leather reinforced with bronze strips that he wore, was not known to the Scout captain. On seeing him, however, Methen's breath hissed between his teeth. He pushed forward to stand arm to arm with Rahotep.

"You dare to defy our lord!" the stranger was demanding with heat as Rahotep's party advanced.

"Not so." That was Pen-Seti speaking in a rush of words intended to overwhelm his hearers. "The message which you bore hither was for the Lord Ptahhotep. To the Lord Ptahhotep has it been delivered. Your mission is accomplished, Lord Nereb, as you may truthfully report to him who sent you. That the Lord Ptahhotep may no longer be interested in the affairs of Nubia—or of those of Egypt—is no man's fault."

"Aye, your message bore my father's name—to my father's tomb it has been taken." Unis smiled slyly. "Thus all dispute is ended, for that which has been sealed unto the Lord Ptahhotep is his alone."

"You hold by the letter and defy the spirit!" The strange officer's gaze went from face to face, resting for a second or two longer upon Prince Teti. "Beware lest Pharaoh takes another view—"

"Do you speak in the name of Apophi?" retorted Pen-Seti. "For to our knowledge the king of the Hyksos holds the north, and what that alien despoiler of the gods orders is no concern of ours!"

"I speak in the name of the Pharaoh Sekenenre, the Beloved of Re, who, seated upon the great throne, holds forth the flail for his enemies, the crook for his people. I am the mouth of the Lord of the Two Lands, a runner for the Son of Re—"

Teti yawned and allowed his gaze to wander to the far wall, where he stared with the intentness of an artist at a very ordinary painting of birds among marsh reeds.

The audience, if audience it was, came to a sudden end as Unis, looking past the stranger, caught sight of Rahotep. His sly smile contorted into a scowl. And so marked was his surprise and displeasure that the Lord Nereb half turned to see who stood at his back.

"What do you here?" spat Unis.

"My duty, brother. Is it not seemly that a man's son follow him to the tomb in all honor?"

"My father is buried. You are overlate in your duty—"

"Your messenger was late, brother, so late that he did not arrive at all. Perhaps he was met by a Kush arrow instead of by my men. At Kah-hi, the raiders sniff close to the trails. But nevertheless I am here."

"Where there is no place for you! Return to your Kah-hi from which you had no right to depart without orders."

Rahotep walked forward. The leopard cub opened its eyes to stare at Unis unblinkingly. When its master stopped a spear-length away from Unis, it mouthed a hiss. Rahotep surveyed his brother slowly, from the perfume-matted ceremonial wig to those plump feet that had never done a full day's march, and back again—just as he might examine a recruit being paraded before him for the first time. Five years ago Unis had been one of the powerful adults whose assurance had made his younger brother feel inferior. But at this meeting Unis no longer held that advantage.

"We have not seen your arrows in flight among ours, brother." Deliberately he used the familiar address of equality, knowing how it must rasp the other. "He who gives orders to a warrior wears also the plume upon his own head—"

33

"Impudent fool, you speak to the Viceroy!" Pen-Seti's long neck bobbed forward. His shaven head with its beak of nose had the outline of a winged carrion eater. "Guard your tongue, lest this noble lord forget the tie of blood—"

But Unis had been stung. He was in no mind to let another speak for him. His fleshy fingers darted out and snatched from his half brother's hand the captain's baton.

"No officer are you in my service, Rahotep! Look now to your own holding, Shadow Hawk!" He laughed with the same old high whinny.

"Now"—one word tumbled over another from Unis's lips, so eager was he to be done with them—"the audience is finished." He turned to Prince Teti. "The pleasure garden awaits us, Lord." With his hand familiarly on the Nubian noble's arm, he went out of the hall.

Kheti snickered. "A duck waddles poolward, Lord. Have we now *your* permission to go elsewhere?" He accented the deference to Rahotep.

The young captain laughed shortly. "Since I am no longer your officer, it would follow that you no longer need my permission for any act." He flexed his empty hand. It felt odd. To leave his baton in Hamset's holding would have been right and proper. To be so summarily deprived of his command by Unis aroused a smoldering anger he was not soon to forget.

"It takes more than a fancy stick in your hand to make an officer, Lord. And it takes other than the Lord Unis to break one," the Nubian replied calmly.

"You are also son to the Lord Ptahhotep?" It was the Lord Nereb from the north who broke in eagerly.

"This is the Lord Rahotep, son to Ptahhotep and to the Lady Tuya, heiress of the Striking Hawk Nome," Methen began, but Rahotep would have none of that.

"I am Rahotep, but beyond that nothing now, not even a captain of Scouts."

"You remain the son of Ptahhotep," persisted the officer. "Are you of a like mind with your brother, that Pharaoh does not rule in Nubia now?"

"If there is again a Pharaoh—Is rumor true then, has a

34

prince of Thebes taken the double crown and would move against the Hyksos?"

"It is true. He has sent forth his messengers to summon an army. But here I find only a dead man to answer—"

"Your message has been rightfully delivered to Ptahhotep, in whose name it was sealed." They had forgotten Pen-Seti, but the priest's glare went from the royal messenger to Rahotep. "Anubis guards His own." He pulled his shawl about his bony shoulders and strode off.

"There was authority for raising troops in the name of Pharaoh in that message?" asked Methen.

"To my belief, aye."

Rahotep smoothed the fur between the cub's ears. The little one gave a muted purr. Rahotep was beginning to think, to form the shadow of a wild plan. A shadow plan to serve a shadow lord. But dare he attempt it? He smiled at the Lord Nereb.

"Within these walls *my* hospitality is limited, Lord. But still have I some claim on shelter. Will you be my guest this night?"

3

Into the Jackal's Jaws

There were four of them in that small, windowless room, and outside its single door lounged two of the archers who had accompanied Rahotep from Kah-hi. An elderly man in the dress of a scribe sat on the one stool, his back against the wall, his tired face very sober. Hentre, who had faithfully followed his nomarch's fortunes to the end, who had remained in a foreign land to serve his lady and her son afterwards, was realizing in that moment the slowness of age just when he wished to give his best.

"The message roll was sealed into a jar—"

"And placed within the tomb chamber itself?" Rahotep demanded impatiently. If that had been done, there was no hope at all for his sketchiest of plans.

But Hentre and the Lord Nereb shook their heads in a duet of negation.

"I arrived too late," the royal messenger said. "The Lord Ptahhotep's inner tomb chamber had already been sealed."

"So the jar was set in the mortuary chapel before the eye

window of the Watcher." Hentre took up the report once more.

"In the mortuary chapel—" Rahotep moved on his pile of mats, his eyes closed as he tried to pull from the depths of memory a vision of a place he had only visited once and then so worn with grief that he had had little attention for his surroundings.

The local tombs of noble families were cut in the cliffs on the western wall of the river valley. There was a settlement there of those whose lives were spent in serving the dead, the embalmers, the coffin makers, the professional mourners, the priests of Anubis, the guards who warded off tomb robbers.

Ptahhotep's tomb was a fine one, with separate chambers for members of his immediate household, and a maze of passageways, most with dead ends, designed to thwart robbers. But flat against the cliff, blocking off the sealed and concealed entrance, was the mortuary chapel where sacrifices would continue to be offered in the names of those who slept within.

"It must be done tonight." The captain opened his eyes.

Hentre stirred and held up a protesting hand. "They will be alert for such a move, Lord. It will but give them the excuse they seek to pull you down—"

Rahotep got to his feet. "I go as a son to visit his father's tomb. I go alone—what evil can they possibly impute to that?"

Methen nodded, but Hentre still shook his old head doubtfully.

"If you go alone, Lord, they can and will impute any manner of evil to you—and who may bear witness on your behalf? Let me—"

"Not so!" Kheti, too, arose and stretched wide his arms. "I am my lord's shield bearer in battle, and this is in a manner a battle. Do you go now, brother?"

"I go alone," the captain repeated stubbornly. "Ptahhotep's son am I. If I take what has been sealed unto him, the Watcher may understand. If we come in a body to steal—then we are in a measure what they would term us—despoilers of a tomb."

He threw that squarely at Kheti. The Nubian gave lip service to Amon-Re, but as a Nubian he called upon the god of his race—Dedun—in moments of stress. His customs, save where they were overlaid by the uses of the army with its Egyptian influences, were not basically those of the Two Lands. But he could understand the belief in the Watcher, who dwelt within the tomb but looked out upon the world through a chapel window. Rahotep thought that what he intended to do, though it would be close to sacrilege and could so be claimed against him, might be condoned by that Watcher within—just as he was also certain that this was his task alone, a duty that could not be shared.

And so in the end he managed to break down Kheti's resistance, though the Nubian insisted upon escorting him as far as the outposts of the necropolis, the place of the dead.

There were flickering lamps in some of the village houses. But the cliffs, with their awesome array of tombs and chapels, were a black line across the sky, merging one darkness with another.

"The patrol drinks deep tonight of the funeral wines, as is their due," Kheti said. "The Lord Unis may have treated the Lord Ptahhotep with unseemly haste in escorting him so swiftly to his other home, but he did not skimp on the feasting. And there may come other things out of the desert to seek the bounty of the offerings. Loosen your dagger, brother, and look twice at any shadow—"

Rahotep clung to the shadows, but he did not slink. Should he be discovered by a priest of the patrol, he determined to demand an escort to the chapel. Such ill fortune would prevent his plan from working, but it might save his life.

The necropolis was as barren as the desert. No wind whispered in a palm crown or rustled through grass. The shadows of rocks lay as long black fingers and threatening fists across his path. A jackal bayed the rising moon. Rahotep's right hand rested above his heart, pressing painfully into the flesh the hawk amulet he wore on a chain about his neck. Anubis, the Seeker, the Jackal, who guarded the doors of the West, this was His domain. But Horus, the Hawk, flew over the desert lands, where the Jackal must pad in the dust. And tonight Rahotep believed he had more to fear from the malice of men than the displeasure of any Great One.

His sandal soles scuffed as he came upon stone pavement, the road leading up to the chapel. The scent of incense, of dying flowers, hung here, growing more noticeable as he advanced. Ahead was the gleam of a lamp, one of the small saucer type for the table of sacrifice. He hesitated for a long moment, listening. So small a lamp must be refilled often, which meant an attendent priest—unless such a guardian had shortly left. And there was no way of entering the chapel save by the road he was on—no hiding place from which he could spy. Rahotep kicked off his sandals, not only for reasons of reverence; bare skin on stone and sand was noiseless.

The captain stood now between the two slabs of red granite forming the door sides. The smell of the offerings was almost fetid in the airless interior. And the morsel of light played upon the painted walls, giving life and color to a face here and there or meaning to an inscription. But he could see no priest on duty.

Slowly Rahotep faced the west wall, his eyes in the restricted light searching for the square opening that must be 'there. His mouth was suddenly dry and parched. He rubbed his damp hands over the kilt on his thighs. So had he felt upon the occasion of his first assault of a Kush village. But he moved forward.

And his change of position showed him a glint of reflection from within that window. Because he had to, Rahotep raised the lamp from within a nest of withered garlands and held it high enough to see those stern features of a well-known face.

The sculptor Ikudidi was a true artist. He had wrought in stone not only the outward form of the Lord Ptahhotep as he had been in the prime of his vigorous manhood, but had also caught the quality of the man himself. Rahotep's breath caught in his throat. This—this was his father!

Then, in a flick of the wavering lamp light, that moment of recognition was past. He saw nothing but an outstanding work of art; the man was gone.

The inlaid eyes gleamed in the light; the lips were set in a serene thread of half-smile. Ptahhotep, as he had been, watched those who came to pay him remembrance. But Rahotep, shivering, put back the lamp, noting only half-consciously that it was close to winking out entirely. He would always believe that more than just the graven Watcher had greeted him for that revealing instant.

To the stone face he gave a warrior's salute to his commander. Then he looked about him for what he had come to seek. Hentre had described it—an urn taken hastily from the stock of a dealer in canopic jars. It would have a jackal's head for a stopper. There it was, between two wine beakers on the altar. His hand had fallen upon it when he was startled by a shout of outrage and anger from behind.

Reflexes trained to hair trigger alertness by his border life saved Rahotep in that instant. He sensed rather than saw that figure springing at him from the doorway. And he had just time enough to counter that rush with a wrestling trick taught him in archers' exercises. Linen, a priest's shawl or long skirt, tore with a loud sound. And in the moment the lamp went out.

Rahotep exerted his full strength and hurled the other from him. He groped on the altar, spilling from it in his haste the offerings, his fingers dabbling in foodstuffs and dead garlands. Then he had the jackal's head under his palm, and a second later the jar was tight in the circle of his arm.

But his assailant had been quick of thought, too, for his voice, raised in a call for help, rang out from the door of the chapel. That would bring the guard, and Rahotep would have no defense against evidence of the despoiled altar.

The captain threw himself at the door, guided by a shaft of moonlight. But the priest was valiant, strong in his righteous anger. He was waiting, and hampered by the jar,

Rahotep could only chop with the edge of his flat hand at the other's neck, a barbarian trick, one Kehti had learned from a river sailor and that he swore might be fatal.

A sharp pain scored Rahotep's shoulder. But the priest had gone down, his dagger clattering from his hand on the pavement. And, before the tomb guardian could stagger up again, the captain was running, heading away from the road of the dead toward the open country with only the vaguest idea of the territory ahead.

There were torches moving in the tomb servants' village. Rahotep listened to the shouting of the guards contemptuously. Had he been in command back there, there would be far less noise and more speed in spreading out a net of men to snare a fugitive. But he should thank Horus that they were such bunglers.

For several minutes Rahotep ran lightly, the impetus of his initial good fortune carrying him on. Then he was aware of blood flowing down his side, a sticky flood over his crooked arm and the jar he cradled. His bare foot came down upon a sharp stone, and the pain made him flinch, twisting his ankle awkwardly so that his smooth lope was reduced to a hobble.

All about him were tempting hiding places, but he did not know the ground as well as those who pursued him did. He might well take shelter in a trap. It was better to keep moving, even at his hampered pace. His path took him away from the cliffs, angling toward the river. Now he caught a glimpse of torches bobbing before him there. Would they uncover Kheti? He doubted whether any tomb guard could match the Nubian Scout in trail lore, especially at night. But he was also certain that Kheti would not leave the vicinity of the necropolis until he was sure of his captain's fate.

Meanwhile, Rahotep leaned against a rock outcrop and forced himself to logical thinking. He dared not return to Semna in his present state. And to approach any of the villas of the nobles on the outskirts of the fort-city was to ask for arrest. As far as he knew, only Methen and Hentre within the territory would give him aid or shelter, and neither could protect a fugitive against the power of Unis.

His progress was in a broken zigzag as he made his way from one projecting bit of stone to the next. And the intervals in which he paused to steady himself against each outcrop grew longer in spite of his determination to keep going. That line of torches along the river reached now almost to the outer gates of Semna. In a few moments that refuge would be closed against him. Rahotep flogged his memory of the great fort, of the outlying villas, of all that lay before him in the general northern direction. And his uncertainty grew. If he kept on, he would be herded away from the river, backed into the scrub land that bordered the desert proper. Then they could track him down at their leisure.

He pressed his right hand tightly against the throbbing slash on his shoulder, trying to stem that steady flow of blood. The priest had not killed, but he had struck better than he knew. Now when Rahotep watched those torches, they seemed to swing and circle like awakened birds in the air, and his lungs labored with the effort he made. But still tight against him he held the sealed jar.

As he wedged himself in an angle between two blocks of stone, using their strength to remain on his feet, he heard something new—the angry chattering of a baboon warning against invasion of its hunting lands. Rahotep shook his head—a baboon? The haziness that had first attacked his sight now jumbled his thoughts. A baboon—that had some meaning.

Then he fought his weakness, the fuzziness that wreathed him in. Kheti! Kheti's warning from the time they were lads evading Rahotep's scribe-tutor. And he hissed softly in return, a warm relief flooding through him. A shadow that had more breadth and strength than any real shadow flowed up to him, and the firm grip of strong hands closed about him. He flinched from the touch on his shoulder.

"Be easy, they have marked my hide somewhat," he said, half laughing in sheer relief.

Kheti's answering comment in Dedun's name was more curse than petition.

"Do you know where we are?" Rahotep asked.

"Near to the shrine of Amon-Re, brother. But they are between us and Semna or the river."

"Amon-Re!" Rahotep straightened. A hope, small and weak, but still a hope, came to life.

Amon-Re was the patron of Thebes, and the priests of His shrine had had, in the past, strong ties with the northern city that had been the capital of Egypt. Would they not favor a Pharaoh ruling there now?

Anubis was strong, but Amon-Re had greater power. It would depend upon the high priest—a timid man, or one who did not wish to dispute Unis and Pen-Seti, would be of no service. On the other hand, a Voice of Amon who was jealous of his own might might welcome a chance to stand up to Pen-Seti. It was a gamble to be sure, but this whole venture was a throw of Senet sticks in the sight of the Great Ones.

"We shall go to the shrine—" Rahotep pushed himself away from the stones. He reached for a hold on Kheti's shoulder to steady himself, and then urged the other to move. Who was the Voice of Amon now? So much rested upon that single question. In the five years since he had left the Viceroy's court there could have been many changes.

The shrine light in the temple was larger and brighter than the lamp of the mortuary chapel. But the shadowy interior seemed as deserted to Rahotep as he staggered up the steps with Kheti's support, to waver over the pavement of the main aisle.

In the chapel he fronted the graven image of the Watcher. Here he faced a more than life-size crowned king, the Double Crown on His head, the staff with the sun disc in His hand. And to that representation the captain made homage weakly, his knees on the cold stone, pushing the jar before him into the full beam of the light from the altar.

"Who are you who bring gifts with bloody hands into the sacred places of the Great One?" What Rahotep had taken for a second statue moved forward with a slow sway of priest's shoulder shawl.

"Khephren!" He identified the priest almost stupidly.

44

"Aye, Khephren. And you, who steal through the night secretly, what do you here?"

Rahotep answered with the sullenness of complete despair. He had made his cast and the sticks had fallen against him. The Voice of Amon was Khephren, a man of austerity, of great and noted learning, but also one who of old had divorced himself from all connection with the rule of Nubia, who visited the Viceroy's court only upon the demands of ceremony, and who had never been known to take a hand in any internal dispute.

"I am Rahotep, son to Ptahhotep."

"And by this evidence a despoiler of tombs." The Voice of Amon indicated the canopic jar, the remoteness of his voice chill with disgust.

"Not so," Kheti replied when Rahotep found it hard to summon the words. "The Lord Rahotep but went to reclaim the Pharaoh's message that our Lord's call for service might be known. He robbed no tombs, though there will be those who will raise that cry against him. And he has taken a hurt that must be cared for—"

"It seems that there is some strange tale in this," Khephren returned. "Let this robber of tombs speak in his own defense."

Somehow Rahotep found words enough to give a bald account of the night's happenings. Perhaps the very baldness of his tale was convincing, for Khephren heard him to the end without any interruption.

"And you came here then—why?" he asked at the end.

"Because He - Who - Travels - the - Sky overwatches Thebes, and Pharaoh is His son. Should a father turn against a son?" Something put those words into his mouth. Then the walls of the shrine tilted in a queer fashion, and he slipped sideways until Kheti caught him.

"Priest," spat the Nubian, "my lord dies if he is not given aid. And then perhaps others shall die also—"

Khephren's rigid features did not change. He stood above Rahotep now, more merciless in judgment than the statue of the god behind him. For a very long moment he looked down at the wounded man. Then he clapped his hands, the sharp sound echoing thinly through the temple. Men came out of the shadows and Rahotep struggled in Kheti's hold. They would be thrown forth from the shrine now, abandoned to the hunters.

"See to the youth's wound," Khephren ordered. "And"—he stooped to pick up the blood-stained jar, handing it to a subordinate—"place this on the high altar under the protection of the Great One, not to be taken from His care until I so will it."

Rahotep relaxed in the Nubian's hold. For the time he had won his gamble. They had been granted sanctuary under Amon-Re.

Some time later he lay on a high, narrow couch, clenching his fists, as the temple healer searched the slash and used the fiery palm spirit on it liberally before he bound it up. Rahotep was refusing the sleep drink of poppy seeds the other prescribed, intent upon keeping his full senses, when Khephren entered the small room. The captain levered himself up on his elbow.

"What is your will with us, Voice of Amon?" His uncertainty made his tone harsh and demanding.

"Say rather, boy, what is Amon-Re's will with all of us," the high priest rebuked him.

Even in his weakened, dizzy condition, Rahotep sensed that there was more to this than the conventional answer of a priest. He watched the stern face with the narrowness of a war captive reading either life or death in the movement of his victor's eyebrows. So he noted that the Voice of Amon was clad now not in his ordinary dress of linen shawl and skirt but in the inner and outer kilts of high ceremony, his shawl replaced by a leopard skin, one of its dangling, gold-taloned paws clipped to his jeweled cincture. High feast day, Rahotep wondered dazedly. Yet it was not dawn—or had the night worn away so swiftly?

Khephren made a gesture and four of the underpriests crowded into the room, taking up the bed on which Rahotep lay as if it were a noble's litter. Kheti stood away from the corner, where he had been squatting, as if to raise protest, but his captain signed him to silence. Something was afoot, but Rahotep was beginning to trust the high priest. He had done all that he could do. The outcome would be the affair of Amon-Re and His Voice.

The bed was borne out into the space before the altar. There was the grayness of predawn outside the outer ranks of pillars. When the priests put down their burden, slightly to the left of the Amon image, Kheti went down on his knees beside the bed, lending his shoulder to Rahotep's support so the captain could see clearly those gathered there.

Pen-Seti he had in a measure expected, also Unis—with a backing of guardsmen and Anubis priests. Drawn up opposite them was an even smaller group consisting of Methen, Hentre, and the Lord Nereb, with two of Rahotep's archers to back them.

Khephren took his place before the high altar. In his hand a sistrum of gold wires and turquoise beads swung to make a sweet tinkle. One of the lesser priests flung powder on a censer, and the blue curls of incense twined upward like lazy serpents.

"Voice of Amon!" That was Pen-Seti, his silhouette against the wall behind him that of a bird of prey. "Release unto us these despoilers of tombs, these blasphemers of the Great Ones, so that Anubis may deal with them as is lawful."

Khephren's face was expressionless, but Rahotep, watching, caught the faintest of eye flickers in his direction, and now he believed he knew what the high priest had been suggesting earlier. He hunched himself up against Kheti and stretched out one hand to the altar where the blood-stained jar still rested undisturbed.

"I appeal to the judgment of Amon-Re. May the Great One, in His everlasting wisdom, decide the truth or falsehood of my deeds!"

"To Amon-Re has this man appealed, to Amon-Re the judgment!"

Pen-Seti's lips twisted, his hands jerked at his shawl. To a lesser man than Khephren he might have voiced the protest now to be read in every line of his body. But somehow here and now he did not quite dare to challenge the other. There had never before been any trial of wills between them, but over the years the Voice of Amon had achieved a position that overawed his fellow priests.

"To Amon-Re the judgment!" That full-voiced agreement came from Rahotep's own party, and a few of those among Unis's followers nodded in a surly fashion.

Khephren twirled the sistrum, and two of the Amon priests brought forward a small wooden shrine, immeasurably old, immeasurably sacred, for it contained "Amon-of-the-Road," the Amon of travelers, which had been brought out of Thebes by that first Pharaoh who had added Nubia to Egypt.

The Voice of Amon prostrated himself before the shrine and then arose and broke the seal of its fastening. From the interior he brought forth and held up in both hands over his head the ancient statuette. And those watching, nobles and guards alike, went to their knees, shading their eyes with their right hands.

Rahotep heard through the silence the faint sound of Khephren's unsandaled feet upon the stone, knew that he was approaching the bed. Yet the captain kept his head bent, his eyes covered. There was a hiss of indrawn breath, a faint murmur, and Rahotep dared to look up.

Khephren stood beside him. Drops of sweat beaded the priest's forehead. He had the look of a man strained to the utmost of physical endurance. And slowly his arms were sinking as if the worn wooden statue he had held at arm's length above his head had taken on the weight of the great granite image behind the altar.

Down, down—Khephren's arms were at shoulder level, lower, lower—the whole body of the priest was being pulled forward by the weight of what he held.

Before it quite reached the ground, the high priest put forth a great effort and swung his body partly around. He faced away from Rahotep, inching toward the Anubis priests. As he progressed, he once more began to raise the statue, until, as he faced Pen-Seti, he again held the image high above his own head. For a long moment he stood so, but the image did not waver. Then he spoke.

"Amon has given judgment. The youth is Amon's. And his task is approved by Amon!"

He turned again with a swift tread to replace Amon-of-the-Road within the small shrine. Then he went on to the high altar and took up the canopic jar. With a swift movement he smashed the clay against the stone and drew forth a roll of papyrus. Slowly he unrolled it, viewing them all.

"This is the word of Pharaoh, of the son of Amon-Re, of him who holds the Flail for our enemies, the Crook for his people. Let our ears be open to the word of Pharaoh by the will of Amon-Re!"

4

What is Thebes to Us?

Rahotep tried to give his full attention to the words that came from the high priest's lips. The roll was, as they had believed, an order for Pharaoh's Viceroy to send north certain regiments settled in Nubian posts for generations—The Pride of Amon, The Protection of Ptah, The Spears of Sekmet. From what old records of vanished dynasties had they culled those names, Rahotep wondered dreamily? Maybe once they had garrisoned Semna, and Inebuw-Amenemhet at Kerma, but no longer. And Unis, hearing that roster of regimental names, was moved to laughter.

He smiled genially now at Nereb. "Pharaoh in Thebes is to be served," he said mockingly. "Summon up The Pride of Amon, The Protection of Ptah, The Spears of Sekmet, and I, myself, shall equip them from my storehouses. Aye, provide their officers with chariots, their men with fine bows, their quivers with a wealth of arrows. Summon them before us, messenger of Pharaoh, and all shall be done even as I say it here in the Holy Place of Amon!"

Puzzled, Nereb looked to Methen for explanation. The veteran was studying Unis grimly, but it was with the grimness of one who has been outwitted. Now he answered the northern officer.

"That roll was compiled long ago. We have not heard of such regiments here since before the Dark Years when the Hyksos came upon us. The troops of Nubia are mainly native auxiliaries and the Border Scouts."

"Aye," Unis added. "Call up bones from the tombs to march north if you will, he who speaks for Pharaoh. But otherwise you will get no such men from the Land of the Bow."

"But you have men in plenty." Nereb raised a last protest. He must have known that he was making it in vain. "Is not this the Land of the Bow? The fame of your archers has spread far! Give me a company of your archer Scouts, a force of your fortress spearmen, to equal those which Pharaoh asked of you—"

Unis shook his head slowly. "Pharaoh asked of me three regiments by name. Those three I have not, nor can any living man lead them forth. The Land of the Bow is defended by her sons; we have the Kush ever raiding to eat up the land. Against the Kush shall our arrows fly. What harm have the Hyksos ever done in Nubia that we should march against them now? I ask you, Lord, what is Thebes to us that we should spill blood in her service, in her far-off wars!" There was a murmur of assent from those about him. Pen-Seti displayed his agreement with vigorous nods.

"Pharaoh commands—"

Unis corrected Nereb. "A prince who has his throne in Thebes commands—but does his force reach over all of Egypt? Apophi of the Hyksos will have a few things to say concerning such a claim. Not one man goes forth from Nubia to fight for Thebes."

Rahotep pulled himself up and found words at last.

"Not so, brother. One man goes forth—"

Unis swung about so fast that the transparent pleated upper skirt he wore whirled out like the scarf of a dancing girl.

"Speak not so loud, tomb robber!" he snapped. "You are as a fly crawling upon the floor—buzz and a sandal shall crush you. But go north if you will; we shall be well rid of you!" Pen-Seti touched his arm, the priest's shaven head close to the other's elaborate wig as he hissed some suggestion, his fanatic's eyes hard upon Rahotep.

"Two men." That was Methen. And Kheti, grinning, smacked his lips together as one might when facing a feast. "Eleven more, all archer Scouts," he added to the tally.

The archers who had come with Methen gave their consent to that eagerly.

Unis had his temper once more under control. He ignored Rahotep but spoke to Nereb. "You have had your answer, Lord. We regret we cannot send the regiments your Pharaoh has asked for—there are no such men within the borders of Nubia. Also, since you bear no orders for recruitment, that you cannot do. It would be well for you to hasten back to Thebes lest your lord depend too much on service he will not get and so go rashly into some enterprise—"

Nereb flushed, reading well the insolence beneath that. But the exactness of the royal orders had tied his hands, and he was forced to stand silent as Unis and his party left in triumph.

Methen moved to the side of the couch. "You are badly hurt, boy?"

"A small slash only." Rahotep was quick to make light of the wound.

"He has lost much blood," Kheti corrected. "Lord Methen, it is in my mind that if we would keep to our purpose and get us to Thebes, we must do it speedily before those others can think of some net to take us in."

Methen beckoned to the northern officer. "Just so. Kheti, send one of these guards to bring their fellows here prepared to march. If they are all like minded to take service elsewhere—"

The Nubian underofficer chuckled. "Lord Methen, they are fighting men. What matter if they pad the border sands or the northern plains? And I think that I smell more

53

loot in this foray against the Hyksos than can be found in any Kush hole!"

Nereb came up as Kheti sent one of the archers back to the fort with orders to round up his fellows and collect the baggage they had brought from Kah-hi.

"Now"—Methen spoke to the King's messenger—"do you accept us for service under Pharaoh by the rules of the warriors' code?"

Nereb looked over his shoulder to the Voice of Amon.

"Will he who speaks for Re witness in the place of Pharaoh?"

Khephren did not reply at once. It was dawn now, though the first rays of the sun were not above the eastern hills. And the priests of the temple were assembling for the morning "Awakening Hymn." Their leader fingered the roll of papyrus.

"The time is the time of Amon-Re," he said. "Await you upon Him."

Sistrums chimed; the trumpet of the Great One called from the portico. With the others Rahotep bowed his swimming head and tried to fit one word of the chant to another. But he was glad to have Kheti settle him back upon the bed as the incense arose and the bright streamers of the rising sun cut the sky.

Sometime later—time was dim now—something was placed beneath his hand. His fingers identified the impress of a seal in wax. And he repeated stumblingly the words of an oath, seeing Nereb standing in the place of his future commander, Khephren as witness. He heard other voices saying the same words—Methen, Kheti, the slightly awed tones of the archers. It was done, they were no longer Scouts of the border, but men of an unknown Pharaoh ruling in a city they had never seen, tied to a purpose Unis and his court believed to be without hope. Were they fools, Rahotep wondered, fools or the wisest men in Nubia? But who could look through a Great One's eyes and know?

The small side court of the temple was remarkably full as Kheti assisted Rahotep through its door shortly after the following dawn. Untidy bundles holding the personal possessions of ten archers were stacked against the outer wall, while Methen was superintending the activities of two Kush slaves transporting his own chests. Today the veteran wore not only his "gold of valor," gained in the battles of his youth, but he went in full military dress, the baton of a regimental commander flourished in his hand to give point to his orders.

The few articles Rahotep had brought from the south by donkeyback were in a plain small chest beside Kheti's bulging bag of spotted cowhide. The captain's most cherished belongings, his bow, his noble's armlets, and the leopard cub were either on his back or under his hand.

Kheti seemed dissatisfied. "It is ill for the Hawk to go so meanly before the Pharaoh. Look upon this northern lord. If that is how they sport their gold in Thebes, we shall be as field workers instead of warriors—"

He indicated Nereb who stood talking with Methen. The wiry royal officer not only bore himself smartly, but, also as Kheti had pointed out, his body armor made Methen's uniform as out of date as the decrees of the builders of the pyramids. Where the Scouts and the Nubian soldiers went bare above the waist save for crossed shoulder belts in times of ceremonial parade, Nereb was encased in an armor of leather and bronze. He did not wear the sphinx headdress of linen, but a cap of bronze over a wig of short tight curls, to which was clipped a single nodding plume.

Rahotep laughed. "Scouts travel light, Kheti. Have we not always boasted that in the face of those who man the forts? Let Pharaoh know that we shall fly bird-free to scout out a path for his troops, and he shall look no more than to remark our skill. Ah, the time has come to leave. Bid the men take up their packs."

The captain had made his farewells, and his thanks, to Khephren. And the Voice of Amon had once more been the austere man he had known in his early boyhood. A little subdued and chilled, sure now that loyalties to Thebes rather than any personal interest had brought him the high priest's help, Rahotep was glad to be out of the temple, eager to face a new venture.

He was still uncertain enough on his feet to be glad of Kheti's hand beneath his arm. But the temple healers had assured him that his wound was closing properly, that the rest on board the river ship would restore him, so that when they reached Thebes, he could march his men ashore with much of his old energy and strength.

The captain brushed aside Methen's suggestion of a litter, preferring to leave Semna on his own two feet, even if he had to have Kheti at his side. Nereb matched his step to the young officer's slower pace as they went down to the waiting ship. The northern officer laughed harshly as Rahotep commented on the craft.

"I return as I went—with one ship!" Nereb was bitter. "And I had thought to head a fleet to Pharaoh's aid! If all his messengers have served him so ill, then indeed will Thebes have cause to weep."

"Not so." That was Methen. "You return with a company of picked Scouts, Lord, men trained to their duty by constant warfare in a harsh land."

"Thirteen men—" Rahotep was inclined to share Nereb's pessimism.

"One man, with his spirit bent to the task, can plow the desert and raise a vineyard. From small beginnings do armies grow. Let each messenger of Pharaoh bring back but thirteen such men and there will be a regiment of seasoned warriors."

The party on its way to the quay was brought to a halt by the sharp impact of something thrown on the pavement before them. It was a crude reddish bowl as the captain could distinguish by the shards into which it had splintered. One of the archers picked up the largest fragment, passing it to Rahotep's waiting hand.

He saw a sentence scratched in a temple scribe's hematic script: "Rahotep, born to the Lady Tuya and the Royal Son Ptahhotep, shall die."

A cursing—such as he had used against the Kush. He did not realize that he had read that aloud until he heard Methen's sardonic comment:

"So Rahotep shall die? So shall every man who walks Egypt when his time comes and it is Re's will to summon him before the Judges."

His hand struck the fragment of bowl from Rahotep's loose clasp, and then deliberately he kicked it and the other shards from their path. "Anubis curses, but Amon-Re smiles. And do the gods ever take as great an interest in the affairs of men as their mouth pieces would have us believe? Let them keep their warnings for the barbarians and the Kush!"

Kheti laughed and planted his sandal on one small piece, grinding the clay to dust against the stone.

"Arrows fly, spears have points, fever comes up from the river marshes, and a man can die of belly ache safe in his bed. Dedun shall have a fat ram and we shall see what will come of it. Ah, Lords, this is a fine ship we go to—"

It was a ship such as they seldom saw on these upper reaches of the Nile. The carved head, turned inwards on the prow, was the Ram of Amon, and the cabin was hung with walls of painted linen, which could be rolled up for the cool of river breezes. At this season the Nile moved sluggishly, starved for the flood of waters that later would swell the current. The brittle, searing winds from the south teased the sail, but it was the current, not those unpredictable gusts, that would take then downstream.

Someone waited for them on the quay, standing a little to one side as if his natural humility made him wait for their recognition. Rahotep dropped Kheti's arm and went up to Hentre.

"You go with us also, old friend—"

The elderly scribe smiled wistfully. "Not so, my son. A handful of wornout brushes and a palette that has served a man for almost a lifetime cannot stand for spear and shield. And it is the weapons of war not the arts of peace that are needed now. I am too old to be torn from my rooting to seek a new growing place—"

"But—" Rahotep began a protest, realizing what it might mean for Hentre to remain in Semna. The scribe's sympathies were widely known. He had made no effort to conceal his allegiance to the Lady Tuya and then to her son. And Unis was petty-minded. Hentre *must* go with them now!

"There is no need to fear for me, young lord," the scribe hastened to add, as if he read Rahotep's thoughts as fast as they crossed the captain's mind. "I have taken service with the Voice of Amon, and Re shall portect His own. I but come now to wish you well and to bring you that which is rightfully yours. When the Hawk was slain by the Hyksos, making his last defense against those who swept over his land, I was one of those who stole away his body to lay it in safety. And thinking that one of his line might indeed again raise his standard, I brought away from his entombing this which such an heir could use as valiantly as did my lord—" From beneath his cloak Hentre brought out a packet done up in a twist of time-yellowed linen. "Wear it on the day when you go up against the Hyksos, Lord, so that he whom I served before will, by the grace of Re, see it flash in battle once again!"

Rahotep put aside the wrappings to find that he held a fine archer's bracer, shaped to cover the hand, with a chain to go about the thumb and a thong to lace it in place at the wrist. This was fashioned of rare silver, and it was engraved with the Eye of Horus, the Winged Hawk of his mother's nome, and the Feather of Maat—the Truth of the Gods. Since this had been shaped to fit the hand of another, Rahotep slipped it on experimentally, believing it would not fit. But the cold metal was smooth against his skin as if it had been forged to his measure. Hentre smiled happily.

"It is just so, Rahotep, that I have many times seen your mother's father—my good lord and friend—fit that into place. Aye, even on that last day when all of us knew that there was no hope of victory! But no barbarian called it his spoil, and now it will gleam again among the arms of Pharaoh's following. Hail Hawk!" He gave Rahotep the salute due a nomarch.

The young captain laughed ruefully. "A nomarch without a nome, heading a party of eleven archers into a misty future, Hentre. But my thanks be unto you, not only for this"—he rubbed the bracer—"but for all else you have done for me since I was a child in the Women's Hall of the Viceroy's palace, tumbling over my own feet. And for what you did for the Lady Tuya, whom you served exceedingly well!"

So it was Hentre's figure Rahotep watched recede into the distance as the ship *Shining in Thebes* cast off its moorings and passed into the pull of the current under the careful direction of the bow pilot. A gong sounded and oarsmen bent to the task of adding speed to their going. Behind them first the quay with Hentre, then even the towering walls of Semna grew smaller and were gone as the turns of the river took them out of sight.

Once this waterway had been thronged with river traffic. The cargoes from Nubia, gold, ebony, ostrich plumes, aromatic woods, and fine skins had gone north, while south had flowed in exchange the finished work of city craftsmen. Now trade was dead. No one moved a cargo willingly into Hyksos territory, except as tribute wrung from nomes by threats. Nubia's wealth stayed at home. Consequently, there was a sad lack of the manufactured articles she needed.

In place of the laden cargo boats, they passed the rafts of herders taking their charges from one side of the river to the other in search of better pasturage. And these half-wild rovers looked upon the energetic downstream swing of the oared ship with amazement.

If the simple people of the land were amazed, their lords were almost uniformly hostile. When *Shining in Thebes* tied up at quays and Nereb tried to bargain for extra supplies, he was met coldly. For the most part he had to deal with insolent overseers who might not laugh openly at Pharaoh's seal on a royal order, but who, trained by years of outwitting tax collectors, were able to evade any direct compliance with official demands. But there were wild fowl among the reed banks, and Hori of the archers proved himself adept with a throwing stick. They might not feast upon roast goose, but neither did they lack something to add to the hard snail-shaped loaves of bread.

No more recruits were added to Nereb's party until they reached the boundaries of old Egypt and came into the domain of the Elephantine lords. The nomarchs of Elephantine, while not yet ranged openly under the Theban standard, were inclined to join in support of Sekenenre. Two regiments of spearmen marched on board transports, making an armada behind the swifter *Shining in Thebes*. Meanwhile, Nereb, impatiently pacing the confined deck space of his ship, talked and Rahotep and Methen listened.

To the veteran, much of this was already an old story. To Rahotep some of the information was puzzling. The rest he grasped because of his interest in the north. But most of all he listened eagerly to all Nereb had to say about the Hyksos military might.

When the invaders had lapped over the Sinai causeway into the delta lands two hundred years earlier, they had come as a destroying wave into an Egypt already war-torn and divided by puppet kings and rebel nobles. Nobles drew back to their nomes, holding what they might, trying to take more from weaker neighbors. They had not joined together to fight a common enemy.

The chariots of the invaders swept like locusts across a field of new grain. And, like those avid insects, they left but the bare earth behind them. In the delta they built Avaris, that city that was mainly a fort such as Egypt—or Nubia—had never dreamed could stand. From it they ruled not only Egypt but also the lands of the Asiatics, until a man wondered where they had *not* set up their false god and their frowning cities.

Every Egyptian, from the delta to the Third Cataract in the Kush lands, knew that old tale of destruction and death. But it was from Nereb that the Nubian party heard for the first time of the Theban challenge.

"Chariots," said the northern officer. "We have horses. We have bought them, traded for them, stolen them!" His teeth gleamed suddenly in a smile as if he remembered some foray of his own. "The Royal Son and Heir, Kamose, is a master of chariots, training his own horses, schooling young officers in the art. Look you, a smashing line of chariots to front your attack, and then footmen to follow after—"

"Archers on the wings!" Rahotep could visualize that in part—though he had seen only one chariot. And his examination of that had been limited to a passing stare.

"Archers?" Nereb did not appear to be impressed. "Archers could not stand up to the barbarians' charge before—"

Methen laughed softly. "Ah, but, Lord Nereb, the Captain Rahotep speaks of archery as it is not known among us in the north. Show the lord your bow, Kheti!"

The Nubian brought out his weapon and strung it. Nereb tested the strength of its pull, ran a questing hand down the curve of the arch, which was built of layers of wood and horn glued together.

"You have not seen such a weapon at Thebes," said Methen. "Nor could any archer of the north loose a shaft from it, for the desert archers are trained to launch their arrows to the mark from the month they first stand upon their feet. Moreover, Lord Nereb, they have yet another trick to aid them besides the excellence of their arms." He looked to Rahotep, and the captain took the hint.

"Hori, Kakaw, Intef, Baku." He named some of his men.

Glad of the chance to vary the monotony of sailing, his small force assembled on the narrow deck in line, their bows strung, blunt hunting arrows to hand. One of the rowing oars splashed on the river surface, sending a covey of waterfowl flapping up into the blazing sun. As one, bow cords were drawn, and, almost as one, the arrows were released at a snap of Kheti's fingers.

Fowls fell. And Nereb uttered a short word of surprise. They had been aiming at birds. But supposing such archers had been sighting against a troop of charging chariots?

"Had the Hyksos urged their forces into Nubia," Methen said, "perhaps they would have discovered that their horses and chariots might not have won the day. We have brought you archers, Lord, such as Egypt has not truly known before. Also they have as keen noses for a tangled trail in tracking as they have keen eyes for an arrow target. Pharaoh may not have his three regiments, but you do not return to him quite empty-handed!"

"So it would seem." Nereb was watching the crew of the ship retrieve the dead waterfowl. "Such archery as that I have not seen before. Nor has our lord."

"Plant your archers on the wings"—Rahotep took up the argument where he had left it before Methen's practical demonstration—"and lead your enemy between them—"

Nereb hooked his fingers in his dagger belt. "The prince must see this and speedily. Aye, perhaps I have brought Pharaoh some good out of Nubia after all and am no failure in his service."

5

Kamose, Commander of Chariots

The fleet of ships came into the quays before Thebes in mid-morning, Nereb's smaller vessel leading. Behind the city of the eastern bank stood the limestone cliffs, already faded from their early morning red-gold to a dull, whitish-brown overlaid with a gathering heat haze.

But it was Thebes itself that held the full attention of the party from Nubia. Semna was a great fort with its attendant administration courts, the villas of its officials. Elephantine, the Ivory Island, had been a fine sight. But this was Thebes, for centuries capital of Egypt. And to the men from the border, it was as unknown as the courts of the Minoans in the salt sea.

Soft fur brushed the underside of Rahotep's chin as the cub he held made a jealous bid for his attention. The captain was struggling not to reveal his wonder at the sight before him as a crewman tossed a mooring rope to the quayside and the *Shining in Thebes* was brought into her berth.

The larger troop vessels, which had joined them at

Elephantine, were maneuvering to land, the men crowding their decks, when there was a stir ashore. Merchants gathered up their wares and hastily pulled back from the road, hearing a shouting from the town, the scurrying of burdened work slaves.

Two spearmen, their heavy pikes at carry, their shields between their shoulders, came as outrunners, and behind them was a light chariot, the stallion that drew it snorting impatiently as the driver kept him to a trot. It was clearly a war chariot. Strapped to the sides of the light equipage were cases of arrows, and a standard pole was mounted beside the young man who stood on a swaying platform, his body weaving expertly to balance against the movement of his unsteady flooring.

A company of spearmen, which Rahotep was forced to approve, followed at a steady lope. They had neither the height nor the heavier build of his archers, but any officer could appreciate that these were seasoned fighting men. Did they represent a picked corps, the well-trained personal guard of a high ranking commander, or were they representative of Sekenenre's whole force? If the latter were true—the captain's excitement grew—Out of Thebes hundreds of years earlier had poured such a force under Sesostris, the conqueror of Nubia, the subduer of Kush. If another Sesostris had arisen here—!

The chariot came to a stop at the end of the dock, and one of the spearmen darted forward to grasp the reins the officer tossed him. Nereb had leaped ashore and gone to meet the newcomer, but the impatience of the latter was such that that meeting occurred halfway down the quay.

As the young charioteer's head moved, Rahotep saw a wide strip of patterned linen drooping from the side of his headband. And he did not need to witness Nereb's low obeisance, the prostrations of the commoners along the dock, to know that this was one of the royal princes.

But it was a prince impatient of ceremony, for his staff of rank touched Nereb's shoulder, excusing the ceremonial greeting, and it was apparent he was asking a flood of questions. Then he looked to the *Shining in Thebes*.

Rahotep was ready. His archers were drawn up in a line behind him, Kheti a little to the left. And at the rattle of his sistrum they gave their native salute, the deep-throated roar of their war cry carrying across the river, into the town, until the buzz of life there stilled for an instant in wonder.

Then Rahotep made his own salute, echoed by Kheti and Methen. And he waited with bent head for acknowledgment. It came quickly, called across the short space between deck and shore.

"You are seen, Captain!"

He straightened to face the prince. Seen so closely the Royal Son was younger, younger and somehow frailer than he had seemed when in command of his chariot. He might be Rahotep's age, or perhaps a year or two older. His thin young body moved tautly, almost awkwardly, as if he had to force it to his will. The flesh on his face was close to the delicate bone structure, but his eyes were intent, old, measuring, as he surveyed the men from Nubia.

Those eyes examined the line of archers, weighing, speculating—as if each man was checked, assayed, and fitted into some pattern known to their new commander alone. Rahotep was certain that not a single foreign detail had been missed—that the size of those bows and the lean fitness of the men who bore them had been noted. And when that stare reached him, he braced himself to meet it unmoved.

"These are Border Scouts, Captain?" The clipped northern speech was spare and to the point.

"They are, Royal Son. All veterans in that service."

"We have heard of the Scouts." That was a quiet, almost colorless statement, but it warmed Rahotep. His men were accepted with the recognition they should and did merit.

"You will remain unattached until Pharaoh commands you—"

Rahotep could not allow his instant disappointment to show. So they were not yet accepted into the army after all. It would depend upon Pharaoh's decision. And his thoughts went on to practical matters—where could they find quarters in the city when they had no official standing? Or should they remain on the ship? But he continued to stand at attention with his men while the prince spoke to Nereb, then moved on to inspect the regiments now disembarking from the ships of the southern nomes.

Rahotep dismissed his men before he spoke to Methen. "So we are not after all in the service of Pharaoh," he broke out hotly. "These northerners perhaps class us with the barbarian Kush—"

"Hold your tongue!" Methen bade him as sharply as he had a decade earlier when he had been putting a boy hardly out of the Women's Hall through his training. "Our Lord uses his tools handily. You have not been passed over—to the contrary, you will appear before Pharaoh personally—a great honor. That was Prince Kamose, the Royal Heir, and the commander of the right wing of the army. And has he not said that you shall rest under the orders of Pharaoh? Walk carefully, Rahotep. There were dangers in plenty in Semna—there may be more waiting in Thebes for the unwary."

"Prince Kamose knows men when he sets his eyes upon them, Lord," Kheti agreed. "He is no fortress soldier, but one who runs with his men in the wastes. There shall be work for bows, spears, and axes, for those who march at his heels." His head up, he sniffed at the mixed smells from the shore. "All towns are alike, save that some are bigger or older than others. I shall keep a close eye upon these archers, Lord, lest they plan to go exploring for the reason of tasting strange beer or some such foolishness. Do we remain on this ship?"

The problem of their immediate quarters was solved when Nereb returned to the ship with the information that they were to be guests in his father's house until Pharaoh signified their future. So, with slave porters bearing their limited baggage, they marched through the crowded ways about the dockside of Thebes out into the wider avenues and so at length to the walled city homes of the nobles.

Though he was used to the simplicity of the frontier forts, Rahotep had been reared in the luxury of the Viceroy's palace in Nubia. And from the tales of his mother's servants, from the nostalgic reminiscenses of Hentre and Methen, he had built up a picture of the old northern capital that had led him to believe that Semna itself was as a Kush village when compared to Thebes. But reality erred from that picture. There was the setting of wealth, of fine and easy living, but it was only a setting. The jewels it had been fashioned to display were gone. Thebes was shabby, old, a beggarman of cities, shadow capital of a ravished land. And Rahotep, seeing the holes in the time-worn fabric, was as disconcerted as he had been at Prince Kamose's reception of his archers. The wealth of Egypt had been sucked north to the treasure houses of the invaders. There were only remnants left for her own people.

Just as Thebes was a shadow capital, so was Nereb's father a shadow officer of its rule. Sa-Nekluft, Treasurer of the North, Fanbearer on the right hand of Pharaoh, occupied an office without power or duties—for northern Egypt was enemy held and there was no tribute to be reckoned in its treasury, no business to transact in its judgment hall. Yet the very fact that Sa-Nekluft had his skeleton organization argued that time might work on their side once more and the Red House of the north rise beside the White of the south.

The porter admitted them to the outer court with a salute to Nereb, and they found themselves in a garden. Sa-Nekluft's duties kept him in Thebes, but his house was that of a country nomarch. Trees grew in circular beds of watered earth, vines looped in trellises, and fronting them on the other side of a long pool were the two-storied central chambers with a high-roofed veranda extending out toward the water. Thebes was a caldron of baking heat under the sun, but here was an oasis of coolness.

There were bright rugs on the walls between the carved and painted pillars supporting the veranda roof, and the sides of the pool had been cleverly painted above the water line with reeds and dragonflies. The scent of flowers was in the air, and the noises of the city were so faint beyond the high walls that one could almost forget it existed.

A young gazelle picked a delicate path toward them, its wide eyes curious, and a dog-faced baboon, eating a date, made an indelicate comment and hurled the stone with such accuracy that it struck upon Kheti's quiver. Whereupon the baboon screamed in triumph and went to all fours in a victory dance.

The leopard cub, thoroughly aroused by such bad manners, spat and struggled in Rahotep's grip, eager to avenge the indignity upon an old enemy of his tribe. The captain had to use his cloak to bag the fighter for his own protection.

"Belikae!"

The baboon paused, its head turned over its shoulder to survey—a little apprehensively—the man coming along the edge of the pool. Then Nereb strode forward, going down on one knee, bowing his head beneath the sign the other sketched with his hand, before he rose and they embraced as close kinsmen.

"My lord"—Nereb beckoned to the Nubian party—"may I bring before you the Commander Methen, once Captain of the Striking Hawk, the Captain Rahotep, leader of Desert Scouts and son to the Viceroy of Nubia that was, and the worthy Kheti, Leader of Ten among the Scouts, also those archers who have pledged themselves to the service of Pharaoh in the sight of Amon-Re—"

The Nubian force saluted. Sa-Nekluft smiled, making quick acknowledgment of their deference.

"To the Commander Methen, the Captain Rahotep, and those of their company, welcome, three times welcome! It has been long since those of the south have come to serve under Pharaoh in this city. But neither has it been forgotten how well they served in the past! This roof is your roof as long as you have need—"

He clapped his hands and gave swift orders to the serving man who answered. The archers were to be quartered with his own guard, and Kheti was introduced to his officers, while Rahotep and Methen were accorded the welcome of honored guests.

Though the magnificence about him might be faded, the appearance of wealth but a slicking of paint across sun-dried and powdery wood, yet Rahotep was ill at ease as he rummaged through his chest of possessions, hunting for the best of his limited changes of apparel. His single piece of "gold of valor," granted him on the occasion of a successful border foray the year before, was a cuff bracelet, a plain band of gold with the figures of lions raised above a background of minute bits of dark blue lapis lazuli. And he could wear the twin upper armlets of his rank, simple gold rings inset with the hawk of his mother's family in green malachite.

But for the rest he had only a warrior's dress, not even the transparent overskirt of a nobleman. Well, what was he but a warrior? He would proclaim his calling openly. But he took care in donning the finely pleated kilt of linen, the cross belts for the upper body, and in adjusting his sphinx headcloth with determination that its ends lie smooth and even on his shoulders. A last searching examination of his person in the bronze mirror showed him a figure fit to appear at a military inspection, if not in the company of noble feasters.

Though the last buckle was clasped, the last stiff fold in place, Rahotep still lingered in the guest chamber, reluctant to venture out into the bustle of the great hall where Sa-Nekluft was entertaining. Had the captain been sent directly to the barracks, he would have been far happier. But to plunge so directly into a life of which he knew very little, of which, in the person of Unis, he knew little good, was an ordeal that awakened in him those same uneasy symptoms he experienced before a dawn attack. And because he recognized those, he moved to attack—or rather to face those in the great hall.

Luckily he counted of low rank among the present assembly, and as such, he would not be given one of the seats of honor with his host at the upper end. He hesitated a moment in the doorway, trying to mark down some seating mat behind a pillar or in a corner from which he could spy out the land and yet not be noted. But he was not to escape so easily, for Nereb appeared out of nowhere to hail him.

After one swift glance at the northern officer's dress, Rahotep felt more keenly than ever the pinch of his own poverty, for the Theban wore not only a gold circlet of rank binding in his ceremonial wig, but a wide collar, armlets, and belt ax, all gold and gem-set. On the other hand, his kilt was the short one of a field soldier, though its front lappet was ornamented.

"Captain, General Amony has come and would speak with you."

With a swallowed sigh Rahotep followed the other on a path threaded between occupied seat mats to the upper end of the hall, where the stools of lesser nobles and the high chairs of the chief guests stood in an irregular half circle, each with a small table loaded with delicacies to hand.

In passing, Rahotep marked Methen seated on a stool and deep in talk with an older man in the dresss of an Amon priest and an even older one with the look of an administrator-scribe. Then they reached the high seats, and Rahotep bowed to Sa-Nekluft. Beside the treasurer sat a thick-bodied man with a width of shoulder almost that of a Kush warrior. His short soldier's wig was crowned with the circlet of a general, and his arms and chest glittered with what could only be gold of valor, since the bee and lion designs were repeated over and over in bracelets, armlets, pectoral, collar, ax, and belt. He was holding a goblet as the two young men advanced, and he did not put it down but surveyed Rahotep levelly over its rim as he drank.

He smacked his lips as he held it empty. "Truly drawn from the jars of the gods, Lord Treasurer. A mouthful of that washes away all dust of the road. So—this is your archer?"

Since he had not yet been named to the general, Rahotep stood to attention, looking beyond the man to the carpet stretched across the wall behind him. But he knew that he was being examined from head to foot and back again critically, and he willed himself not to flush under that cool evaluation, which was more searching—and perhaps more hostile—than that he had met from the prince that morning.

"Present him!" The order came as a growl, and Rahotep dared not relax outwardly, though he knew a tiny thrill within. The general was accepting him as an officer of the forces, no matter that his rank was humble.

"The Captain Rahotep of the Desert Scouts, out of Nubia, General."

Nereb obediently made the introduction, and Rahotep saluted with palms at knee level.

"Nubia," the general repeated thoughtfully. "Frontier service against the Kush, Captain?"

"Aye, lord."

"Fal-Falm, Khoris, Sebra, Kah-hi—" That listing of forts came as a volley of arrows, and Rahotep replied as quickly, masking his amazement that a general in Thebes would be able to name such obscure frontier posts.

"Fal-Falm, Lord, and Kah-hi—"

"Nereb tells me that you have brought a detachment of your men with you—"

Now Rahotep did flush, forced to admit to one who commanded his thousands the smallness of his own force. "Ten only, Lord—and my Leader of Ten—they are all volunteers from Kah-hi—seasoned trackers and Scouts."

"Aye." The general was frowning. "That was a bad business, Sa-Nekluft, the naming of regiments in that order."

The Treasurer of the North nodded. "They *would* consult the old rolls in spite of all advice—"

General Amony snorted with the contempt of a man of action for bureaucratic officials. "Pen fighters! Everything must be done as always it has been!" He clasped the goblet, which he had been turning in his fingers, down on his table, and a serving man hurried to fill it. "So because they consult old lists we lack men. But"—he took up the staff of office lying across his knees and tapped the palm of his left hand with its lion head—"'the power of righteousness is that it endures.'" Then his fleshy lips shaped a smile. "Surprised, Captain, to hear a warrior quote the Great Elder? But it is true. And this time when the Flail is lifted in battle, it will take more than the mistakes of scribes to hold back our chariots and the arms of our bowmen. Also I do not think we shall ever get three regiments from Nubia unless we pluck them forth with our own fingers! There is mischief brewing there—" His eyes, under their heavy, drooping lids, were intent upon Rahotep with the fixity of an inquisitor.

"You are Ptahhotep's son, Captain?"

"His second son, Lord, not his heir."

"So—well, I knew your grandfather, the Hawk, well. We were shield brothers when we were in the House of Captains as lads. He was first a warrior, and his last stand against the Hyksos has made a tale of valor for the camps to sing. He would look with favor upon a grandson who was a soldier on the Kush frontier and has now taken service with Pharaoh. To my mind he has left you a good heritage, boy."

Rahotep understood. The burly Amony was not referring to the vanished nome where his grandfather had ruled, but to the blood in his veins, the determination that had held him to his duties at Kah-hi in exile. It was the same kind of determination that had led the Hawk to struggle—if hopelessly—against the invader.

"He revolted too soon." Amony now gazed down the hall as if he saw not feasting but a sight far more grim. "But when that Hyksos lordling made a southern journey and demanded the Lady Tuya for his House of Women, then did Re-Hesy call out his men and raise the battle standard. He was crushed as millet is crushed in the grinder—too soon. Now those serpents have ruled in peace so long that they grow fat and sluggish, lolling in their high seats undisturbed, counting out their tribute tallies unquestioned, pinching out the lives of men between thumb and forefinger, bringing the blood and defilement of their devil god into sacred places."

"To all things there comes an end in the chosen time," Sa-Nekluft broke in. "Egypt has lain under shadows before and arisen mightier than ever."

Amony nodded, his hand going out once more to the waiting goblet.

"Captain"—there was dismissal in his tone—"I would see more of these archers of yours, but this is not the hour for the display of skill such as Nereb has described to me. We can use you—of that there is no doubt. And to the Hawk's daughter's son—!" He raised his goblet to his lips, and Rahotep seized hurriedly upon another Nereb handed him to return the toast.

"To the Lord General," he murmured as the tartness of the liquid spilled across his tongue.

Somehow he took the proper two steps backward without stumbling over any mat or bringing up against a stool, and then he was glad when Nereb steered him to the left, where, behind some pillars that provided an effective screen from their elders, he was brought into a gathering of nobles and officers closer to him in age and not so far above him in rank. Had he not been sponsored by a commander of Prince Kamose's guard, he wondered if he would have met such ready acceptance in that group where clothing and arms so far outshone his own. But it seemed that here also Nubia was a magic password, and while some of the brightly clad courtiers were seemingly bored by the military talk of the officers, there were three or four who ringed Rahotep in, questioning him about frontier warfare and the methods of Kush raiding.

"Barbarians," commented one of the nobles scornfully. His already large eyes were rimmed with malachite, and his beringed fingers smoothed his transparent shoulder cloak into the proper folds whenever he moved and dislodged their careful display, "Savages—"

"But fighters!" Nereb corrected as he clapped his hands to summon a servant with food for Rahotep and himself. One of the officers leaned forward to address the captain.

"Your men are all archers? And their bows are of unusual size. What is their far range—"

Nereb laughed and cut in before Rahotep could

answer. "Would you know more than our lord, Seker? The captain and his command have not yet appeared before Pharaoh."

"War—always battle and the range of spears, the massing of chariots," cut in the young man who had commented upon the barbarian Kush. "This is a feast and not the barracks of the guard. And what is that?"

He pointed so dramatically at a spot halfway down the hall that all the group followed the line of his finger with their eyes. Something small and black, almost a blot of shadow, had detached itself from a pillar and was making its way determinedly among the clusters of occupied mats in a series of small rushes, crouching low at each halt.

Rahotep got to his feet even as a lady leaned forward, her lotus wreath drooping askew from her wig, to investigate the creature that had at that moment taken refuge in the lee of her somewhat substantial person. She reached out a plump hand with an exaggerated coo of delight and then gave a small shriek, which was neither coy nor affected, as Rahotep closed the distance between them in a few desert-trained strides.

He scooped up the leopard cub and made his apologies and explanations to the lady. She sucked a slightly clawed finger and smiled up at him, after a frank appraisal of his person, accepting his words with a very gracious smile, which faded quickly when he bowed himself away, the cub in his arms, now padding a playful paw at his dangling throat amulet.

The young men hailed the captain's return with amusement and would have passed the cub from hand to hand, but, as usual, he snarled and swiped out warningly with unsheathed claws. Rahotep excused himself.

"Bis must be returned to safe keeping. He is not yet mannered well enough for company."

But when the captain passed into the corridor leading to his room, he was in no hurry to finish his errand. The warring scents within the hall, the chatter and drone of many voices, the strangeness of the company, made him restless. Still holding Bis, he went on into the garden,

74

busied in trying to sort out his impressions of the crowded day. When a low voice addressed him from behind, he reverted to frontier alertness and spun to one side in a half crouch, his dagger ready in his hand.

There was a dry chuckle from the man who had hailed him.

"I assure you, Captain Rahotep, I am no assassin. Rather am I messenger. You are summoned—"

"By whom and to where?" Rahotep countered. He was flustered, but he did not want the other to guess that.

"By one who has the right to command all within the boundaries of the Two Lands!" The note of humor had gone out of that voice now. "Come at once, Captain."

6

Eyes and Ears for Pharaoh

"Cover yourself, the head also!"

A hooded traveler's cloak of the desert country was held out to Rahotep. But he was not ready to be so easily ordered about by a stranger. With Bis purring against him, he did not take the covering, but asked again, "Where do I go? I do not follow a no-name so quickly. In whose service are you?"

The other clicked his tongue impatiently. He stood, as Rahotep had already noted, carefully in the half shadow, out of the full beam of the door torch. But now he held his hand palm up into the light, and on that palm lay a flat seal. Rahotep bent his head to see it closer. There was no mistaking the curve of the royal cartouche—Pharaoh's messenger—though why he should be so stealthily summoned after this fashion, the captain could not understand.

"I must return Bis to my quarters first—"

But the messenger flung the cloak about Rahotep's shoulders. "You will have to bring the beast with you.

There is no time, and we must not be seen leaving, boy! Come!" His grip closed about the captain's arm and tightened, urging him toward the wall. Reluctantly Rahotep obeyed.

They came to a smaller gate half hidden behind a row of bushes and so out into a narrow lane. A chariot waited there, with a man, who wore a servant's waistcloth but bore himself as a warrior, holding the reins, while a companion nursed a traveler's torch.

Rahotep's guide jumped to the floor of the vehicle, and the captain at his gesture followed a little gingerly. It was a bit like standing on one of the reed rafts used for bird hunting in the river marshes, he decided, bracing his body against the sway of the plaited floor as the groom sprang away and the driver loosened rein. The groom and the torch bearer sprinted ahead as Rahotep's companion handled the nose ropes skillfully, bowling along between the blind outer walls of the noble houses of the quarter. Rahotep knew so little of the city that he could not guess in which direction they were heading. But if he was indeed obeying a royal summons, and no one would dare to use the Pharaoh's seal except by his order, then they should leave Thebes altogether for the country beyond.

Though the princes of Thebes were lacking in the wealth of their ancestors, when Sekenenre's father had assumed the throne with hope for his country's freedom, he had followed the ancient custom and had erected his own royal dwelling palace beyond the old town. His son, confirmed now in the semidivine rule, still lived there, but in time would build for himself another House of the Two Doors.

Rahotep was right in his guess at their destination, for they were outside the city. The driver let out the horse in a dash, which made the captain shut his teeth hard and close a fist about the side of the chariot bucket. Ahead was a dark bulk of building with a trace of lamplight showing faintly through window lattices. But they did not head for that. The chariot swerved, bearing toward the east in a sweep, which took them behind the building to a length of wall over which dropped the long leaves of palms.

A groom sprang from an angle of the wall to catch the reins, and the driver dismounted, jerking Rahotep's cloak in a silent signal to accompany him. They were before a postern gate, and a figure stood there holding a small lamp in one hand and shielding its fluttering flame with the other. Rahotep saw it was a woman and, by the glint of jewelry at her throat and wrist, no common servant.

She edged back, her lamp a beacon to bring them on, and then the door curtain fell behind them and they were in what Rahotep judged to be a garden. The lamp flitted ahead, and they paced single file behind it to a house. Then they were in a corridor with painted walls and a score of lamps to light it.

The woman who had guided them was of middle age, her elaborately curled wig encircled by a band of gold ribbon. As she moved, double ankle rings set with inlays of dragonflies in light green chimed faintly together. A fan hung from a cord about one wrist, and Rahotep's eyes widened, remembering his mother's stories. This could be no other than one of the senior ladies of the court, a fanbearer to one of the Royal Wives, or to one of the Royal Daughters! But why—

He studied the details of the corridor down which he walked. A painting of flowers in a garden with delicate winged butterflies at play over them caught light from the lamps. The lady reached a door at the far end and turned to face Rahotep and his companion, a critical gleam in her eyes. Rahotep's guide pulled the cloak from the young man's shoulders and pointed to the captain's sandals with a swift motion.

Rahotep kicked his toes free of the thongs. One did not wear foot covering into the presence of a superior. Bis moved in his hold, and he looked down at the cub in perplexity. If he left the small feline here, it might wander into the garden and be lost. But if he was going to an audience with Pharaoh, dare he take the cub with him?

The lady waved them on. Rahotep tried to fit the squirming cub tight against his side and hoped for the best.

He ducked beneath the door curtain and stood in a miniature copy of a great hall. The same dividing pillars, the same wall coverings, the same high seat dais at the far end as could be found in all noble houses, yet this one was both richer and on a smaller scale than any he had seen. And noting the serving maid adding fuel to the pottery brazier in the floor, the other girls standing in attendance about the group at the high seat, he halted with a sudden sense of foreboding. He was in the Women's Hall of some great noble—or could it be the House of the Royal Ladies?

Fully alert, he used a Scout's eye to catalogue the room and the people in it.

As yet it appeared that he went unnoticed, and he had those few moments for a quick survey. The two chairs before the end wall hanging were both occupied. And, as he caught sight of the blue-green sheen of the Vulture Crown on the elder woman, Rahotep bit his lower lip. One of the queens—Teti-Sheri the Royal Mother, or Ah-Hetpe the Royal Wife?

He was able to see them better as he advanced a step or two. She of the Vulture Crown must undoubtedly be the Queen Teti-Sheri, while the other, leaning over to move a piece on the Senit board, was much younger. A fragile circlet of gold wires studded with tiny blue and white gem flowers caught together with inlaid lotus blossoms held in place the long locks of her own wavy hair. Yet there was such a marked kinship between the finely cut features of both women that their blood relationship was plainly close.

The flower-crowned royal lady made her move and laughed, lifting her forefinger in a concede-defeat sign to the boy hunched over the board as her opponent. His sturdy body was in contrast to the willowy elegance of the ladies, for he had the broad shoulders, the stocky build of a wrestler. And his face, now expressing concentration as he looked upon the spindles of his board army, was not handsome, for his upper teeth projected slightly, raising his lip, and his nose was broader and lacked the straight line seen in both feminine faces.

But Rahotep had very little time to study the party as the lady who had led them to the hall moved swiftly toward the queens, where she "kissed dust" in the ancient form.

The Queen Teti-Sheri straightened in the embrace of the cushions that filled her chair. And Rahotep went down in the full obeisance in his turn as those keen eyes, rendered larger by the darkened lids and corner lines, fastened on him. He crouched on the pavement and then gave a little gasp as Bis broke from his nervous grasp, flopped on the floor, and eluded, with his usual speed and grace, the wild grab the captain made in his direction.

The younger royal lady laughed again, but there was no mockery in that amusement. Rather it was an invitation to them all to join in her fun. Rahotep, scarlet under his weather-browning, heard the tread of feet but dared not look up to see who was approaching.

"Rise, kinsman!" It was a deep young voice, richly masculine, that gave that order, and he felt the tap of an honor stick on his shoulder. His head went up to see that the boy from the Senit table stood there smiling.

And, strangest of all, Bis, who steadfastly refused to show any friendship with any human other than the captain, who rubbing catlike on the other's ankles. Then Rahotep noted the prince's tassel on the band confining the other's thick brown curls and knew this to be Ahmose, the younger of the Pharaoh's sons.

Rahotep arose, astonished, as the sense of the other's greeting words struck home. And he moved shyly behind the prince to the queens.

The Royal Mother Teti-Sheri was watching him eagerly, studying his face as if she sought there some feature she had once known.

"So you are son to Tuya." She motioned him further forward when he paused at the proper distance. And then, noting his bewilderment, she explained. "Did you not know that the Lady Tuya was reckoned among our household when she was but a little maid? How else should it be when the Lady Heptephaas of the royal line was her mother? Ah, that was in the dark days when no man knew whether he would live from the Coming of Re in the morning to His Departure at night. The Hawk made a marriage for Tuya with the Viceroy of Nubia for her safety, for a prince of the Hyksos looked upon her and finding her fair, demanded her for his House of Women. So she departed from us—and we wept—" Her words fell into silence like the fading note of a silver-stringed harp.

Rahotep's hands tightened behind his back. Never had his mother mentioned life at the court of Thebes. Had that been because she dared not let herself remember—in a house where the Lady Meri-Mut ruled—a happier day? Looking now upon the Royal Mother, the captain did not doubt that her household was far different from that of his father's half-Nubian First Wife's.

"Tell me of Nubia, son of Tuya!" The Queen was alert again, and as Rahotep hesitated, not knowing whether she wanted to hear of his mother's unhappy life there or of the land itself, she prodded him into speech with a skillful question. So that, as time measured by the water-jar clock dripped away, he realized she was wringing out of him information he had not even known that he possessed, squeezing him dry as a man squeezes dry a grape skin.

And, gathering confidence because he did know those answers, he dared to glance once or twice beyond the Royal Mother's chair. A rug hung against the wall there, but now and then it stirred slightly as if it did not cover wall but some alcove or doorway. And he was convinced that while the Queen Teti-Sheri, the Royal Wife Ah-Hetpe, and the Prince Ahmose listened to him openly, there was another listener behind that rug and that he spoke to a larger company than he saw.

"This Prince Teti—would he raise his own standard?" asked the Royal Mother.

"It is so rumored, Royal Lady. But rumors are not always rooted in the truth."

She smiled. "You are cautious, Captain. It is a good trait in one so young. The Prince Kamose had heard tales of the skill of your archers. It is likely that they shall be asked to display that same skill before our Lord. Meanwhile, know this, child—the favor that was Tuya's is also her son's. Now bring me this Nubian leopard which the Horus Hawk showed you"—for that story, also, she had had out of him. "I would see him the closer."

Her change from the exacting inquisitor to the gracious lady was so sudden that Rahotep blinked, but he obediently looked about him for Bis. Then he started. The leopard cub was installed under the chair of the Royal Wife and he was very much engaged. By some means known only to himself, Bis had stolen a section of roasted pigeon from a small table laden with delicacies. And this he was devouring with great gusto and dispatch.

Ahmose, following Rahotep's horrified gaze, broke into laughter. His mother, startled, leaned over the arm of her chair, striving to see what they were all looking at.

Teti-Sheri echoed her grandson's mirth. "A thief in the palace! A looting warrior!" She stooped gracefully and snapped her flat fan against Ah-Hetpe's chair. Bis, clinging to his pigeon, backed out to where Rahotep could seize him. But when he would have pulled the remnant of bird away from the cub, the Queen Mother shook her head.

"Let the bold one keep what he has taken. A good omen for you, Captain. When the occasion warrants it, be as bold as Horus's gift, for the time has come for boldness and an end to lurking!" It seemed to Rahotep that her eyes went to the rug as if her words were meant as an encouragement to someone else also.

Shortly thereafter he was graciously dismissed, and his return to the house of Sa-Nekluft was engineered in the same manner as his earlier departure. If the treasurer or his son knew about that secret expedition, they said nothing, and Rahotep gathered, without its being told him, that the whole surprising episode was to be kept to himself. Later he found his way to Methen's room and, under the pretext of learning more about Theban life and the undercurrents to be found in the city, asked the veteran questions to build up a background into which he could fit the personages he had met that evening.

Methen·spoke of the Royal Mother with the deepest respect. As the Heiress she would have been queen whatever betided, but she had been queen in fact as well as in name. To her influence was attributed her husband's resistance to the Hyksos, and now her son's open rebellion. The Royal Wife Ah-Hetpe, her daughter, was of the same independent mind. Sekenenre, himself, though as yet untried in any great battle, had the foresight of an able administrator, and his son, the Prince Kamose, was a leader of value—

"And the Prince Ahmose?" questioned Rahotep.

For the first time Methen shook his head. "Ahmose is very young, unproven. It is rumored that he has petitioned Pharaoh for a command in the campaign. The Prince Kamose, as Royal Heir, is the one men look to for leadership."

But when Rahotep was stretched on his couch late that night he wondered. He had felt the impact of the Prince Kamose's personality there on the quay true enough. But there was something elusive in that Royal Son, a consuming fire within his slender body, as if he were a flame igniting a palm frond, burning fiercely, yet as quickly gone. But Ahmose was different, the same drive and purpose but on as solid a base as the young prince's stronger body. Kamose could fire men to victories, but he would waste himself cruelly in the process. Ahmose would set to battle methodically, as a man would follow a trail, and in the end the same victory would be his and he would still be fresh.

Rahotep swung his feet from the couch and sat up, staring into the dark. How he knew this, or why, he could not have explained. But in that moment he was certain that if he had any choice in the future, it would be to serve under Ahmose. And, as if he had made the necessary decision, he straightway found the sleep that had eluded him earlier.

The summons to assemble his men and march them to the field of warriors came early the next morning via Nereb. Since the heat of the day was such that the sun punished those laboring under it, any training must be held before Re's Boat was in mid-sky. The northern commander had put aside his dress uniform and appeared in the simple kilt of a field officer, marching beside Rahotep as a guide.

Yellow dust was churned up from the broad expanse of the level, sun-baked soil where chariots seesawed into line. The impatient stallions reared and squealed, and then, at the flash of their commander's baton, thundered across in a spearhead formation led by the vehicle of the Prince Kamose. Rahotep, watching that charge, could now well understand the downfall of Egyptian arms when such an advance had been turned on spearmen and bowmen by the Hyksos who had poured into the Two Lands generations earlier. But also he could estimate, with eyes narrowed against the sunlight, how a company of well-placed archers could deal havoc. A horse, even when galloping, was a larger target than a man. Pick off the horses and your chariots would crash and foul against each other. Your spearhead would crumple in upon itself.

Kheti's archer-wise eyes had marked that as quickly. "A volley from the right and left, Lord," he remarked, "and those wheels would cease to turn. Though I grant you they have speed, and the archers would have but a single chance and needs must be well placed to do it!"

Nereb turned to them with an intent look. "You both believe that your archers could break such a charge?" he half challenged.

"It is as Kheti has said. The ground must be right, the archers posted properly, and it must be well timed—there would only be an instant or two in which all would be just right. But—given those instants, aye, even a gang of Kush raiders could cause you trouble. Nubian bows have both the power and the range."

"You may have to make good that boast," warned the other.

"It is no boast, Lord," Rahotep returned. "I have seen Hori of my command drive an arrow clear through an oryx while it fled. And all of my men are proven marksmen."

85

Nereb left them to report to his superiors, and it seemed that they were not to have an early opportunity to prove their skill and so win formal admission to the ranks before them. The archers grew restless, grumbling in half whispers. And those whispers became pointed criticism at the performance of a company of bowmen using the shorter bow of the north and shooting at targets the Nubians viewed with open contempt. Only his presence, Rahotep knew, kept those comments from being voiced aloud.

He was heartily tired of breathing dust, baking in the sun, and standing without employment, when a runner dodged around a company of spearmen, to reach the Scout archers.

"Lord," he panted to the captain. "Pharaoh would look upon you—come!"

They followed the messenger at a jog trot in a zigzag path to avoid chariots and footmen, until they came up before a platform on which was a folding stool under a sun canopy. Two fanbearers kept the sultry air moving over the blue war helmet of the man who sat there. Captain and archers alike, they prostrated themselves before the Lord of the Two Lands.

"Pharaoh would see the power of your arms, Captain. Let your men fire at the targets." It was the Prince Kamose who advanced to relay the order. And Rahotep, not daring to look up at the face beneath that blue helmet, worked his way backward through the dust until it was permissible to rise and face the stuffed cowhide bags being set up on the range.

He frowned at the shortness of that range and, forgetting everything but the necessity of doing their best, waved the targets back and yet back again, though the men setting them were agitated at his gestures.

"Each man will fire in turn," he said to Kheti, "and then two volleys together upon signal."

"Even so, Lord," the other agreed and passed along the order.

One after another the Nubians stepped to the line, the

huge bows were bent, and arrows sang through the air, to be buried feather-deep in the hide targets. Kheti took his place, and, last of all, Rahotep, the silver bracer winking on his hand. Though his bow was less than these his men carried, it was made to the same pattern and his aim was as good.

Then, as one man, the archers drew into a level line, Kheti at one end, Rahotep at the other. The captain threw a quick glance along the line and then his lips shaped a whistle. Twelve arrows flew almost as one, and all twelve hit the targets. A hum of comment arose from the watching officers and men, but a messenger came from Pharaoh's platform.

"It is Pharaoh's will that you fire against moving targets now," the officer told Rahotep. "They shall release birds from a net. Let your men be ready."

What followed was much like the exhibition they had given Nereb on the Nile ship. None of the birds got across the field to freedom. And Rahotep was given orders to approach the platform once again. He stood with bowed head to hear the Lord of the Two Lands speak for the first time.

"It is pleasing that Captain Rahotep and his men be taken into our service. Let them be enrolled as Scouts attached to the troops of the Prince Kamose."

"Life! Prosperity! Health!" Rahotep voiced the conventional answer. "May the Son of Re live forever!"

He was turning over in his hands with a vast pride the new Captain's flail that had been presented to him, admiring the lion head on its butt, when a chariot pulled up in a puff of dust. Its driver, controlling the impatient horse with ease, leaned over the rail to call to Rahotep.

"Captain!"

He recognized Ahmose, the prince's broad face framed by a linen headdress as simple as his own but bearing the royal *uraeus*. He saluted with his newly won baton and hurried closer.

"Tomorrow we hunt lions in the desert strip. Since your men are noted Scouts, let them display their talents in that

87

manner—as well as they have shown their marksmanship here today." He smiled. "It is in my mind, Captain, to attach to my heels a cub like unto yours—if we can flush out any such. At any reckoning, we should have good sport—very good sport—" He spoke the last words slowly as if they might convey some double meaning. Then he released the reins and whirled away.

"That is a great lord, brother." Kheti had come up behind his commander. "A true warrior by his looks."

"That is the Prince Ahmose"—Rahotep corrected him with a hint of sharpness—"the younger of the Royal Sons."

"So?" Kheti watched the rapidly dwindling chariot across the training plain. "Well, still I say he is a warrior before he is an officer—or a Royal Son. What wished he of you, Lord?"

"That we go with him tomorrow for the hunting of lions. He desires to see our Scout craft—"

Kheti nodded. There was satisfaction in his tone as he replied: "And so he will, Lord. I trust that one may someday come into Nubia—for Teti will not find him an easy mouthful in any feasting! Aye, Scouts we shall be, and if any lions lie in this land, they shall come forth for his sport!"

The archers, now accepted into the royal command, were given a section of the barracks, a small side building opening on a court, which offered them semiprivacy. Rahotep and Kheti had a room to themselves, and the others spread their sleeping mats in a hall. This was infinitely better than their quarters at Kah-hi, and when they were supplied with good rubbing oil, excellent rations, and not called upon for immediate duty, they chanted their praises of this new life.

Hori produced one of the small hand drums of his people to mark time, and one after another the men joined in the warriors' dance, which was a part of their training, its body movements designed to keep a man both lithe and quick on his feet.

Then, as they flung themselves panting to earth, they were aware of a group of newcomers, some of the spear-armed infantry by their dress. They were escorting a taller man, his skin glistening with oil, only a brief cloth about his loins. Rahotep grinned, knowing well the reason for such an approach—the old challenge to be faced by any company new to a fort. And he glanced around to see Mereruka already rising to his feet, unbuckling his kilt belt, while his fellows sat up alertly, bringing out of their belt pouches small personal possessions that were good items for wagering. Having seen Mereruka in action, most of them indeed having served as his easily thrown wrestling partners, none of the Scouts had any doubt about the ability of their champion.

If these northerners thought their man fit to stand against a Scout, especially one whose skill had enabled his comrades to beggar most of the frontier posts of the Kush border, they had better take second and longer thoughts. With sighs of pure happiness the Nubians settled down to what they knew would be a profitable evening. Truly Dedun smiled upon them this day!

7

"Lion" Hunt

The hunting party set out from the barracks before dawn, in order to be well on its way before the full heat of the sun hit the desert lands. And for the second time Rahotep shared a chariot, holding on with one hand to the rim of the bucket as Nereb, at the reins, rocked them along in the wake of the prince's more resplendent vehicle. His men were pattering on ahead with the houndboys, having been given a good hour's start on the drivers.

"A bull of Min's temple herd was pulled down by lions this month," Nereb said between jolts. "There is a pair of young males seemingly without fear of man."

As Nereb spoke, Rahotep was assessing the equipment lashed to the sides of the chariots. Throwing spears—aye, a trained hunter used throwing spears against lions—and the bow case and quiver were also usual. But he continued to use his eyes and make no comments on the two shields that the pressure of Nereb's knees kept in a standing position before him. Nor had the captain missed the fact that Nereb's spearmen had padded off along with the houndboys earlier. They might be required as beaters, that was true. On the other hand, there was surely no need for them to perform that duty in complete battle array.

As the chariots made a turn from the Theban road onto a wide expanse of black baked clay, which, when flooded a month or so later, would be productive fields, Rahotep approached the subject indirectly.

"How far south do the Hyksos hold?"

"From a day's journey north of Thebes our people still pay tribute. But their first fortress is again a sunrise away. Twenty years ago Thebes loaded tribute ships and invader princes sat in government here—"

"You expelled them? Why did they not then return in force?"

Nereb smiled, an odd cold smile. "They did not go, they died. Their god turned his face from them and there was a plague. What man can raise bow or spear against the sickness that strikes between sunrise and sunset? Their king sent a message unto the Lord of Thebes saying he was awakened by the snorting of the hippopotami of the river and that we should clear our land of anything that displeased him. So with those who returned his governor's body to him, we sent also the hides of hippopotami. But it seemed that with those hides went also the curse of Amon-Re, for the sons of Set sickened and the plague struck into their ranks, though it did not harm those who obeyed the true gods. And fearing the illness, the barbarians made a decree to withdraw from the south until the danger was past. Only it seems that that time has not come yet. There are tales that in the lands of the Semitics there has been much trouble and that the King of the Hyksos needs must turn his attention to putting down rebellion there." Nereb shrugged. "It matters not how it has come about—plague, curse, or trouble beyond the rim of the world, but they have given us a space in which to set about the preparations for their undoing."

There were odd gaps in Nereb's story to Rahotep's mind, a certain evasiveness on some points. Also he noted that they were now traveling a northward route. But he shelved his suspicions when they came at last to a wide waste area where dried reed beds and papyrus thickets stood brittle and sere on the parched land. Smoke, black and thick, curled up from isolated points in a semicircle and moved slowly forward through the crackling reed forests, marking the advance of the beaters with their torches, the smell of which was designed to rout out any lion that was lying up after a good night's hunting.

The dogs, freed from their leashes, were yapping excitedly, their paths through the dead and dried wilderness marked by the wild waving of yellow reed crowns. There was a deep, coughing roar. Nereb had pulled the reins of his chariot horse about his waist as he would do in battle, leaving his hands free for the throwing spear he drew from its carrying thongs. Rahotep, a little uneasy as to marksmanship from his unsteady footing, selected an arrow and set it to bow cord.

Their chariot was to the left of that driven by the prince, and on the opposite side of Ahmose's position was a stranger to Rahotep, an older man in civilian dress who had a driver to manage his horse while he handled a short spear. By custom Ahmose would be allowed the first cast at any lion breaking between either chariot, and the prince had followed Nereb's example of reins about the waist, a war bow in his hands.

The horses had been well trained, holding their places without movement, their heads high, their ears pricked forward a little as if to catch any sound from the reeds. Again that cough, deep, resentful. And above it the yapping of highly excited dogs and shouts of men.

Papyrus plumes were agitated, snapping off as the smoke of the torches showed the path of the beaters. But there was no other sound from the aroused lion. Had they not known the habits of the beast, those waiting in the chariots might have been disastrously off guard when a tawny shape, magnificently maned, snarling with rage, burst through the last screen of dried herbage in a bound, which carried it between the chariot of the prince and the one in which the civilian balanced his spear.

93

A bowstring twanged sharply, and the lion came to earth in a smashing somersault, tearing at the brick-hard clay with frenzied claws.

"Ho!" They raised the cry of congratulation, and Ahmose, with a boy's glee—the very first really youthful gesture Rahotep had seen him make—waved his bow over his head, while two of the spearmen trotted forward with a rope to drag the trophy to where it could be skinned.

But the beaters had disturbed a second beast in the reed jungle. There was another roar, and then a flurry among the reeds. The yap of a dog became a scream of agony. Against all nature some lion must have turned at bay, refusing to be driven from its chosen place, and was now about to fight it out with the men on foot. Rahotep levered himself up an inch or two against the side of the chariot, striving to see more of the melee than just the wildly agitated reed tops.

Such dried-out land contained, as he well knew, traps. Hard as the sun cooked the earth's crust, there were places where some moisture lingered underneath. And anyone breaking through the flinty upper surface might well be engulfed in the mud beneath, entrapped past his own efforts to escape. Rahotep had seen a cow so caught once—until it had had to be killed because it could not be drawn forth. Intent upon a lion at bay, any one of the beaters might be so caught before he realized his danger.

The chariot horses were affected by the clamor, and both Nereb and the prince put aside their weapons to control the nervous animals. Ahmose's black reared with a scream of stallion rage until Rahotep feared for the safety of the light vehicle it drew. The prince was talking to it soothingly, his voice steady, as he gripped the reins with sure knowledge.

A shout arose from the reeds, and out of that dried morass shot a dun-brown streak, skidding almost under the feet of Nereb's horse, sending it plunging ahead. Rahotep's grasp on the rim of the bucket was broken with that jerk, and he fell backwards, landing on the ground with force as the chariot bowled away, the horse momentarily out of control.

Gasping, watching the sky spin dizzily from right to left and back again over his head, the young captain suddenly knew that he had not landed flat upon the earth after all, that under his shoulders something squirmed vigorously, squalling in rage and fear. Hardly knowing why, but with some dazed memory of past wrestling bouts in which he had striven so upon the ground, Rahotep threw himself over and flattened down that wriggling body, feeling coarse fur under his hands and the hot breath of a flesh eater upon his face.

He held on because he had to. Only so long as he kept those kicking limbs pinned to the ground could he hope to escape a wicked mauling from the claws. Luckily his captured beast was but little more than half grown, or he could not have held it for more than a moment past its initial surprise and panic.

The captain was holding on grimly when another form plunged through the dust. Rahotep sat up, coughing hollowly, his eyes streaming, as he made futile motions to rub them free of dust. Kheti's big hands, with the full weight of the Nubian's great strength, pinned the snarling young lion flat. He grinned at Rahotep through a mask of dust and sweat.

"Ha, brother, this is a catch! Somewhat larger than Bis, but of the same spirit. Did he mark you?"

Shaken, Rahotep inspected the damage. His kilt bore a ruffle of tatters down the thigh, but there was no mark on the skin beneath to overlay the older scar there. He had indeed been lucky, for it was well known that a lion's claws were unclean and the wounds dealt by them healed slowly and painfully, if at all.

Two of the spearmen came running up, a coarse net between them. And by the efforts of all four the lion was made captive just as the prince reached them on foot. He touched Rahotep on the shoulder, bringing the captain around to face him.

"Have you taken a hurt, kinsman?"

Rahotep laughed, a little unsteadily. "By the favor of Horus, no, Royal Son. And it seems that you have now the cub you wished to serve you. Nay"—he inspected the still writing body more closely—"more than a cub. If one taken so well grown can ever be tamed—"

"Never have I seen or heard of such a happening!" The concern faded from the prince's face. "It shot under the chariot close to the ground, and in the same moment you landed full upon it! Who would believe such a tale if he did not witness it with his own eyes? Truly you are one favored by some Great One—"

But they were not yet done with the hunt. Perhaps the vocal fury of the captive drew its companions from the reeds, or perhaps they only fled before the beaters. Two more tawny animals erupted from cover, another yearling cub and a lioness.

The cub ran straight, a flitting brown shadow, belly fur brushing the ground between leaps. But the female showed fight, speeding for the men clustered about the captive. There was no time for protocol of the hunt. Kheti's ax went up, a spear pointed—and both weapons struck home.

Ahmose drew a deep breath and stirred the now limp body with the toe of his sandal. Then he eyed the reed screen.

"It would seem that there is more than one surprise for us this day. But since even the favor of the Great Ones can wear thin in time if one stretches it too far, it would be well to be satisfied with one's luck to this point." He signaled for the groom to lead up his chariot.

"Nereb"—he hailed the other vehicle pounding up to join them—"so that red one of yours has answered at last to his nose reins? But then, I do not think even Moonrunner"—he drew his hand in open affection down the arching neck of his own horse—"would stand for a lion beneath his feet, a living lion, that is. You were prudent to stand aloof, Sebni." He spoke now to the civilian. "Horses and attacking lions do not love one another—"

The man in the third chariot smiled thinly. "So it would appear, Royal Son. And may I suggest that it would be well for you, Prince, to be more prudent—"

There was a chill in his tone that matched the thinness of

his smile. Rahotep eyed him covertly, surprised by the underlying note of disapproval in his speech. Could he be a tutor, attached by court custom to the prince's household? But surely Ahmose was of an age to claim, as a man and a warrior, freedom from such restraints.

Sebni, too, could not be old enough to have fostered the prince from infancy as the overseer of his household. Though it was difficult to judge the courtier's age, the man could not have been more than ten years older than the prince he served. And he was not the type to fit well among a fighting man's company—not with his fine robes and air of fastidious detachment. Who was he and what position did he hold that he accompanied Ahmose in a sport he could not find to his liking?

But as the houndboys, beaters, and the rest of the huntsmen drew in, Rahotep recalled earlier suspicions. This indeed was an over-manned party. The number of beaters was twice what was needed, and all of those he saw were seasoned fighting men. Only Sebni, his charioteer, and the groom and two runners who had trailed the civilian on the field were nonmilitary.

As he reclaimed his bow from the trampled dust, thankful to discover that that had not been a casualty of his mishap, Rahotep wondered anew at the purpose of the party. They had hunted lions, true enough. He flexed his bruised arm ruefully. He'd remember that hunt with a twinge in his healing shoulder for some days to come. But he couldn't escape the belief that the hunt was only a screen for something very different.

And he was sure of that when, instead of returning to Thebes with their trophies, the prince detached a runner to the nearest village to bring up men to take care of both dead lions and the captive until their return.

As they pushed on, still northward, Ahmose did not repost the beaters, or send men to quarter the reed beds. Midday and the heat found them in the lee of a ruined temple, and they sheltered from the sun in the nave of the sanctuary that had been despoiled by the Hyksos many years earlier. They had bread and onions, which were common field fare, along with a thin warm beer—such rations as might be served out on the march, but certainly not the usual food of the court. And Rahotep was not surprised to see that Sebni made a pretense of eating, but no pretense of enjoying the few bites he choked down, while the prince, on the other hand, munched away with the same hearty appetite as the archers and spearmen whose food he shared in equal portion.

The Nubian archers were trained to keep apart when they stretched out in strange surroundings to take what ease they could, their bows to hand, their belt axes turned so that they could be seized upon at the first alarm. Kheti nodded in one corner and at last snored peacefully. But Rahotep could not find any position that eased his bruises, and at last he gave up all efforts to rest and sat with his back against the wall, gazing toward the mutilated inner shrine, trying to reconstruct the place as it had once been.

Then his hand was on the hilt of his dagger, though he did not turn his head or breathe any faster. That faintest of sounds from the corner of the wall against which he rested was warning enough to one who had lain in spy outposts above a Kush hold. Someone was approaching from that direction and taking every precaution against sound—such stealthy creeping was a warning in itself. The captain moved away from the wall and brought his knee to the floor so he was half turned in a crouching posture to face the skulker.

But at first sight of the other he remained where he was. Ahmose, regarding the captain so ready on the defensive, blinked and then smiled. He beckoned with a finger, and Rahotep slid around the corner as the prince retreated, until they stood together in what had once been the inner sanctuary of the temple. Why the prince should take such a way to speak with him secretly, the captain did not know. But that it was of importance he did not doubt.

"Can you bring out your men without its being noted? Much depends upon leaving here unobserved—though I have those to cover our trail as best they can."

"That I can do, Royal Son," Rahotep replied confidently. He dared ask no questions as to why this was necessary.

Ahmose's smile grew wider. "We go to a task which, I think, will please you and your men well, kinsman. I had thought to take those of my own command, but now I would see how the Scouts work alone. However, we can only go unremarked—"

"By Sebni, Lord?" asked Rahotep.

"By Sebni!" The answer was delivered grimly, and the smile disappeared from the prince's full lips. "Be swift, Captain. Bring your men this way without notice if you can."

Rahotep flitted back to the group of archers. He knelt beside the nearest. As one hand slid over the man's mouth, his other tightened on the bowman's upper arm and shook it ever so slightly. Eyes opened, looked at him with quick consciousness, and Rahotep released the alerted man with a small gesture, so that the archer turned to arouse his next comrade after the same silent fashion.

The priests who had once served this forsaken temple had had their own private passages, a fact that Ahmose appeared to know. Almost, Rahotep thought, as if the Royal Son had made previous exploration here with some plan in mind. One by one, the archers stepped through a low door, bending nearly double, into a windowless, narrow space that must run between double walls, until they moved out into the sun through a square from which a block of stone had been recently removed.

Ahmose, himself, was the last through. And he moved briskly with little of the caution he had displayed inside the temple.

They had come out behind the building, well away from where the horses had been picketed and the chariots parked. To the captain's surprise, Ahmose made no move in that direction but, motioning them to follow, led the way directly from the temple toward the barren hills, which, with their yellow-brown walls, marked the end of cultivated land. They entered a gorge that cut back into the desert like the pointing finger of a hand, and there the prince met a man who arose out of the ground—or dodged into their path from behind the fallen rocks.

The newcomer wore only the twist of cloth that was the usual garb of a field worker, but he saluted Ahmose as if he were one of the prince's officers.

"They have gathered the horses by the river, Royal Son. There has been a delay in the coming of the ships—" He accented the word "delay" with a meaning laugh.

"What forces have they?"

"Fifty. Mostly slingers, a few bowmen—but only officers' chariots since they return by the river. They are picked men though, Lord, and not to be lightly challenged, for they are led by the Commander Horfui—I have seen him with my own eyes!"

"Fifty—and Horfui—" Ahmose drew his hand down his chin as one who is working upon a problem. Then he turned to the yet unenlightened Rahotep.

"They say that the archer Scouts not only hunt the desert for raiders, but that they like high odds when the sticks are tossed in the battle game. How be it, Captain? Dare we go up against fifty of the Hyksos under a commander who has won his gold of valor a hundred times over?"

Rahotep made an answer dictated by the belief he had had in this leader since his first meeting with Ahmose.

"Prince, I do not think that you go into this without a workable plan—"

The Royal Son nodded. Rahotep thought the prince understood his trust in him. He began to explain the ordering of a battle plan, squatting on his heels so that he could trace in the dust, with the end of his baton, a crude map.

"The Hyksos have come to gather their horses—those which are put out to pasture on the lands of those subject to them, to be fed and tended until they are needed. They have them here, at the wharf of the old nome. But the ships to take them north have been delayed. Should the horse lines be raided and as many driven off as possible, it would cause great difficulty. So—I think they shall be raided! And this very night. They will not expect trouble from the desert side, since their patrols make a curtain between the Two Lands and the Bwedanii, and to their minds there is no danger to be faced from us—" He said the last words with controlled anger. "Thus if we circle about, coming in upon them from the northeast after nightfall—"

Rahotep could grasp the possibilities. It was the sort of foray that suited the Nubians, not too many generations removed themselves from the activities of the Kush they had more recently fought to control. Cattle raiders, border thieves—they knew the tricks of old on both sides of the Pharaoh's law. And he caught fire from the complete confidence the prince displayed.

The small force circled out into the desert, striking away from the temple in an eastward line and then slowly turning back toward the river. Once in the line of march, Rahotep found himself being edged into command, the prince leaving to him the ordering of the Scouts. But Ahmose watched keen-eyed as the Nubians fell into action such as they had known hundreds of times before. He copied their loping stride, showing that while he was a master of chariots, he did not disdain the pace of the infantry.

It was after nightfall, and they had kept to a brisk pace that had covered ground when they saw the torches of the Hyksos' camp. The missing cargo ships had not yet arrived and the horse guard was still waiting with the herd picketed out in lines along the bank. The failure in transportation must be making problems for the enemy. They would have to feed the animals, keep them secure, and stand guard, though both the prince and his spy seemed certain that the Hyksos did not fear an Egyptian attack here.

The captain split his already small party into three. Kheti with three Scouts was to angle south and work his way up along the riverbank. His party had two purposes, to take care of any sentries who might be posted there, and to secure one of the torches that were fixed at the end of each picket line.

A second force with Rahotep himself in command, was to duplicate the same maneuver to the north, while the remainder of their party was to gather, as well as they could in the dark, all the dried grasses, reeds, and other combustibles they could lay hands upon, making up fire arrows ready for use.

Much of that journey on the riverbank had to be done on hands and knees or on the belly, serpent fashion. Rahotep hoped fiercely that the presence of the camp had frightened away any crocodile that might choose to rest along here. He had no desire to meet that death unaware. And he kept sniffing for the warning musky odor of the reptiles.

Instead he breathed in the strong smell of horses, a scent from cooking fires, which made him run his tongue across his lips enviously, and then the aroma of body oil warmed by flesh. At that moment Hori rose from beside him and threw himself forward. There was a queer little catch of breath, close to a sigh, out of the night, and Hori lowered a body carefully to the ground. The archer hissed a signal, and they moved on, Rahotep detouring about the form of the sentry who had never known from whence his death had come or why.

There were men passing up and down the picket lines, carrying hides of fodder to their charges. Most of them were Egyptians, slaves, he judged. He drew close to Hori, stripping off his headdress and his arms belt, pressing these into the archer's hand. The Nubians with their superior height and darker skin might be noted by any keen-eyed officer. But the captain would merely be another Egyptian laborer among all the rest.

Rahotep dodged into the edge of the lighted camp area, then walked forward at a slow pace, as if both sullen and weary, toward the last torch that burned nearest their lurking place. He dared not be furtive or hurry, and his palms were sweating as he worked the lighted brand from its pole holder, expecting any moment to be hailed. Then, holding it so close to him that it scorched his skin, with his body between it and the camp, he struck out once more for the dark, leaping for the dip in the ground from which he had emerged.

8

Pharaoh's Guardsmen

Arrows bearing tufts of flaming stuff arched in the air above the horse lines. The picketed animals went wild with fear, their terror fed by the shouts and excitement in the camp. Men milled about aimlessly for those first few moments of surprise, but a volley of shouted orders told Rahotep that an officer, or officers, was keeping his head with the steadiness of a veteran.

The raiders had only those first few moments, while the surprise had confused and immobilized the men by the river, in which to deliver their blow. But the archers went into action with the same practiced dispatch with which they would have handled a Kush village. Four of them kept those blazing arrows in flight; the rest infiltrated the picket lines.

They slashed at the restraining nose ropes of the horses with their daggers. And the ensuing confusion of freed and frightened animals added to the general uproar. Though he knew very little about the handling of horses, Rahotep snatched at a dangling rope and held on against the pull of the half-seen animal it had tethered. Luckily the horse was not a fighting stallion, and when the captain retreated into the night, it obeyed his tug readily enough.

In this noisy confusion his sistrum could not signal, so Rahotep threw back his head and, with the full force of his lungs, gave the eerie war cry of a desert raider, such a paean of victory as the Bwedanii voiced when sweeping over a caravan. Let the Hyksos believe that the desert rovers of the waste country had somehow broken through their patrols to raid.

Running, with the horse he had brought out of the camp thudding close beside him, the captain headed eastward to that pinnacle of rock they had earlier marked for a rallying point. And now, in the moonlight, he could see that it was no natural outcrop of stone, but a headless, battered figure, some memorial to that Egypt the invaders had tried to stamp into the dust.

Rahotep was not the only one to return with a horse. In spite of their awe of the animals, three of the archers, among them Kheti, had brought with them four-footed loot. And two of the figures coming in led a double catch. It was when one of them spoke that Rahotep knew him for the prince.

"We have stirred up a nest of scorpions—it is best that we leave it behind us with speed!"

The captain glanced back. Torches were flaming into life, and there were greater spots of illumination where some of the fire arrows must have ignited stores or fodder. A war horn blared out an imperative summons. They could see men assembling, armed and ready. Rahotep, wise in such attacks, spoke to Ahmose as if they were but fellow officers.

"Prince, if they think that we are Bwedanii, they will strike eastward and not to the south where they might cut us off. So let us first lay a trail in that direction—"

"So be it. But they will be eager to reclaim the horses, and those we need. They are worth more now to the forces of Pharaoh than all the gold of Nubia!"

"Only let us reach the desert sands, Royal Son, for in the

sand spoor may be more easily left to read falsely."

Ahmose was plainly reluctant to march out of their way, but the wisdom of the captain's argument could not be assailed. Only on one point did he remain firm.

"We have taken five mares—and those are above price, for the Hyksos will not trade mares or let them out of their hands if they can help it. Those must not be lost. The stallions are another matter, and also they are more difficult to lead."

"Prince." That was Kheti, respectful enough, yet with the experience of an accomplished raider to back his advice. "Let us muddle the trail a bit, and when we reach the right place where tracks can be hid, then let the mares be taken while we head on with the stallions. If they can smell out such a track as we shall leave for them, then they are indeed hounds of the Dark One and not men who can be slain with axes! And against the Dark One who can strive?"

So it was done. The moon was both a help and a hindrance, for, while it made clear their own road, it might also betray them to the hunters. Thus they laid a pattern intended to confuse, in spite of the need for haste, setting to use every bit of cover the country afforded—which was precious little—until they came to a line of irrigation ditches, now largely clay-bottomed gashes.

"Your road with the mares, Royal Son." Rahotep pointed to the nearest ditch. "A path may be worked from one to another which they cannot spy out with ease until Re gives morning light, and there are hours before that."

The prince laughed. "Well enough, Captain. How do we spearate? Amten and I can manage to lead two each, but we shall have to have at least one more man to take the last."

"Kakaw"—Rahotep told off the best of the trackers—"Ikui, Mereruka, Sahare—you are now men of the Royal Son and under his orders. Prince, I shall join you when we are sure we bring no trail of trouble behind us."

"See that you do join me, Captain!" That had the sharpness of an order. "This has been a good twisting of the sons of Set, but it is not to be a battle. Commander Horfui is no green young officer to be affrighted by a hail of arrows in the night. When he drives forth, it will be for the taking of heads—" Grimly he mentioned that notorious custom of the invaders, the mutilation of their prisoners, that the captives' hands and heads might be offered to their dark god in his shrine of abominations.

Having seen the prince's party turn southward by the net of ditches, Rahotep led his own men to the east, bringing with them the three stallions. Two of the horses, luckily, were young enough to manage easily, but the third was ready to cause trouble, trying twice to rear and stamp upon the man who held its rope. Only Kheti had the strength to handle it. The Nubian underofficer hissed to it, mimicking as best he could the sounds he had heard used by the army grooms as they hitched, unhitched, and cared for the chariot horses. Perhaps it was that which at last made the animal answer the pull of the rope. But as they started on a steady ground-covering lope toward the limestone cliffs and the eastward boundary of the Nile valley, it ran almost abreast of Kheti, as if it, too, could sense the pressure of their flight and was now willing to join in it voluntarily.

The sun was up before Rahotep, under the press of its heat, realized that in their hurried plans they had forgotten one important item—water. Each archer carried slung on his hip the small water bag of the frontiersman. But they had drawn upon those the day before with the belief that their contents could be renewed without difficulty. Now none contained more than a mouthful or two, warm, unappetizing, with the strong smell and flavor of the container. And if they combined it all, the supply could not suffice one of the horses. Any trade-route well of the desert would have its garrison. They must cut back to the bottom lands and the river and do it soon.

Kheti and Rahotep backtrailed for a space, climbing a hillock to look over the countryside. They sighted a detachment of warriors doggedly following the trail they had left, just as they had planned.

"Wah!" The Nubian gave credit where it was due. "They know the desert land, brother. See the pace they set."

"So now it is for us to spread wings and fly," commented his captain dryly. "Have you a magic for the growing of feathers, Kheti?"

The Nubian chuckled. "Nay, but a magic for the growing of new feet, as you shall see, brother. Let us go!"

They returned to find the Scouts slashing at their water bags with their daggers, having poured all the remaining liquid into one container. With the flatted pieces of hide they had the means of confusing their back trail—an old Kush trick. And only those who had fought against those wily raiders and knew all their methods would be able to guess what had been done.

In turn two archers formed a rear guard as the small party made a sharp turn to the south at the edge of a bare space where no prints would normally show. As they kept to the sand, those in the rear beat at the loose earth with their leather flaps, erasing the tracks.

And it seemed that their ruse was successful, for, though they had to slacken their pace for the sake of the horses now suffering from heat and lack of water, they saw no other signs of pursuit. If they could reach the river without any interference, their expedition could claim a clean victory.

Grueling hours went by. It was a long time later that the largest stallion's drooping head came up. He sniffed eagerly, his nostrils flaring red. Then he gave a high whinny and reared, tearing his lead rope from the astonished archer's grasp. And his fellows bucked and plunged until the men, in self-defense, had to free them.

"Water!" Kheti's voice was a hoarse croak, and they quickened their own pace, though there was no hope of retaking the now galloping animals.

They came down a cut in the limestone escarpment and saw that this was one of the places where the horny hills that walled the valley pinched in upon the bottom lands. The oily sunken stream of the Nile curled through baked mud flats less than a quarter of a mile away.

But they saw something else. A cluster of domed storehouses stood there, the harvest center of some nome. And back to back among these a party of bowmen were making a stand against odds. They were besieged by a small squadron of chariots, now driving in a ring about the buildings, while those who manned them used spears and arrows against the defenders. And so fast did that circle of vehicles move that it was a moment or two before Rahotep could see that there were only four of them, each with both a driver and a warrior.

One of the horses in that mad whirl gave an uncanny scream of pain and terror, and rose, pawing the air, the shaft of an arrow protruding from its barrel. It crashed back upon the chariot it drew, smashing the unfortunate driver in the wreckage. The warrior passenger sprang free at the last moment, just escaping by inches another form of death as a second Hyksos vehicle, unable to avoid the wreck, crashed into the crumpled chariot and still kicking horse.

There was a shout from the besieged bowmen. And two men who tried to crawl out of the tangle were shot. It would appear that the party by the storehouses was giving excellent account of itself. Only the enemy was about to receive reinforcements.

Those four chariots, which had pinned the bowmen down to their improvised fort, were but the scouts of a greater squadron. The drum of unshod hoofs on the baked clay, the rattle of turning wheels, the war cries of drivers and warriors, came like a roar from the north as another body of the Hyksos swept down, just as a scythe might slash across a field of ripe and ready grain.

The lead chariot had a standard planted in it from which whipped the coarse strands of a horsetail dyed black and red. And it was plain that the warrior in it, a throwing spear ready in his hand, was no common soldier of the host.

An arrow from the storehouses sheered off part of that flaunting plume. Two more horses in the charging line went crashing down, and one of those also fouled its right-hand neighbor in the bargain. But in return one of the archers reeled back with a spear in his shoulder.

The three stallions that had broken free from Rahotep's men came pounding across that end of the battle ground with but one thought—to reach the water beyond. And when one foolhardy charioteer attempted to drive between them and that water, they crashed him.

Rahotep's sistrum swung in a buzzing circle, and his men spread out in a gradually widening line. The chariots were now between them and the storehouses—they were beginning the same sort of encircling movement their scouts had used to keep the fugitive footmen pinned down. He glanced along the line of his own men. The range was great, almost beyond their best efforts. But to go farther into the plain was to ask to be ridden down before they had struck any sort of blow at all—as the Egyptians had been beaten in their first battles with these foes.

Arrows rested on bow cords. His line of archers was as steady as it had been before the Pharaoh two days earlier. The captain gave the order to fire. And the first shafts were still in the air as archers reached for their second. The rain of arrows clipped into the outer circle of chariots, bringing down both horses and men.

That sudden attack from a new direction came as a complete surprise, and the moving line of Hyksos tangled. It was then that their commander proved his worth. The chariot with the standard slewed around under the expert management of its driver and a shouted stream of orders sent men spreading out and away, breaking up the knot in which the arrows had been striking home.

Though they had now lost their initial advantage of surprise, the archer Scouts still possessed their training and their hard-won battle knowledge. Those by the storehouse were letting fly enough shafts to sting the enemy steadily from the other side.

There was one point in the Hyksos commander's favor—he cut off the party by the cliffs from the water they must have—he might even force them back into the desert lands for a distance they might not be able to retrace. Then the other party at the storehosue could be picked off with ease as their arrow supply was exhausted.

"Arrows?" Rahotep shot that demand at Kheti. He had some ten shafts left in his own quiver, but he knew that, in spite of his training and will to battle, he could not possibly equal the Nubians in the effectiveness of their shots.

"Eight!" "Five!" "Nine!" The count came back to him, man by man.

"Now if Dedun but smiles." Kheti bent his giant bow. "Let this fly straight, O Guardian of the Upper Ways and the Lower Paths!" His aim had no fault but that of ill luck, for the commander of the Hyksos was saved from death merely by the action of his horse. That animal swerved to avoid a broken chariot and Kheti's shaft went between the officer's outflung arm and his body, instead of into the flesh below the short ribs as intended.

Perhaps his leader's near escape disconcerted the driver, for the horse plunged forward in a mad dash straight for the waist-high wall that bounded a now barren threshing floor. And seeing no avoidance of a crash, the Hyksos officer leaped free, landing on hands and knees within the storehouse enclosure.

He was on his feet again with the litheness of a man well schooled to chances of battle, only to front a shorter, younger man half crouching behind the shelter of a shield, a mace swinging in his hand.

The Hyksos officer gripped a battle ax, though he had no shield, and his footwork was clever and quick. But he was not speedy enough to sidestep the rush that drove him away from the open space and the backing of his men, back toward the knot of the besieged.

Deprived of their leader, the enemy tried to re-form, to start the drive toward the cliffs and Rahotep's party. The drive began, and then it broke, for the Nubians held their fire until their captain's signal and then tore the air with a volley aimed breast high at the animals.

Men jumped or fell from the chariots; some gained their

feet to come on at a run, with ready slings and spears.

"Down!"

They had met that kind of warfare before. The line of bowmen fell to earth escaping the ragged shower of those mixed weapons. Rahotep winced as a sling stone struck the cliff wall and ricocheted against his tender shoulder. He dropped his bow; his dagger was out and ready, as were the belt axes of every second man along that line. Then they were on their feet, springing out to meet the rush of the Hyksos while the other four archers covered them, picking off attackers.

The captain saw a bearded face, a horn-set helmet, looming over him, and ducked to avoid the thrust of a spear, stabbing up almost from knee level under the other's guard. The man roared in sharp pain and dropped his spear, clasping his hands to his middle as he went down. Rahotep stumbled, recovered, and leaped to the right as he caught sight of another metal blade.

"Ho!" That was Kheti's shout. "Back, brothers, back with you!"

Rahotep retreated with the others, their weapons to the fore, as snarling leopards might retreat to gather distance for another spring. Over them whistled arrows.

Three of the attackers were down and still. A fourth drew himself along by his hands, his legs trailing behind him. Two more pitched to the ground under the volley Kheti had directed. There were shouts, but the Hyksos drew back. The savage fury of the Nubians in battle was new to them.

Archer and spearman glared at each other across the black earth beaten into dust by their trampling. For the moment their own portion of the fight comprised the whole world. But they were shaken out of that preoccupation by the skirl of the same commanding horn Rahotep had heard sound in the horse camp. And, startled by the urgency of that call, he looked up—to see a haze of dust in the south and, through its curtain, horses coming at a gallop.

His first flare of despair changed to wonder and then to

a warm rush of exultation as he sighted the standard in the lead.

"Scouts!" He turned to his own small command. "Out upon these sons of Set! Let them taste blade and bow!"

But the Hyksos, already disorganized by the mishap to their leader and sharply bitten by such bowmen as they had not met before, were withdrawing. Some five chariots turned northward, their drivers lashing the horses into a gallop.

Rahotep led his men across the flats as the rescuing Egyptian force broke into two parties, the larger pursuing the fleeing Hyksos, the other wheeling to the storehouses, while a second dust cloud heralded the arrival of footmen to police the field and drag the wreckage apart in their search for surviving enemies. His own command gained the small domes just as a figure, disheveled and bleeding from the shallow gash across the upper arm, put out a hand to the wall of the threshing floor and so pulled himself up to his feet.

"Prince!" The captain vaulted to the wall and supported the other who grinned at him through a gray mask of dust.

"Behold how we hunt lions of another sort, kinsman—" Between panting gasps Ahmose got out the words, pointing to the man lying at his feet, his head back at such an angle that the oiled and curled beard pointed an accusing finger at the opponent who had brought him down. "Horfui does not ride again, and in Avaris there will be a gnashing of teeth—for this commander was the guardian of the south!"

Steadying himself with a grip on Rahotep's ready arm, the prince leaned over to pick out of the churned-up chaff and debris a fine belt ax, hefting it critically in his hand to test balance and grip, before he thrust it into his own belt, following the custom of one victorious in a personal battle duel. It was a beautiful copper weapon with a cedar handle, overlaid in gold and electrum, the head decorated with a griffin design set in carnelian and turquoise, showing plainly when the dust was rubbed from it.

"No Hyksos arm this," commented Ahmose. "It came from someone of the People of the Sea, some noble or prince of Minos. Perhaps it was Horfui's by right of war—as now it is mine."

"Yaaahhhh!" That was the victory shout of the troops. The chariots that had fled had been rounded up. A handful of men surrendered; the rest went down fighting. Then a plumed horse galloped to the storehouses and the Prince Kamose gave his reins to another, coming to join his brother. Ahmose greeted him with a wide smile.

"Here lies Horfui, brother. It is well?"

The elder prince showed no signs of elation as he regarded the dead Hyksos commander. But when he spoke it was with quiet commendation.

"It is well, my brother. Horfui was a mighty man in their ranks. This time his daring betrayed him—to our profit. But not always can daring win for us. Had not your messenger reached me—then what would have chanced with you?"

Ahmose shook himself as might a hound emerging from a swim in the river. "We have proved ourselves to some purpose—" He looked out over the tumble of chariots and dead horses and men. "Give me these archers, brother, and I shall undertake to go up against Avaris itself!"

Kamose's lips curved in a faint smile, and for a moment the weight of responsibility seemed to slip from him. There was a warm affection smoothing the usual sharp urgency of his voice as he made answer to the impulsive offer.

"In time, impatient one, in time. For this day the toll is sufficient. As for the archers"—he looked past the younger prince to Rahotep and the men who had followed him to join their fellows by the domes—"I will agree that the account they have set on the tallies is high. Captain!"

Rahotep saluted.

"Pharaoh shall hear of your stand. He has given you to be my men. Now I shall give you back to him for his own guard. Deal with him as you have dealt with my brother and your days shall be long and full of honor—"

"May the Son of Re live forever!" Rahotep acknowledged the promotion.

To be attached to the person of the Pharaoh was such an

honor as no humble officer of a barbarian frontier force might hope for. But it was one he did not wish. A man ambitious to rise in royal service might well relish being under the royal eye, but Rahotep wanted army service in the field, even if it meant again the stark frontier posts of the south. He was ill at ease in the stultifying ceremony of a life for which he had not been trained and which to him was almost as alien as the life of Avaris or of a Kush village.

Kawak, the archer who had been speared in the defense of the domes, was not dead. Kheti and Rahotep, with a knowledge of rough field surgery that had come with experience, agreed together that he had a good chance of survival could he be transported to Thebes without delay or too much handling. With permission from the Prince Kamose, they commandeered a cargo boat that had followed the Hyksos' ill-fated expedition with supplies. Loading the archer and three other seriously wounded on board, they trailed the land forces back to the city.

Their spoil was mainly horses. Ahmose had held on to the mares taken from the picket lines. In addition, the fruits of victory numbered ten trained stallions. Six of these were in harness, and they and their chariots were simply incorporated into the Egyptian force, while in the core of the company of spearmen was their handful of prisoners, all of common rank. The archers had shared among them the weapons and ornaments of those they had slain.

"A good fight." Kheti sighed with satisfaction as he sat cross-legged beside Rahotep on the deck of the boat. "This is a lion hunt well to my liking, brother. May we have many such."

Rahotep shook his head. "Think you that the Pharaoh's guard forays into the desert."

But Kheti remained cheerful. "These Pharaohs of Egypt do not send their men into the fight and lurk themselves behind shields—the first blow they strike with their own hands. I have heard their warriors speak of that, brother. When a town is to be taken, the foremost upon the siege ladder must be a Royal Son. When wheels turn and horses race, then does the blue crown advance at the crest of the attack. These are *men* that we serve, Lord, and the guards of such will see action aplenty."

Rahotep eyed the force paralleling them in march along the bank. Aye, by tradition those of royal blood must be leaders in body as well as in mind and spirit. But the foreboding he had felt within him since the Prince Kamose had named him to the guard remained, a cloud he could not throw off.

9

The Jackal Barks

The glory of Sekenenre's court was faded, slightly tarnished. But to one who had heard of the magnificence of the earlier Pharaohs merely in old tales, who had spent all his recent years in the stripped bareness of frontier posts, the outer courtyard with its red granite pavement, where were ranged the Royal Bodyguard statue stiff, and the inner audience hall with its seven-stepped black throne were at first overwhelming. Only later did they become the core of a growing and eternal boredom.

Pharaoh was more a prisoner of his divine duties than any Kush slave toiling in the mines. The hours of his life, from his ritual arising to his bedding at night, were rigidly numbered, and there was an assigned rite or duty for each. Even the food that passed his lips and the drink carried to him in the selected wine jars were prescribed by the physicians of the household as to kind and quantity. He was no mortal man but the symbol of the link between Egypt and the Great Ones, and as such he was allowed no personal desires at all.

Or was he? No one could live long within the confines of any household—even a household as diverse and sprawling as the royal court—without hearing as many or more rumors than those which haunted any camp or barracks. Hedged about by age-old ceremony and pressured by rite and custom as the Pharaoh might be, he still had some free choices to make as Sekenenre himself was in the process of proving, to the confusion and covert opposition of some of those about him.

When this Pharaoh had stood for the first time in the sanctuary of Amon-Re, grasping the Flail and Crook and fronting the image of the god whose earthly representative he was, what had he said? The words were carved now for all men to read, and they were bold words for a shadow king on the shadow throne of a torn-apart kingdom.

"Re made me the herdsman of this land, for He saw that I would keep it in order for Him; He entrusted to me that which He protected."

And to Sekenenre that guardianship was not a passive thing; it was a duty that led him to front the might of the Hyksos, to pit the small remnant of what was once Egypt against the fury of a well-entrenched foreign empire. But if Sekenenre saw revolt as his sacred duty, there were others who did not, as Rahotep had come to understand.

Wearing the scarlet-and-yellow-striped headdress of the guard, with the insignia of their service emblazoned on their leather lappets, the ten archers served their tours of duty with other detachments under the Chief of the Guard and the nominal command of their own captain. If by royal favor they were accepted in theory, the facts of the matter were not quite the same, for ambition led a man into court service, and it also nourished intrigues and hidden maneuvering for royal notice.

To have a body of Nubians from what was considered in Thebes a province not only barbarous but suspect as to loyalty, under a landless officer, come into close service under Pharaoh was more than many a young, or not so young, Commander of a Hundred, or Commandant of Chariots, could accept with grace.

Rahotep walked softly, as any Scout in enemy territory.

He might be new to court life, but he was not new to the atmosphere that clung to the dark corners, having contended too long with something very like it in the household of the Lady Meri-Mut. His early schooling at Unis's hands made him sense quickly veiled animosity and recognize slights for what they were. He learned more of the subtle forces warring among the officials and the household from day to day.

One by one he sorted out and marked those he believed to be the hard core of resistance to Pharaoh's will. There was the Vizier Zau, who reminded the young captain only too strongly of Pen-Seti. Not as old as the priest of Anubis, perhaps, but truly a man of intellectual powers, a worthy administrator, precise in the detailed handling of executive duties, able in a post that was intended to take much of the burden of rule from the shoulders of Pharaoh. Within those limits Zau was all any ruler could ask of the gods. But his limits were too narrow, and Rahotep pieced together words, half-understood whispers, small actions, which made him guess that Zau was sincerely convinced that the Two Lands must not break the pattern-of-things-as-they-are, and that the Vizier believed Sekenenre's proposed vigorous action was courting disaster for the land. A fanatical man completely sure of his own righteousness, he was as dangerous as Pen-Seti—more so because of the power he held beneath the royal seal.

To Zau Rahotep added Sebni of the Prince Ahmose's household. Though the younger prince appeared to go his own way with some freedom, Rahotep knew now that the scribe Sebni had been set in the Royal Son's following to act as a restraint and a curb. Only Ahmose's own strong will gave him the power to flaunt the scribe—as he had done during the lion hunt.

There were others; the captain could recite names. Some were men of power holding hereditary offices from which they could not be removed without some proof of open treason or incompetence. The Treasurer of the South, Kheruef; two judges; General Sheshang; and a few high-ranking priests.

Perhaps his own dealings with Pen-Seti, his danger in

the necropolis of Semna, had made the Scout officer especially wary of the Temple of Anubis and its priesthood. But Rahotep believed that he had no lasting prejudices against the followers of the jackal-headed god—that Seeker who was set at the portals of the other world to guide the wandering spirits to judgment. Once in Egypt the priests of Anubis had truly been "seekers," students of knowledge—not only for its own sake as scholars, but for the general benefit of the people. They had trained forelookers—those who could see a little into the future—and cast horoscopes of men, striving to avert danger and ill to come, advising and helping when it struck.

But the wisdom of any god must filter through the minds and emotions of his or her servants. While those servants were in themselves true worshipers, not misusing any power for their own gain, then did the immortal knowledge come clean and fresh. But when those servants turned from the inner laws of the Great Ones, claimed advantages to themselves, then what they had to give was muddy and befouled. There were two faces to learning, one bright, one dark. And to seek out the dark deliberately was to turn from the service of Amon-Re to that of Set.

So Rahotep, standing at attention to the left of the throne during the "small audience" of the early morning, surveyed Tothotep, High One of Anubis, and disliked what he saw. The cold serenity of Khephren was here, but with it something far more deadly smouldering underneath. Yet he could not mistake, even though it was not directed at a captain of the Bodyguard, the impact of the man's personal power.

And Sekenenre gave close attention to Tothotep, whereas he brushed aside the veiled protests of Zau. On one of his rare off-duty periods Rahotep commented on this privately to Methen. The veteran officer of the Hawk had been given the drilling of newly raised spearmen and so was stationed at the Theban barracks. Now, as he lounged at ease with Rahotep on a reed raft as they fished, he frowned.

"A man does not shout aloud his presence when scouting a Kush encampment," he observed obliquely.

"Nor does he walk barefoot among serpents!" Rahotep countered. "I am no simple savage to be befooled by traders. But I must ask some questions lest I paddle unknowingly into a nesting place of crocodiles. Is it because I have no cause to remember those of Anubis with liking that I distrust their high priest here?"

"No one speaks ill of a temple." Again Methen talked around the question. "But any Pharaoh's face turns to the Jackal with respect, for there is an old bond between them, one not spoken of openly in these days. My younger brother was of that shrine. When the Hyksos overran the Hawk Nome, his throat was cut on his own altar as a pleasing gift to Him Who Dwells in the Darkness. But thus it is that I know some of the secrets of Anubis. And the greatest of these is that in the ancient days the Jackal held Pharaoh's life between His jaws—and more straightly than the gods hold the lives of us all."

Rahotep sat up, setting the light craft to bobbing under them. "How so?"

"Long ago—before the pyramids were built, before Menes united the Two Lands, North and South, making them one, then did Pharaoh live only as long as he was strong and vigorous. And when he aged, the Jackal came to him—for those who served Anubis cast his horoscope and so foresaw his death date. They sped him toward his horizon so that a younger and more virile man could occupy the Great Throne. To the Jackal alone—and those who served Him—was given the power of Pharaoh's fate. And now His priests still cast the royal horoscope. Also they have the power of forelooking so that they may warn of ills to come."

"I would not like to stand opposed to Tothotep," Rahotep said slowly.

"Neither would I. You wish now that the prince had not shown you the favor of court promotion?"

Rahotep, having ventured one confidence, now released a flood. He needed both reassurance and advice.

"I hate the court—it is no better than Semna. Also I feel now that I am but a piece in some game played by those hidden from me. Were we from Nubia put where we stand to be a defense—or a weapon? I am as one treading a strange path with a cloth about my eyes!"

There was no sign of sympathy on Methen's face. Instead, his features had taken on the expression with which he had so often met unnecessary stupidity in the past, giving Rahotep a momentary but nostalgic memory of less complicated days.

"Do you wish to return again to the House of Captains as a boy, refusing to play a man's role? Is it time for you to awaken and be true to your inheritance. You are not a simple soldier of the forces—you are what you were born to be—the Nomarch of the Hawk. What matter if there be no nome under that standard now? The day will come when it is restored, and you must be ready to take your place as its ruler. Use your eyes, your ears, your mind, and do not act the sullen child whose playthings have been stolen from him. This is more your life than that of Kah-hi. Learn, learn so that when the right time comes, you shall be prepared to act! You compare yourself to a piece in a game—prepare to play such games yourself. On the border you strove to think as the Kush in order to entrap them. Here you must be taught a new way of survival. Do you understand?"

The veteran's momentary anger changed into a serious pleading. It was as if he were pointing out to the younger man a path that must be dutifully followed but for which he could not be the guide.

Rahotep laughed shortly and bent almost double to present his bare back to his companion.

"Use your flail, Commander. Is it not rightfully said, 'A boy's ears are on his back, he hears best when well beaten'?"

"As long as the beating is from my hand, then it is well. But, oh, Rahotep, walk carefully, lest the beating be another's!"

"And those words shall I wear as a shield on my arm. Be sure I have ears to hear that!"

Thereafter he tried earnestly to follow the veteran's advice, knowing it to be good. Though the life of Pharaoh was so hedged about by ritual and ceremony that he seemed more the symbol the priests claimed him than a living man, yet Sekenenre was no puppet. He lacked the boundless, exuberant energy of his younger son; he even appeared to lack the force and drive of his heir. Yet, as Rahotep came again and again into his presence when on duty, the captain began to see and appreciate the way this frail, dedicated man was working to achieve his own ends.

Physically the Pharaoh had that delicacy of form that Kamose had inherited. His features were finely sculptured, almost feminine in their beauty. But his mouth and jaw were firm, giving a truer clue to his inner strength. He was a master of chariots, and Rahotep guessed that he only approached a measure of happiness when he was freed from the confines of the court to lead his army in the field, where custom not only allowed, but decreed, that he take an active and vigorous part.

The dry season was nearing its end, and the Nile was showing the first signs of the approaching flood. Rahotep had been a month of long days in royal service. And, as the river darkened and began to swell, so did tensions within the court heighten.

The captain was on duty the night that the Queen's scribe Pepinecht, that same stranger who had guided him to the Hall of Royal Women on his first night in Thebes, came to him with an order that bypassed the Chief of the Guard and yet was given under the royal seal.

"A week from now Pharaoh must travel for the measuring of the river rise. Tonight there will come those to read what lies before him. Admit them."

To Rahotep that statement meant little. But when later he was making the rounds of the archers he had posted at the inner doors of the private quarters, he witnessed the arrival of a party of priests from the Temple of Anubis. Tothotep, wearing his robes of ceremony, was accompanied by a thin, dried wisp of a man whose ascetic face was like a single sheet of papyrus through which shone torch light. This elderly priest carried carefully in his two hands, breast-high, a bowl of blackened silver, and by that token Rahotep recognized him as a "seer," one of the small number of those who could by some Great One's favor look into the past or the future.

The Royal Mother and the Royal Wife were borne through the halls in their carrying chairs. Once within the inner chamber where the priests had gathered, they dismissed the majority of their attendants, and it was the servants of the Jackal who drew across the doorway the woven curtains, closing the room.

Still through the fabric the scent of incense found its way, nor did the curtains deaden a low monotonous incantation, intoned with the intention to seal the seer from the world and enable him to open his eyes elsewhere. Rahotep had seen the process once before—in Semna— though at that time the results had been negative.

The seer would stare into the depths of the god's bowl, while on the water that filled it floated a film of oil. Were Anubis willing, that film would form a picture—or some sign to be interpreted by His priests.

Sound and scent together were intended to dull the outer senses. The captain paced down the corridor, taking care to pause before each of his men to ensure that they were still alert. But he was before the door of the chamber when the chant ended abruptly and through a thick silence the tremulous voice of an old man mumbled. Rahotep could make out no separate words, but then there was a sudden, sharp exclamation, uttered by a woman.

Other voices were raised, and Rahotep could hear the anger in one, well controlled though it was. That was Tothotep! Then the calm tones he had heard pronouncing judgment, uttering decrees, brought silence again.

"So be it! What Re gives is also His to take away. But while I live, I shall do what I believe to be His will. Does a warrior in battle wrest away a comrade's shield to cover his own body? Even the Hyksos do not so. Sekenenre shall live so that no man after his departure to the horizon can say: 'This was no fit lord, but one who cowered in the sun, fearing the dark.' Nothing is altered, nothing will be altered in my plans. I have spoken!"

When the priests of Anubis came forth, one of them led the seer, steering him by the arm, for the man tottered along as one who is blind, a pallor of shock drawing his face yet closer to the likeness of a corpse. Tothotep came last of all, and in the compression of his lips, the jerk with which he set straight his cloak of leopard skin, Rahotep read the extent of his anger.

It was by some evil chance that in that same moment the high priest fronted the captain almost squarely. And that which lay like coals of a smothered fire deep in his eyes was not good to see. Pen-Seti had been feared, but this man was greater than Pen-Seti, just as the emotion he aroused was more terror than fear. For what seemed a long moment ripped free from normal time, they stood face to face, and those dark eyes raked the younger man as if Tothotep were by some means transferring to this lesser object all his rage and frustration. Rahotep knew that no good would come from that meeting, chance though it was. Again he was plagued by the thought that he was being moved here and there, will-less, by those to whom he was only a mindless piece on a game board.

The high priest did not speak, nor did Rahotep as he stepped aside to let the other by, and then hurried on to answer a beckoning hand from the doorway. It was the same senior Lady of the Household who had escorted him to his first meeting with the queens. And now, adding to her orders to recall the carrying chairs, she said in a half whisper:

"When you are off duty, Captain, the Great Lady would speak with you. Come to the wall door."

The incense was gone, the palace itself settled into the usual calm of the night, and then he was free. Almost timidly he rapped on that portal through which Pepinecht had ushered him. And within, the scribe waited, to lead him to the small hall.

But this time the two queens sat alone. There were no tables piled with feast dishes, no gaming board set out. He had an odd, fleeting impression that he was walking into the quarters of some commander in chief. A glance at that back wall, which had been cloaked with a rug on his first visit, showed him now a curtained door. As he "kissed dust" before the royal ladies, both the scribe and the lady of honor withdrew out of hearing.

"Captain." The Royal Mother's hands rested on the arms of her chair. Now they tightened their grip. "Is it yet known what has passed this night? There are ears, aye, and eyes, too, in the walls of Pharaoh's house, and tongues to relay ill news quickly."

"Royal Lady, if aught is known it has not come to my hearing!" He spoke the truth with all sincerity.

She watched him with the narrow-eyed intentness of a hawk. Then she glanced at her daughter, the Royal Wife. That younger face so mirrored the elder that it was uncanny. And in that short space when their eyes met, some silent message was exchanged.

"Listen well." Teti-Sheri's voice was only a fragile husk of a murmur. "This night He-Who-Speaks-for-Anubis brought his seer and it was foretold that if Pharaoh goes up against the Hyksos, then his time will be cut short and he will depart to the horizon—"

"Be it not so!"

She waved aside his shocked protest. "So must say all those who love Egypt, for Pharaoh plans to throw off the shackles of the invaders and do it now. The longer men lie in chains, the more they forget the sweetness of freedom. There are those who come in time to look upon their chains, their cages, as places of safety in an uncertain world."

Unconsciously he nodded agreement, remembering speeches he had heard within the courts of Thebes.

"Therefore they will fasten upon such a dire fore-telling—" She hesitated, visibly of two minds about proceeding.

And a flash of sudden and terrifying insight made him add, to his own horror, "Perhaps thinking to make it true by the efforts of man—"

The Royal Mother sat very still. On the wall the black shadow of her vulture headdress had a questing look. But the Royal Wife stirred, her hand half raised from her lap as if to ward off some blow. Then Teti-Sheri smiled, but there was nothing joyful in the curve of her lips.

"Tuya may take joy in the new Hawk; his wits are not dull. Think so, kinsman, but also keep those same thoughts locked within your head. A warning to a soldier in time is as good as an extra company at his back. Take care, and again I say to you, take care! You and your archers stand outside the old patterns of our life. For that very reason you may be able to better fulfill your duty and see that our Lord departs not before his time—"

"There is this also." For the first time Ah-Hetpe spoke. "Because you are from afar, there will be those quick to blame you in preference to friends or kinsmen should aught go wrong. And it may be that no saving hand can be held out to avert disaster—"

He had it now! All his formless and vague fears came into sharp focus. To the queens, he and his men, without local ties and uncorrupt, might be salvation in face of a palace plot. To any plotters the Nubian company would be convenient scapegoats. He must indeed walk blind-folded a path in a crocodile swamp. Something of that realization must have been visible in his face, for Teti-Sheri smiled again, but not with the icy remoteness he had seen earlier.

"Serve us for but a little time, Captain. When our lord goes up against the Hyksos, and he *will* lead out after the Blessing of the Waters, then their chance will be past. And if they strike, their serpent fangs will only close upon stone."

But that was a promise that held but small comfort, Rahotep decided bleakly, as he sat on a stool in his quarters, gazing a little absently at Kheti whom he had summoned for a conference he did not know just how to begin. He might have known that his foster brother had already gathered some of the threads of the tangle into his capable hands, for the other spoke first.

"The Jackal had barked to some purpose tonight, brother. Already tongues wag concerning a warning."

"Aye. And that I have had doubly. We must be truly on

127

guard until after the Blessing of the Waters—"

What more he might have added was not to be said. Nakh-hof, second in command of the guard, stood in the doorway. His face in the lamplight was greenish beneath the brown, oily drops that ran down his cheeks, and he held himself erect with an effort.

"Captain!" His voice was a half cry of pain. "A bad sickness has struck. Half the guard cannot leave their sleeping mats. Take your men and cover the chamber of Pharaoh until I can send you relief!"

On their way from one corridor to the next Kheti spoke hurriedly to Rahotep.

"A sickness which strikes so speedily and fastens upon the men of the inner guard is indeed an odd one. Mayhap one who barks is concerned."

That it was a sickness and a grave one was manifest, Rahotep discovered when he posted his men in place of those who had, for the most part, to be carried away by their comrades. He hoped that the warning he gave secretly to each archer would be enough to keep the men alert and ready for trouble.

The night wore on, and it began to seem that he might have been unduly suspicious. It was less than half an hour by the great water clock before the Pharaoh would be aroused for the dawn greeting of Amon-Re when a cry broke from the inner chamber.

Rahotep raced down the corridor reaching the curtains just as the door guard burst through them. He bumped against that archer, for the room beyond was almost completely dark and the man had paused inside to get his bearings. In the corner where the Pharaoh's bed stood half concealed under a canopy, there was a struggle going on, and Rahotep leaped for the disturbance, shouting at the same time for a light.

He threw himself on a tangle of fighting men, his hands slipped on flesh that had been thickly oiled. Then they met hairy skin, an animal's pointed ear! Pharaoh was fighting for his life against some monstrosity that mounted a beast's head on a human body!

The captain struck out with his fists, blindly, with all the strength he could muster. Something grunted as a light flared in the doorway. The monster wriggled toward the corner. Rahotep took a step forward in pursuit and came down on one knee as his foot caught under a second body. He groped and his fingers closed about metal.

A torch had been brought in behind him by Nakh-hof who had somehow miraculously recovered from his severe illness. As its smoking radiance was swung under the bed canopy, all the crowding guard could see clearly. Rahotep knelt by Sekenenre. The Pharaoh was moaning faintly, and in his upper breast a dagger had been thrust, a dagger whose hilt was now in Rahotep's hold. Save for those who had just entered, the room was empty. To these witnesses he was an assassin caught in the act!

10

Slaves of Anubis

Rahotep pressed his forehead tight to the unyielding stone of the wall against which he lay. Something in that small, self-imposed pain helped to clear a path through the fever haze that imprisoned his body, a path for ill-assorted, broken thoughts and half memories. He was shut in this box of utter black, as if his abused body had been sealed, while still living, into the sarcophagus of a tomb. Yet—his breath caught in the half-sob of a child who had wept himself into exhaustion—for Rahotep, son of Ptahhotep and the Lady Tuya, there would be no tomb, save one the river crocodiles would grant. He would be a long time in dying, and afterwards there would come total oblivion instead of any afterlife. Or would the Judges of the Dead be more merciful than those of the living?

Much of what had happened since Nakh-hof had come upon him with the unconscious Pharaoh, the assassin's weapon in his hand, was mercifully a blur. He had been brutally flogged and questioned through that flogging. When he found no one would listen to his story or his protestations of innocence, that they sought only for a confession of guilt, he had kept silence to the end.

There was one moment he remembered with brutal clarity, when his own captain's flail had been broken ceremoniously across his battered face before the assembled guard. And he had another memory picture of his archers, stripped of their arms and proud insignia, being herded away to the slave compounds, the unconscious Kheti, who had resisted injustice to the end, being dragged along in their midst. After that he had awakened here. Though where he was he did not know, or greatly care any more.

He moved a swollen tongue between torn lips in a vain quest for moisture. Water! A picture of a scummy pool in a dying stream on the Kush border haunted him. He longed for that water. Green with weed, evil-smelling, thick with insects though it was, he desired it avidly. But though he lay in a cell that was dank and chill, there was no water. Perhaps he had already been condemned and was walled in here for all time, shut in with a curse that would imprison his spirit with his moldering body. He had heard dark tales of such punishments. And surely no greater crime could be charged against any man than that of raising a dagger to the Son of Re!

There came periods in which he escaped the dark, the cold, the pain, and ran with the Scouts once more in the open wastelands, or climbed down the cliff to the ledge where Horus had guided him to find the leopard cub. Then once more he would awaken to the cell and the hopeless present.

He was shackled by an ankle ring, he discovered. And the chain leading from that ring was fastened to a bolt set in the stone of the wall. But the mere fact that he was so chained destroyed his worst fear. Had he indeed been walled up and forgotten, they would not have bothered to shackle him. And so, heartened by that one small fact among all his fears and forebodings, Rahotep began to explore his quarters with his outstretched arms.

Pain came at the slightest movement of his flayed

shoulders, but he persisted, driven by an inner core of stubbornness. His groping hands found no break in the walls about him on three sides. The length of the chain—though he lay full length on his belly and stretched out his arms to their fullest extent beyond his head—prevented him from locating the fourth. But his questing led him to a jar and a plate.

Gasping with eagerness, he pulled the jar to him slowly, fearing to spill even a drop of the precious liquid he could hear sloshing in its depths. He drank sparingly of the musty water. But with every sip he swallowed he believed he could feel new energy flowing into him. The plate held a three-cornered loaf of coarse bread, the husks of grain rasping in the stuff—common slave fare. He ate part of it slowly, wincing at the pain in his lips, choking upon the bites he forced down. But he did not eat it all, though his middle pinched with hunger. There was no sign he might be given other supplies. Best make this last as long as possible. Rahotep sat up straight, not daring to touch his lacerated back to the wall, and chewed carefully.

The food had strengthened him in the belief that he was not to be left there forever. And putting the horrors of the immediate past to the back of his mind, the captain began considering what could be done here and now to help himself. His body was bare of any clothing. Even his throat amulet had been taken from him. He had no possible weapon and he was chained.

Chained! His fingers went to that ring on his ankle, moved along the links to the ring that anchored him to the wall. That had been set deep in the mortar where four blocks met. He tugged at it, already knowing that it would require more than Kheti's strength to loosen it. But mortar—

Once more he groped on the floor, found the plate on which the bread had rested. It was, to the touch, a rough thing of baked clay. But it might be a tool of sorts. At any rate he would not sit in the dark making no effort at all, awaiting death with a broken spirit!

Deliberately Rahotep broke the plate, and was left with

two jagged, pointed shards. With one of these he began what he knew was an impossible task, picking with that fragile, crumbling clay point at the stone-hard stuff in which the ring was set. He might as well attempt to drain the Nile with his cupped hands, something within him commented bitterly. But he kept on, though the clay powdered away with every stroke.

There was no night or day, no hours to be marked in the dark. He could have been there for a longer or a shorter time than he guessed. Sleep came. Rahotep drank sparingly of the water when he awoke, stiff and sore, and ate a mouthful or two of the bread. Neither supply had been replenished, and he congratulated himself on the foresight of rationing what he had found.

The last fragment of the broken plate was powder and his fingertips were raw with rubbing the most infinitesimal bits back and forth around the ring. He thought he could feel a slight indentation there, but it was all lost effort. And now he sat quietly, cradling in his hand the one remaining bite of bread.

He was rising that to his lips when there was a burst of blinding light above the level of his head. His hands over his eyes in instinctive protection, Rahotep flattened against the wall where his chain was fastened. He had been so long in solitary darkness that he first did not understand the promise of those sounds from overhead. Sluggishly they fitted into a pattern in his ears, began to make a measure of sense.

"Lord Rahotep—?" There was a familiar slur softening that urgent call. Then a second voice, pitched low, but with the carrying snap of an officer, brushed aside the first inquiry.

"Rahotep! Brother!"

The captain pulled a name out of his memory, said it aloud in that husky whisper that seemed all that was left to him for a voice.

"Kheti!"

"Aye, brother, Kheti. Hold that torch lower, fool! Nay, *after* I am through this hole—not before!"

A body squeezed with some effort through the square opening some eight feet up on the far wall, hung for a moment by the hands, and then dropped to the floor. Rahotep's eyes still smarted in the light from the torch extended through the wall hole, but he forced himself to look about the stone cell that had held him—for how long?

"I am chained—" His husky whisper echoed oddly from the bare walls.

Kheti was already down on one knee examining the links and the ring to which they were fastened. He gave a test jerk to the fetters and then shook his head, turning his attention to the ring about the captain's ankle.

"This may be broken, brother. Brace yourself!"

In spite of the pain in his back Rahotep stood against the wall, his arms outspread to balance himself, as Kheti inserted both thumbs into the ring. Muscles stood out on the Nubian's shoulders, and Rahotep felt his bone and flesh caught in the pressure of those hands.

"Ah—the metal is old and worn—" Kheti grunted with satisfaction. "Once more, brother—"

Rahotep closed his eyes, felt a trickle of cold sweat course down his jaw. Then that terrible pressure was gone with the tinkle of metal against stone. His whole foot felt numb as if the circulation in it had ceased, but he stumbled forward without question as Kheti led him across the cell to stand under the opening.

"Up with you now!" The Nubian's hands closed on the captain's waist, and Rahotep was heaved aloft. The torch was withdrawn abruptly, and hands came down to catch his upraised wrists. He was pulled up, out of Kheti's hold, dragged roughly enough for it to seem for a moment that he was being pulled in two.

He lay on his back in a corridor so narrow that his shoulders brushed either wall. And those there stood at his head and feet. But Rahotep's dazzled eyes told him that they were his archers.

"How—?" His question was never finished for there was a scuffle and he heard Kheti once more giving orders.

"Close that stone tightly, you pig of Kush! Let these

135

shaven skulls wonder if their own Great One made a meal of the captain behind their backs. That would be a good story to ram down their throats! Lord"—he loomed over Rahotep, giving him an officer's greeting—"can you walk? We know not where this burrow leads, but it must have an end somewhere!"

"Give me a hand up. If I have enough left of my foot bones"—Rahotep laughed a little lightheadedly—"I can assuredly walk. Where are we and how did you come hither—?"

Kheti's hands hooked in his armpits dragged him up, and the Nubian's mighty shoulder was behind the captain as a support until he was able to stand steady.

"We are in some hidden way of these sneaking priests—a long hidden way by the looks of this—" His bare toes scuffed in the thick dust on the floor. "Because we can heft stones past the moving of their slaves they brought us in to clear part of a ruined shrine built in the far past on which they plan to raise another lurking place for their magics. Today Mahu chanced to find in the wall a stone which moved under his hands when he cleared away some rubble. Tonight we broke out of the slave quarters and used that door—"

"But how did you find me?" demanded Rahotep as he followed behind two of the archers, one bearing the torch, Kheti and the others at his back.

"There was much talk of how you were kept in some secret place of the temple." Kheti's tone was hard; the hand he had kept on his captain's shoulder as if to steer him aright tightened. "They were planning a mighty spectacle—"

"With me to play the center of it!" Rahotep finished bleakly.

"That is the truth you speak, Lord. Therefore, when this secret way led into the interior of the temple, as we could see through the spy holes in the walls, we kept outlook for aught which might betray where they had prisoned you."

"Aye," Mahu the torch bearer broke in. "Look you, Lord!"

He swung his brand closer to floor level, and Rahotep marked a handhold carved into the side of a block of stone, apparently to aid in its being pulled forward.

"One of these we opened. We found a prisoner's cell beyond—empty—except for the bones of a man long dead. So each we came to we inspected. And in the third we found you!"

"But we are still in the Temple of Anubis then?"

"We are, Lord." Again Mahu's whisper floated back. "This is an old pile much built over. I do not think the shaven skulls themselves know all its secrets. And if we do not find the other end to this burrow, we can remain hidden for a day, until the chase has spread out into the desert, and then retrace our way through the camp of the slaves."

"Meanwhile, we can learn more of the shaven skulls' secrets," remarked Kheti. "We search now for their treasure room—"

"This is no time to think of looting!" Rahotep half stuttered. The Nubians, as followers of Dedun, would not balk at helping themselves to the offerings of a foreign god. But he was surprised to hear Kheti suggest something so far from their main objective of escape.

"Not loot, Lord!" Hori's tone was one of honest indignation. "We but take what is lawfully ours. These priests pounced upon our weapons as tribute to their Jackal. Give us our arms once more and we shall stand as men—"

A low growl of assent echoed along the line of Scouts. And Rahotep made no protest when they halted now and again to peer through holes in the walls to see what lay beyond. Under those conditions Kheti's search for the treasure chamber made very good sense indeed.

The excitement of his liberation had carried Rahotep along as the swell of the flood waters carried debris downriver. But now his head whirled giddily and he steadied himself with one hand against the wall of the narrow passage, concentrating upon the important business of placing one foot before the other without losing his balance. They halted by another peephole, and through it came the sound of full-voiced chanting.

Foggily Rahotep recognized a word here and a phrase there. The priests were forming a procession for a cememonial visit from Pharaoh. What Pharaoh?

"Sekenenre—?" He looked to Kheti for an answer.

Only dimly to be seen in the limited light, the Nubian grinned.

"Pharaoh is himself save for a bump on the head and a scratch on the chest, brother. Otherwise we all would have been dead long since!"

That the captain could believe. But who—or what—had been the assassin he had driven off—and where had that other vanished to? Kheti, who had been watching through the spy hole, turned away with a sigh of mingled relief and satisfaction.

"There they go, guards and all! Let us hope that they shall be some time braying to their Jackal. What is it, Mahu?"

The foremost archer had slipped along the passage, around a corner where he had to scrape to get his bulk through. Now he looked back at them and beckoned violently.

What Mahu had found was the room they sought. Narrow slits high in the wall brought daylight to the storeroom, and they saw shelves piled with coffers and jars. Mahu pointed excitedly to a rack on the wall wherein hung bows.

"Aye, those are ours!" Kheti confirmed. "Now—how do we reach them?"

He hunkered down on the floor of the passage and ran his hands along the wall, seeking an entrance here such as they had found to the cells. A pleased chuckle told them he had discovered it. And the others crowded back to give him room.

The block, which was a narrow one, came away with difficulty, and the Nubian underofficer surveyed the opening dubiously.

"More a path for a snake," he commented. He made a try, but it was obviously too narrow for him or any of the archers. Rahotep edged forward.

"This task is mine. Let me through!" His words came in a rush, for he did not honestly know if he still had strength enough to do what must be done. When Kheti got out of the way, Rahotep squirmed in. The rough stone of the opening raked his tender shoulders, bringing a sharp exclamation from him. But he persevered and, with a last kick, was through.

Because he did not dare try to get to his feet, Rahotep crawled across the room to the rack. He crouched below it panting, while he nerved himself for the effort of getting up and freeing the weapons. Then he levered himself up with the aid of a coffer. One by one he loosened the bows, pulled the quivers of leopard hide off the hooks. The priests had been thorough in their claims for spoil. He found his belt with its fine dagger and the silver bracer that had been his only heritage from the Hawk slung over a peg at the end of the line and added them to his collection.

It was when he took the bracer that he dislodged a box on the shelf below. The lid fell with a faint noise, and Rahotep stiffened, his breath coming in painful gasps, his eyes on the outer door, bracing himself for the entrance of the temple guards.

But the door remained closed; there was not the slightest sound from without. In the coffer, whose lid he had knocked off, lay a more than life-size, but a very lifelike, mask of a jackal. The animal's own hide was stretched with skill over a light frame of wood and wickerwork, as he saw upon lifting it out.

Plainly it had been intended to be worn over the head of a priest. There was a furred flap to lie about throat and shoulders. Fingering its ears, its furry hide, Rahotep knew now what kind of monster he had found in Pharaoh's bedchamber. A priest of Anubis, wearing such a guise, could well be taken for a messenger of the God, not to be questioned by any man who saw him. The captain longed to take the mask with him as proof of his wild story of the assassin, but it was too bulky, and he set it aside with regret.

Slowly, fighting his spinning head and trembling body every inch of the way, Rahotep crept back to the opening, pushing his loot before him. He was afraid he could not negotiate that small door again. But he thrust his hands through in half appeal and felt a warm, tight grasp close about his wrists, drawing him on.

Of what happened after that he had no memory at all. When he awoke again, he was lying face down on a pile of mats. Flashes of burning agony broke through the steady pain he had known for so long, and he tried to twist away from the grip that held him fast under the torturing touch.

"Quiet, brother!" The words again came out of the air above him, as they had in the crypt where Kheti had first found him. "Give me more oil here, stupid one."

Liquid dripped upon the captain's back and was rubbed in in spite of his struggles. Then a hollow reed was put in his mouth, and he was ordered to suck. He did so meekly. The acid-sweet taste of wine that had been mixed with milk was on his tongue, and he swallowed.

"You will live—" Kheti's tone was meant to be light, but there was relief in it. "Those weals are already half healed and the oil will aid them."

Rahotep opened his eyes and turned his head. Before him was a wall, which had once been painted. Somewhere he could hear the splash of water and the mutters of men keeping their voices low.

"Where are we?"

Kheti came into his line of vision. He held a goodly slice of melon in one hand and was taking half-moon bites from it, licking juicy fingers in between times. Now he squatted so that he was closer to the captain.

"Where are we, brother? Where but in the courts of the Jackal."

Rahotep tried to sit up and fell forward again.

"We've been taken!"

Kheti shook his head. "Not so, brother. We have us a

snug lair. It seems that Mahu was right. In the old days this was a mightier shrine than it now is. And we have chanced upon a court where no one but the lizards and the birds have come for years. The guards are out beating the desert for their Nubian slaves, while we lie up here and are served with their best—for Hori and Kakaw are expert looters of their kitchen. It is a fine joke."

Rahotep began to laugh weakly. The whole situation was beyond any fantasy. It was lifted straight from some tale such as that of "Sinhue the Exile." Either that or he had indeed "passed beyond" and this was life on the other side of the horizon.

But fantastic though the situation was, it was true. The Scouts, because of their training, were able to conceal themselves in that deserted section of the temple that must once have housed many priests back in the days when Thebes was the capital of a wealthy Egypt. They pilfered supplies from the stores and they had a day and night of rest to consider and make plans for their future.

Rahotep well knew that outside this very temporary hiding place their lives were forfeit on sight, unless they could reach the waste places beyond the reach of Pharaoh's law. There was one alternative no one voiced—that of fleeing north and taking service in the ranks of the Hyksos. Rahotep himself fastened grimly upon one target, centering his whole mind upon it as he would aim an arrow at an enemy. He must somehow expose the plot of the priests—if by the favor of Re that was at all possible.

They kept hidden during the day, sleeping by turns with the ease of men who had learned to take rest when and where they could between periods of grueling action. And it was after sunset when Kheti came out of the hidden ways with news.

"Tothotep has visitors. Men gather in his inner apartment."

Rahotep sat up alertly. He was now far different from the miserable fugitive who had been carried there on the night of his escape. Though he moved cautiously and favored his back, his body was clean, and he wore a kilt of linen once more, as did all his men—the pure white of temple livery rather than the striped cloth of royal service. When they made their final bid for freedom, it was their hope to be taken for a detachment of the guard, darkness of night aiding in that deception.

"Whom does Tothotep entertain?"

"The Vizier for one—"

Kheti had said only that much when the captain was on his feet.

"Can they be watched and their words overheard?" he demanded sharply.

"Aye. But this night we must move. The guards sent out to sniff our trail will be returning—"

"Well enough. But also it might do better for us to hear what is said by these men."

Kheti caught at his arm. "You no longer serve the Pharaoh, this king who rewards a true man with the whip! Mix no more in the affairs of these shaven skulls and those who yap with them, brother."

Rahotep jerked free of that restraining grip. "Do you forget our oath before the altar of Amon-Re?" he countered. "Perhaps the Pharaoh believes that I have betrayed him, but before the gods I stand clean, and so I will hunt down those who have befouled our honor in Thebes."

Kheti was scowling. The warrior code of the ancients still had power over soldiers' minds. Even in Nubia a measure of its power held. Reluctantly, manifestly against his inclination, he nodded at last. And he padded with Rahotep along the dusty inner passage until a gleam of light from a spy hole marked their goal.

Tothotep indeed sat on the other side of that wall, while on a chair of honor the Vizier was enthroned, a concealing desert cloak and hood thrown aside. Two other men were there—the General Sheshang, and one who lurked in Tothotep's shadow, sitting cross-legged on the floor in a scribe's favorite attitude, his kilt stretched tight from knee to knee as a writing desk, though he did not hold a brush and his pen case was still slung on his shoulder.

"I do not like it." Zau spoke very low. The two at the spy hole had to strain to hear him. "Those Nubian archers may still cause trouble—"

Tothotep smiled coldly, a smile that was worse than another's frown. "They are a body without a head. Lacking their officer, they will flee into the wilderness, seeking to return to their own land. And from our present news from Nubia, they will find such a cold welcome there that they will trouble us no more, for our messenger has returned but this evening with the news that the Prince Teti has seized the rule. If our guards fail to track them down, it is of little matter to us."

"And their officer?" pressed the general.

Tothotep's expression was now slightly pained. "He is safe in our hands, Lord. At the proper time he shall be served as he merits. All is working as we have wished. And by nightfall tomorrow"—he paused and to Rahotep's sudden discomfort his eyes fastened upon the wall behind which they stood as if he could see through that solid stone and mark them both—"by nightfall tomorrow the Great Seat shall be vacant once again and there will be wailing for a Son of Re passed to his horizon!"

It was as if a serpent had hissed that. The plume in the general's circlet jerked, the tip of his tongue showed, passed across his lips.

"It is a dangerous game that we play," he observed.

"If *you* have made your preparations, Lord," Zau snapped, "then there is nothing to fear. Our lord will be ambushed by the Hyksos in the valley as he returns to camp. His loyal bodyguard will be slain to a man defending his sacred person. And Egypt shall welcome a new and untried young lord who can be more easily brought to listen to the words of the gods! Would you have us ruined, utterly overrun by the northern barbarians? With Nubia gone to the rebel Teti, we have only to cry war to be crushed between two grinder stones. Let Pharaoh lead us into battle against either host and the other will strike so that we end in their slave gangs. Better to pay tribute and give Apophis lip service then to be ground to dust!"

"And that is the Truth of Maat!" Tothotep added.

But the general was still unconvinced. "What if the Royal Heir does not heed your excellent advice in this matter? His thoughts have ever agreed with his father."

"The Prince Kamose is frail of body. There are many plagues that may attack a man."

"And Ahmose?" Sheshang asked doggedly.

Zau laughed. "Ahmose is but a boy. He is under the hand of Sebni whose mind we know well. To him war is adventure. Perhaps he can be persuaded into turning his eyes southward to make a campaign against this Teti. Send him with a force—such a force as *you* could select for him, General, and the Prince Ahmose would not again trouble the Two Lands."

Tothotep arose suddenly. "We cannot fail! It is written in the bowl, the Jackal has signed an end to this reign and we but fulfill the duties of our order!"

Zau drew the edges of his cloak about him. "See that you do your part, General. Let Pharaoh enter the Valley of the Lizard in his chariot, but when he comes forth, it must only be upon a warrior's bier!"

11

Pharaoh Departs to the Horizon

Rahotep fought down the excitement that was making his heart pump too rapidly. His breath came like a runner's. The desert cloak muffled him well from any prying eye, or so he trusted. He had crossed the river from the temple to Thebes without any unmasking. But the hardest part of his exploit was still before him. He must leave the protection of the wall against which he had flattened himself, walk boldly between those sentries at the gate, giving the countersign, and find his way to Commander Methen's quarters without being revealed for what he was—an outlawed fugitive.

With his hand tight about the hilt of his dagger, he approached the gate. It was still early evening, so early that the men who had leave within the city were only now straggling back to the barracks. The captain attached himself to the tail of one such group, a good pace or two behind so that none of the men might be too inquisitive.

Those returning exchanged rude chaff with the sentries, which was abruptly silenced when the officer of the guard appeared. Rahotep cursed his ill luck under his breath. But the officer did not glance at the cloaked figure standing a little to one side—rather he employed his powers of caustic comment on the now sheepish leave men whom he lined up and marched smartly away.

With a vast sigh of relief Rahotep threw back his hood, allowing his warrior's headdress with its improvised insignia to show. It all depended now on whether the sentries could recognize him. But his service with the royal forces had been of such limited duration that he hoped he had more than an even chance of bringing it off.

A spear swung down as a barrier before him.

"Re rises in glory." Rahotep pinned his future to the password that Mahu, scouting the barracks wall, had whispered to him only moments earlier.

The spear snapped up and the sentry saluted. Rahotep was free to enter the barracks court, which to his mind was far too well lighted, with its torches set in regularly spaced brackets along the walls. Luckily he had been several times to visit Methen in the veteran's quarters and needed no guide. The last obstacle, that the commander might not be in his room, remained.

By great effort the captain kept his pace to a leisurely one, though every nerve in his body hammered. He crossed the court and mounted the narrow stairs leading to the smaller apartments where the senior officers had their private rooms. Then he was at the right doorway, a little weak with relief to see that its mat curtain was down. Methen was there.

He stood listening for any murmur of voice that would betray a visitor. And so intent was he on that that he was doubly startled when the curtain bulged near floor level and a flat black shape squirmed frantically under it to fall upon his sandals and claw a welcome at shin height.

"Bis!" The captain went down on his knees, and the leopard cub butted him with his round head on which the ears were now standing pricked. Bis rose on his hind legs to paw at Rahotep's cloak until the captain gathered the cub up and hugged him close. Somehow that wild welcome

146

eased an inner hurt as the oil and tending hands of Kheti had eased his outer ones.

Then the mat slapped up on its roller, and Rahotep, still on his knees, looked up to Methen's wondering face. He saw the older officer's eyes widen as a hand came forward to grasp the folds of his cloak and pull the captain in. It was not until the curtain was safely down again that Methen turned and spoke.

"Where have you come from, boy? What happened that night in the palace?"

The captain sat down on the nearest stool, Bis draped across his lap purring. He told his story, as far as he knew it, starkly as he would report it to a commanding officer.

When he was done, Methen nodded. "You and your men were used to further another's plan," he observed crisply. "We guessed as much but we had no proof. Truly you have been favored by Re. But what are you doing here? The sooner you are away from Thebes, the stronger your hopes of life will be—"

"I have a message," the younger man cut in. Quickly he described the meeting he had spied upon in the temple. "Warn Pharaoh—or else they will succeed this time where they have failed before—"

Methen crossed the small chamber in a couple of strides. As he looked out through the latticed window, he brought his fist down against the wall.

"It is not so easy. I am under a cloud because I have come from Nubia—which is now frankly a rebel state. I would not be allowed near any of the Royal Ones. And"—he turned again, his face bleak—"how do we know who or how many of those in the army are true to Pharaoh?"

"Nereb?" hazarded Rahotep. This aspect of his task had not occurred to him before, and inwardly he berated himself for not having foreseen it.

"He is with Pharaoh. But perhaps through Sa-Nekluft something may be done. Those I would trust with my life are all out of Thebes tonight."

"By purpose?"

"It might well be so. Be sure, Rahotep, I will do all that it is possible for a man to do to warn our lord. But it is in my mind that they may have hedged him about with their own men so that no whisper can reach his ears."

"Then there is left only one other thing. Where lies this Valley of the Lizard?"

"What is in your mind?"

"I still command ten archers—eleven with Kheti—who are the best of all the army. We have most of the night and all the day before us in which to act. Maybe when Pharaoh is attacked, he will find his guard has doubled!"

But Methen was shaking his head. "I do not think anyone on foot could reach there in time. Our lord is already out of Thebes—to appear at the Temple of the Waters. He will not return to the city but will cut directly across country to join the army. And he goes by chariot as does his guard. You cannot use the road the army is traveling, for you would be quickly discovered. To circle through the wild lands will add to the distance you must travel. It cannot be done."

"Nevertheless," returned Rahotep, "we shall attempt it. And if you cannot reach Pharaoh, try to get the ear of the Prince Ahmose. Now show me where lies this Valley of the Lizard and how one may reach it from Thebes."

With a pattern of lines traced in wine on a scrap of linen tucked within his belt, Rahotep left the barracks. Methen had insisted upon accompanying him back through the gates, and one other stalked behind them, although they discovered him too late.

Bis was determined not to be parted from Rahotep now that he had found him again. And when Methen would have picked the cub up to carry him back, the leopard gave such a display of royal anger that for fear of a scuffle they were forced to let him pad along in the captain's wake.

By dawn the Scouts were well into the fringes of the desert lands, and Rahotep drove himself as hard as he did them. If it were humanly possible, under Amon-Re's will, that they reach the Valley of the Lizard, then it would be no fault of theirs if they did not. What they could accomplish there, the captain had only the vaguest ideas as yet. Could they discover and pick off those who lay in ambush before the arrival of the royal party, they would indeed be favored by fortune. But at least they could add to Pharaoh's defenders and so retrieve in part their past disgrace and failure.

In spite of their best efforts, Re's path across the sky was too swift. Knowing that he dared not reach the valley with his men in a state too exhausted to pull a bow cord, himself dizzy with sun and weakness, the captain was forced to grant periodic rests, laying himself flat upon the ground, striving to relax each taut muscle of mind and body, while Bis curled against his side as if, should he stray, he would lose all touch with Rahotep again. Today the cub had suffered Kheti to carry him when he tired, though at ordinary times he did not like the Nubian to handle him.

"Let that one shed his milk teeth," Kheti observed, "and grow to full strength, and you will have a battle-mate second to none! He will follow you to the horizon, for he has set you in place as his lord—and among the cat people that is rare."

Rahotep assented absently. His mind raced ahead, trying to foresee and plan against this difficulty and that. He had utter confidence in his own men. Let them only reach the battlefield in time, and he did not believe that any company in ambush could stand against them. It was only a matter of hours—

Long since they had learned, by bitter experience, the best method of travel through waterless wastes. Though they had left Thebes with a full waterskin for each man, that supply was strictly limited. And they had not been able to lie up in the hottest portions of the day.

Therefore they faced as best they could the force of the sun, as they marched through rocky defiles between the cliffs—cliffs streaked and cracked—detouring around slides of gravel, clay, and boulders. Cliffs and rocks alike threw off a quivering haze of pure heat, which burned a hand laid unwarily on a surface to steady climbing feet. Their only relief was to follow the scanty line of shade up

149

one of the cliff walls where they could find footing.

Time and time again Rahotep made a stiffer climb to a height from which he could view the countryside and then refer to the rough map Methen had drawn for him. And he was too tired and beaten to exult when he at last identified a landmark and understood that they were not too distant from their goal.

Because of the coming floods, the large encampment of the royal forces had been removed from the level fields back into the high lands where the waters did not reach. It was the Pharaoh's plan to march north during the first weeks of the flooding, when the chariot legions of the Hyksos would be prevented from assembling on the plain, which they needed for their most effective charges.

Neferusi, the garrison town held by the invaders, was the agreed-upon objective of the first Egyptian drive. It had been amply fortified after the regulation Hyksos fashion, and for over a century it had been a center for the oppressors' government in middle Egypt.

Thereabouts, all native opposition to the foreign rulers had been crushed generations earlier, and very few men would rally to any invading Egyptian force from the south. The Hyksos would undoubtedly sweep the land bare of supplies and anything that would aid the rebels, and the spearhead attack from Thebes, if it failed, could well be the last—as well as the first—stroke in Sekenenre's war for the liberation of his country.

But all that the best military minds in royal service could foresee had been prepared and the army awaited now only the order to march. If Pharaoh reached his camp unharmed tonight, they would move forward. If he died—as his opponents were determined—the whole delicate structure of the revolt might topple, as clay walls toppled before the push of the flooding river, reducing both his house and his nation once more to a sullen vassalage, with all the patient work to be done again.

The Royal Heir could be prevented from early moves to hold things together by the bonds of mourning custom—which advisers such as Zau and Tothotep would certainly hold him to, making him a prisoner of his kingship until it was far too late to proceed with the invasion of the enemy-held territory this season. And if Kamose proved no tool for their use, he in turn would be swept away. It was all so very easy to do once Sekenenre was removed to his horizon! Rahotep could foresee all this as clearly as if he were a temple seer watching coming events in the bowl of Anubis.

"Lord!" Hori had reached the cliff top before him this time. "There are chariots coming!"

The captain did not disdain catching the hand the other lowered to him, using the archer's aid to gain a better vantage point. Hori was right—a column of dust rolled yellow-white from swiftly turning wheels and churning hoofs, a small squadron of chariots. No, even fewer than that, for Rahotep could count only five in that line. They had been forced into single file by the nature of the country, and the one at the head was distinguished by the two horses, as well as by the standard, of Pharaoh.

Between the Scouts and that advancing line was a stretch of broken country, which turned Rahotep sick with the knowledge that only the wings of Horus Himself could transport them across it in time. But they had to try.

At the risk of bad falls the Scouts advanced at a scrambling run. But they were yet far from the lip of the valley's rim when they heard confused shouting, which could only mark the launching of an ambush. A band of hot pain griped Rahotep's lower ribs as he struggled on, falling behind his men in spite of his best efforts. He saw Kheti reach the rim of the cliff, set arrow to bow cord almost before he halted, and let fly down into the gulf.

Then the captain made a supreme effort and came to a sliding stop beside his Leader of Ten.

Below them was a melee of horses and men. Those who lay in ambush had been too eager, or else their prey had become suspicious, for the royal party was not far into the valley. Lucky shots, however, had brought down both horses of Pharaoh's chariot. And to avoid trampling into that stalled vehicle, the following one had turned to one side, locking wheels with the wreck and effectively bottling the whole passage. But the worst was that some inexpert management on the part of at least one driver at the other end of the line had ended in a second smashup, so that the ambushed were now caught between two stoppers and imprisoned—to be picked off at leisure.

From the heights Rahotep and his men could see those who had set the trap, at least those in concealment on their side of the valley. There were archers among them as the shafts pincushioning the dead horses below testified. But slingers, expert with their deadly balls, were at work now, and Rahotep saw three of the penned guard go down under the skull-breaking shots of good marksmen.

Sekenenre, his blue war helmet-crown protecting him from that rain of death, had leaped to the platform of one of the stalled chariots and from that point was directing the resistance. But how could men fight back against well-concealed enemies stationed above? Shields were up now at the command—forming a roof of sorts. But too many had fallen at the first attack.

One of the long Nubian war arrows sang through the air, and a slinger arose to his tiptoes, as might a man diving into a pool, before his body went limp across a rock.

"Pick your marks!" Automatically Rahotep gave battle orders. "Loose at will!"

There was an angry shout from across the valley. A sling-shot bullet struck a foot below their perch as the enemy posted opposite sighted the Scouts. But now the odds were swinging in favor of the Nubians.

"Five!" chanted Kheti. "Five notches for our shafts, Lord."

They might be able to fire on those who lurked on their side of the valley. But the ones in hiding on the other cliff were almost as well protected from them as they were from the tormented men trapped below. And though five and then six bodies marked the success of the archers' aim, those in the ambush were still in peril, for the others continued to fight grimly to wipe out the royal party.

Only four or five of the guards and officers who had

accompanied the Pharaoh were still on their feet about the chariot where Sekenenre stood. Their useless bows had been discarded; they held axes and maces and the shields, which afforded them a small measure of protection.

The call of one of those war horns Rahotep had heard among the Hyksos at the horse camp blared in their ears. Kheti shot, and a figure perched on the heights crumpled in mid-note. But whatever his signal, it brought to a desperate action the struggle below.

Men arose from behind rocks, from the shelter of stunted brush, and dashed downslope toward the beleaguered party. The Nubian bowmen did what they could, but even a supreme marksman could not have brought all those runners to earth before they reached their goal.

They leaped in upon the small group of Egyptians while Rahotep and half his force went into their own attack, covered by the other Scouts. The slope on this side was less steep, and they reached the choked road only a moment or two behind the enemy.

A bearded man in the body armor of a Hyksos thrust at Rahotep with a spear, and the captain lithely swerved, getting in under the other's guard by stooping almost to ground level and coming up breast to breast. His dagger bit home low and deep, and the other, with a strange look of bewilderment, staggered back and was gone.

"Aaaahhh—" The fierce, throat-rasping battle cry of the Nubians rose above the general clamor, and Rahotep caught a glimpse of Mereruka swinging a slinger up over his head to dash him earthwards with crushing force.

The rage of battle was on them all, and the captain did not really think clearly again until some chance brought him up hard against the wheel of an overturned chariot so that he clung there for support and looked about him dazedly.

The small shield wall of the surviving guardsmen was still up, but he could not see the blue helmet of their leader. Mahu sat against a rock while Kakaw wrapped a strip torn from a kilt about a bleeding cut on his forearm. There were dead men aplenty. And Kheti was superintending the binding of some half-conscious prisoners.

Rahotep stood away from his wheel and moved toward the shields of the guards. Before he reached that improvised fortress, he heard the terrible keening of the warriors. And he knew with a sick certainty that they had failed. Pharaoh had departed to his horizon.

It was hard to recognize the Lord Nereb in the battered figure with a face that was a mask of blood and dust. The young officer sat on the ground supporting Sekenenre in his arms. At Rahotep's feet lay the blue crown. And he needed only a glance at the horrible wounds on the Pharaoh's jaw and head to know that there was no hope at all. No one could have survived such blows.

"Sorrow! Sorrow! Our lord has departed!" A spearman of the royal escort scooped up the bloodstained earth beneath his feet and rubbed it across his face. But Nereb looked across the broken body he cradled to Rahotep. There was no surprise in the measuring stare with which he greeted the captain. It might almost have been that he expected to find the outlawed Nubians there. And for one bleak moment Rahotep wondered if this treachery was also to be laid to them.

"You arrived opportunely, Captain," he said. "We might have had much to thank you for—"

Rahotep brushed his hands across his eyes, trying to wipe away the fog that seemed to come between him and the meaning of the other's words. He strove vainly to climb out of some well of fatigue. This crushing failure, added to all his other misfortunes of the past few days, was too great to bear.

"We strove to prevent this, Lord. It seems we came too late."

"What man could foresee such blackness of treason? We had won the battle cleanly before we lost our lord. It was treason and not lack of valor which—which brought this about."

"How knew you that?" the captain asked, for those in the ambush were Hyksos by dress and arms and he had had no chance to tell his tale.

154

"Look you there!" Nereb did not shift his gentle hold on the dead Pharaoh, but he pointed with his chin to a spot behind the chariot from which Sekenenre had commanded his beleaguered force.

His feet leaden with exhaustion, Rahotep wavered over. Two bodies lay there. The under one was that of an officer with the special insignia of a guardsman—Nakh-hof. And the dagger protruding from his armpit was Egyptian. In his hand was still held a bloodstained mace, while across his knees sprawled his companion in death, one who wore a jackal mask such as the one Rahotep had found in the storeroom of the temple.

Steadying himself with a hold on the chariot, Rahotep stooped low enough to seize upon one of the upright ears of that strange headdress, tugging it from the head of the assassin. He had seen the man who had worn it before. It was that silent scribe who had sat behind Tothotep's stool during the meeting of the traitors he had spied upon in the Temple of Anubis!

"Did these kill—?" he began slowly.

"Nakh-hof struck the first blow—he who was supposed to protect our lord with his own shield. May Osiris judge him fittingly! And the priest struck twice more while I was busy sending the first traitor to his final accounting with Re! Had it not been that this crocodile spawn turned against him, the Son of Re was safe. Your Nubians were clearing the field and the victory was ours. I do not know from whence you came, Captain, or what good fortune brought you so to our aid. But almost did you give life to Egypt, and that you failed was no fault of yours or of those you lead."

"Lord!" Intef of the archers came running, and in his hand he held what seemed to be a mass of fur or hair. "We did not fight Hyksos alone. Look you!" He waved the disgusting handful of fibers under his captain's nose while Rahotep surveyed it blankly, having no idea of its purpose. Then Intef, in his excitement, so far forgot himself as to pull his officer away from the little circle about the Pharaoh and point to one of the tumbled bodies of the attackers. He went down on his heels and thrust the stuff he held against the slack chin of the dead man to form one of those curled beards so strange to Egyptian eyes.

"Thus it was, Lord, until Bis pulled it away. See, the black one seeks the same elsewhere—"

Bis was crouched half across the chest of one of the captives who had been tied up at Kheti's orders. The cub was snarling while the man he sat upon watched with terrified eyes. Bis's ready claws tangled in the wealth of hair upon the prisoner's face and tugged. The stuff came free to reveal very Egyptian features. Egyptians disguised as Hyksos! Had the Nubians not taken a hand in this venture, the Pharaoh's death would have been listed as an act of war and the power of the enemy so made manifest to all the fainthearted. It was a plan that might have been born in the devious brain of Set!

"Hoy!" From the heights came a call from a Scout. He gestured eastward, making the sign for troops approaching. But a second later he added to it the up-pointed finger, which signified that it was a body of their own men, doubtless from the camp.

Rahotep shuffled back to Nereb. They had laid the dead Pharaoh on a bier of their cloaks and shields, his crook sword bared in his hand to show his death in battle. And under the orders of his officer, the wreckage of the chariots was being cleared.

Ahmose drove the first vehicle to enter the narrow file of the valley, sending his horse well ahead of the rescuing troops who strained to match his pace. When he sighted the tangle of the ambush, he leaped from his chariot, running toward them, only to stop short as he caught sight of the bier. The face he then turned to Nereb was no longer that of a boy.

"Who did this thing?" The words had odd little spaces between them as if the prince exerted great control to get them out at all.

Nereb once more pointed without words to the bodies of the traitors, and Ahmose went quietly to look. He said nothing, then or ever, concerning Nakh-hof or the Anubis-masked scribe. But when he came away, he stopped before Rahotep. It was then that Nereb spoke for the captain—as if he feared that the Nubians and their leader might be charged with this crime also.

"These men fought well to save the Son of Re, Royal Son. Had it not been for traitors' blows they would have done it."

Ahmose took no notice. "Methen reached me," he said directly to Rahotep as if they two were alone. "You have done well, kinsman, and we have served you ill. Pharaoh to whom you swore allegiance is dead in spite of your efforts. Is it your wish to depart from our service?"

"Rather is it my wish to follow you, Royal Son, since it is in my mind that what has happened here shall be paid for." Rahotep found his tongue.

"Paid for?" queried the prince. "Aye, a hundredfold, a hundred-hundredfold! This is but a beginning—not an ending!"

12

Re Strong in Judgment

The semidesert village was a poor one, built on a little hillock almost at the edge of the flooded land. Those who normally sheltered there must have had many a lean year when the rising river did not reach this point to renew the grainfields. But there was the well that gave water, and so the archer company could not complain of their temporary quarters, poor though they were—a fact that Kheti pointed out so briskly to the first of the grumblers there that there had been no mutterings since.

They had ample supplies, brought them by night on an ass train driven by men of Nereb's personal following. And they had orders to keep under cover, their duty ostensibly to guard the four prisoners taken in the Valley of the Lizard.

One was an Egyptian, of noble rank Rahotep guessed, though he had been instructed not to question the man. The other three were real Hyksos, for not all the beards worn in that fatal valley proved to be detachable. The Hyksos watched their captors warily, openly suspicious because their treatment had been good so far. After the tales Rahotep had heard of the cruel handling meted out to captives taken by the invaders, he believed he could understand a measure of their bewilderment.

The captain did not know the reason behind his present assignment in this village, but he trusted the prince and did not doubt that Ahmose had some plan afoot. In the meantime, there was no excuse for growing slack, so he drilled his men, regaining in that toughening process his own wiry strength as the gashes on his back healed to scars he must carry the rest of his life.

Part of Rahotep's exercise time was spent with Bis, who was growing fast. Battle lions and leopards were not unknown among the Egyptian forces. Of old, Pharaohs had led charges with tawny felines subject to their command bounding beside them. But such use of uncertain-tempered cats was chancy unless the beasts had been well schooled. So Bis was trained by the use of Hyksos garments from the valley until Rahotep was certain the cub could search out an alien lurker upon order. The leopard was affectionate with the captain, tolerant of Kheti to the point where he allowed the Nubian to caress him now and then, aloof with the rest of the archers, whom he accepted as a part of Rahotep's general surroundings and so a part of the natural way of life.

But with strangers he was wary, crouching with a trickle of growl deep in his throat. And he took the same stance when they held practice in the early dawn, ready to bound forward when the order to attack came. Soon he would be a formidable opponent for any man, especially one not expecting to front a black leopard.

Kheti made him a collar of well-softened baboon hide, ornamented with bits of turquoise and copper in a traditional pattern of the south. And to this he submitted with pained resignation, even allowing a leash to be attached, providing it was Rahotep or the underofficer who held the other end of that restrainer. But he still retained some kitten playfulness, loving to wrestle and conduct a stealthy hunt of a feather lure the captain would trail for him in and out of the deserted village buildings.

So a procession of days crawled by. They had come here under the guidance of one of Nereb's men the evening of the death of Sekenenre, and they had strict orders to remain until they were summoned, guarding the prisoners. But they were beginning to chaff at their voluntary confinement when one of the sentries gave a warning whistle. Men dodged into concealment, and Rahotep wormed his way on hands and knees up the roof stair of the overseer's taller house in time to see a small company of men nearing the village.

Their pace was limited by the oxcart that lumbered in their midst. But though they wore the scanty waistcloths of field laborers, the captain was sure they were other than they seemed. He glanced down at the mud huts. To all appearances the village was deserted. But could they continue to conceal their presence if the cart and men were headed here?

Then one of the travelers advanced and looked up, as if he hoped to be identified by any who watched.

"Methen!" Rahotep ran down the stairs. By the time he was out of the small court and into the beaten mud of the lane, the commander was hurrying toward him.

"Rahotep!" They threw their arms about each other in a kinsmen's embrace, and then the commander looked the younger man up and down, his satisfaction at what he saw plain on his face.

"You have come for us?" demanded the captain.

"Indeed I have come for you, boy. You look well and have done well. Now perhaps you shall do better. You have your prisoners? As if I need ask you that!"

"They are safe and they have been kept apart from one another."

"Wise." Methen nodded approvingly. "I have been dispatched to bring them—and you—to Thebes."

"To Thebes?" In spite of himself, Rahotep could not disguise that note of apprehension, and Methen understood as quickly.

"You need have no fear of that charge still standing

against you, boy. To what you learned, Pharaoh has added much more—"

"Pharaoh?" Rahotep remembered only that limp body in Nereb's arms.

"The Royal Heir"—Methen spoke formally—"has been proclaimed before the face of the gods. Kamose rules the Two Lands. It is in his name that I bid you come to Thebes, that the Son of Re may sit in judgment."

They set off again at dusk. In the oxcart lay their prisoners, bound and then covered with bags so they looked like sacks of grain. To all purposes, their small caravan resembled one bearing tribute for the court, sent under guard from the holdings of some lesser noble. And Rahotep knew that many such would be on their way to Thebes, that the offerings at Sekenenre's tomb might be worthy of a Lord of the Two Lands.

Methen admitted that he did not know what plans the Pharaoh had made or what role Rahotep was to play in them. The rest of his news was almost as vague. With the death of Sekenenre the arrangements for the campaign were at a standstill. The royal army was encamped in the highlands, and rumors were alive there and in the city that the forces would be disbanded, for, after the lengthy ceremonies of the royal burial had been carried to their proper conclusion, it would be too late to move this year.

"So it will happen even as those traitors planned it!" Rahotep burst out with chill disappointment. "They will net Kamose in their rites and customs and he will not be able to free himself—"

"Do not see him as clay to be shaped by a potter," Methen returned. "Aye, now he assents openly to those who would guide him. But has he not also sent for you? Once you spoke highly of the Prince Ahmose. Do you think he is one to forget his father's death? Yesterday he was proclaimed Commander of the Army—since the new Pharaoh is not wed nor has a son. And, after his brother, Ahmose is the Royal Heir—"

The commander fell silent for a moment and then added in a low voice, "There are others beside the prince to be concerned over this matter. The Royal Mother has long urged the war against the foreigners. And she bred her son to the belief, after him her grandsons. She is a lady of power. And Kamose and Ahmose have ever looked to her words with respect and attention. To her influence add that of the Queen Ah-Hetpe, who has been one with her mother in this. It is already said that if Pharaoh goes to war, her hands shall hold the Crook and the Flail for him here in Thebes. Neither of those ladies will surrender her hopes for a free land lightly—especially to such as Zau and Tothotep. Thebes is a city of many secrets, boy, and I think we guard some of them!"

With the slow-moving oxen, the needful detours to avoid stretches where the Nile was already creeping into the fields, it was on the morning of the third day after leaving the nameless village that they came into Thebes. They were expected, for the Queen's scribe, Pepinecht, appeared before them in the roadway as if conjured up by some magic.

"Tribute from the Hawk?" he asked in such a brisk, businesslike fashion that Rahotep was close to gaping at him foolishly. "Head your cart to the right," he ordered without waiting for any confirmation or denial. "The Court of Offerings is already full—you must find a place beyond—"

That "place beyond" was a much smaller enclosure backed upon a wall that Rahotep's knowledge of the royal city led him to believe was that of the garden about the personal apartments of the royal family. At one side was a shed, which Methen indicated.

"Stay out of sight there with your men and the prisoners. I do not know how long you must wait, but do it in patience—"

And Rahotep courted patience through the rest of that long day. Never had he been less inclined to sit on his heels and wait upon the pleasure of others, but it had to be done. Most of the archers went to sleep. Three started a toss-stick game in a far corner, walling in the prisoners they kept ever under eye. Bis snapped at inquisitive flies in intervals of intensive tongue-grooming, and finally followed the humankind into slumber, his whiskers and toes twitching now and then in the excitement of a hunting dream.

No other cart turned into the enclosure. Their oxen had been taken away by Methen and his men, leaving the sack-filled vehicle as a screen before the shed. Kheti lay on his back, his head pillowed on a piece of sacking.

"This is a strange land, this Egypt," he commented. "First we lie in the king's favor, then we are slaves, and now—what are we now, brother? Guards of secret prisoners, awaiting some new change of our fortunes. Let us be simple warriors again, for we know that trade and none can take the knowledge from us—"

"Do you wish to return to harry the Kush?" the captain asked idly.

"Not so. It is in my mind that when these princes eat up the Hyksos, then will they turn their eyes southward. Were I in Nubia, I must bend knee to Teti—"

"Yet have I not heard you in the past speak of the Prince Teti as a mighty man in battle and a good leader of men?"

"However, since that hour I have seen mightier men who shall someday lay their whips about Teti's shoulders should he sit upon some high seat and call himself king before their faces! This new Pharaoh is great enough, brother, but in his shadow stands another man I would follow willingly—"

"The Prince Ahmose!"

"The Prince Ahmose." Kheti agreed. "Those who trail bow or spear in *his* service shall have their fill of action. And if there are those in this strong-smelling city who believe they can drive him with a rope about his nose as they drive their horses, then let them look upon him again with more knowing eyes, for they are no judges of men!"

"For which judgment do I render thanks, O archer of Nubia!"

Rahotep stiffened, and Kheti, his eyes wide with surprise, sat up abruptly. But when they would have made proper obeisance to the cloaked figure, he waved them up impatiently.

"Tell off four of your men who can keep their tongues quiet behind their teeth and let them bring the prisoners," the prince ordered swiftly. "Do you come with me. Bearing your arms—"

"Kheti, Hori, Mahu, Sahare." Rahotep rattled off the names. His underofficer was already moving purposefully toward the captives' corner. As he cut the thongs about their ankles, the captain turned the command of the rest over to Kakaw.

They followed Ahmose through a gate into the garden and then on a path winding between rare shrubs to the center building. The sentry on duty there did not salute, did not apparently notice them, but he stood aside nimbly to let them pass.

Rahotep was able to orient himself now. They were in an outer corridor of Pharaoh's private rooms, heading toward the small hall where Sekenenre had received the Vizier and the highest officials of his court. There were lamps aplenty, and in the corridor outside the curtained doorway were drawn up a double line of veterans of the guard who wore, not the insignia of Pharaoh, but that of the Prince Ahmose.

"Pharaoh sits in judgment," the prince said quietly to Rahotep. "Do you and those with you stand behind this curtain until you are summoned."

They faced an expanse of matting hung as a screen. Ahmose sidled around this to the right, and Rahotep, finding a slit through which he could see the room, signed his men and their captives back against the wall and planted himself before it.

Lamps on small tables and brackets about the chamber gave light for the three scribes who sat ready with writing materials. One of those scribes was Pepinecht; the other two Rahotep knew were attached to the service of the High Judges.

Seated a little to one side was Kamose. He did not wear the double crown of ceremony; a circlet with the *uraeus* proclaimed his rank. It was obvious that he was not present in his person as Ruler of the Two Lands, the dispenser of all justice. The stools of those who faced the rest of the company were occupied by three men who together made a strangely assorted company, though Rahotep did not doubt that they were firmly united in allegiance and purpose.

Sa-Nekluft, Treasurer of the North, Holder of the Gold Seal, was on the right. On the left General Amony sat almost sleepily, his officer's flail resting across his bare knees, for he wore the field dress of an active warrior, rather than the double skirts of a courtier. Between the administrator and the warrior was a third man the southern-born captain had never seen before, older than either of his companions, with a grave but untroubled face of serene self-confidence and authority. He was robed as a high priest, and on his breast was a beautiful pectoral of Amon-Re. This must be the Voice of Amon at Thebes, head of the far-flung priesthood of Amon-Re, Nefer-Rohu, the Beloved of Re, He-Who-Speaks-for-the-Great-One.

Facing these three was another trio, outwardly as confident and sure of themselves, untroubled by what might lie ahead. Zau, the Vizier, had the middle seat, and he was flanked by Tothotep and General Sheshang.

Rahotep had been so busy identifying the company that he almost missed the quiet speech of the Amon priest. Now he listened to it intently, hoping to gain some hint of his own part in any action for tonight.

"Since the Son of Re believes that this too nearly touches his own temper and emotions and that his judgment might be colored so that he would act not as the Voice of Re in giving verdict, but as a man whose anger or sorrow can make him weigh the scales of Maat unequally, we serve in this inquiry under His decree and He will listen but judge not—"

"There is naught to judge!" Zau spoke sharply, but with that inner note that suggested that the former speaker had presumed beyond all rights. "We ask of you why we have been so summoned, secretly, and not before all men? Of what are we accused? Of what can we be accused? We are loyal servants to the Most High One. To Pharaoh shall we appeal for a hearing—"

He was looking beyond the tribunal of three to the young Pharaoh, intently, angrily, willing Kamose to face him and agree with his words. And the new king did turn his head to look at the Vizier, but his face was as remote as the face of the ancient king of the frontier fort on the Kush border. His delicate, almost too refined features—so different from his brother's—mirrored no emotion, only detachment. He met Zau stare for stare, and the second of silence lengthened. It was as if those two fought a silent duel of their own, will against will as it might otherwise be mace against mace. Nor did the younger man flinch from meeting the power of the elder.

It was Sheshang, perhaps the weakest of the rebel three, who broke through that quiet. A man of action, it seemed he could not endure the wait for direct accusation, the chance to defend himself.

"The Lord Zau speaks for all of us," he growled. "Let us be accused openly that we may defend ourselves against lies—"

Tothotep cut in, his very calmness of tone dampening to the soldier's call for action.

"The time grows short. Now that our Lord Sekenenre— with him abide ever the Peace of Re—has departed to the horizon, there must be decisions made for the preservation of the Two Lands. Not only do we know that Nubia has turned against us under that traitor Teti, threatening our southern border, but also a general of Apophis is on his way to Thebes. His party draws near to Neferusi. These Hyksos are fat with easy living; no longer do they yearn for warfare. If we meet them weaponless, they will accept a token payment of tribute and leave us in peace. Is this not a time to unite to face them rather than indulge in quarrels among ourselves?" He was the reasonable man trying to restore friendship among foolish children, and so well did that part become him at that moment that had Rahotep not known that just the reverse was true, he might have been won to the priest's support.

Amony brought his flail down in a slap across his knees. "As the Voice of Anubis says, time grows short. If we are to receive Apophis's general in a fitting manner, we must close ranks. But it appears that we differ as to the manner of the greeting we prepare for the sons of Set!"

Ahmose had taken his stand beside his brother, a little apart from the judges. Now he stirred as if he would heartily endorse that statement. But he said nothing.

"To bring down the wrath of the Hyksos upon Thebes is the act of one courting destruction and darkness." Zau took up the argument with a fanatic's fire. "Pay tribute, lest we be crushed between two shields—Nubia and the invaders! How dare we take the field against such a double set of enemies? Only two, perhaps three, of the southern nomes will support us, in part. Such an army as we can put into the field would be vanquished in its first battle, leaving us to be utterly swept away by an aroused Apophis. Perhaps then Thebes would cease to be—" His voice grew shriller and shriller as he spoke, and now he was on his feet, hammering his fists together to emphasize his points. Where Tothotep had argued with suave reasonableness, the Vizier strove to overwhelm his opposition with the force of his own fears.

It was Sa-Nekluft who replied. "It seems we have been drawn from the path we are gathered here to follow. We are not here to debate the manner in which we are to greet the general of the Hyksos—whom after all these years Apophis has seen fit to dispatch to Thebes—rather are we in judgment upon traitors. Let us now consider the case of Nakh-hof, second commander of the guard, who did with his own hand slay the Son of Re!"

Zau still stood, glaring at the Treasurer of the North as if Sa-Nekluft had swept away from him the power of speech. The General Sheshang stirred uneasily on his stool and was provoked into answering.

"What proof have we of the treason of Nakh-hof?"

General Amony became brisk. "Let the Commander Nereb stand forth and speak—"

"Knowing," Nefer-Rohu added sternly, "that he is

under the Eye of Horus-Re and that his words will be measured against the Feather of Maat, here now, and also in the day when he goes to face the Judges of the Horizon—"

The young officer came out of the far end of the hall and took the Oath of Maat readily. In colorless, formal words he told of what had happened in the Valley of the Lizard.

Sheshang plucked at his lower lip as he listened, and when Nereb was done, he demanded harshly, "So it would seem that his vile Nakh-hof was indeed cursed of the Great Ones and lifted his hand against our departed lord, along with a renegade priest. But what have we here to do with a wickedness that must have been born of disordered wits?"

"Not all the attackers were slain in the valley," said Amony. To Rahotep he now had the look of Bis when the leopard cub had been particularly clever and knew it well. "Let the prisoners be brought forth!"

Ahmose snapped his fingers in the direction of the curtain, and the captain took his cue, marching out his small party. He did not look at Pharaoh, but made his salute to the three judges.

"Rahotep, Captain of Desert Scouts in the service of the Royal Son Ahmose, with captives taken on the field of battle."

General Amony leaned forward to inspect the prisoners. "Senti"—he named the Egyptian among them—"you are far from your command it would seem. When were you relieved from guard duty at the Well of Wali-heti?"

The man stiffened but made no reply.

"And three Hyksos. Yet you also wear their dress, Senti. And I have heard a tale of false beards, which is indeed a strange thing. Why does a Commander of Spears under the Son of Re lead an attack upon his overlord wearing the dress of the enemy?" From the purr of a great cat, his voice became that of a grim avenger. "Guard!"

There was a stir by the door. The men wearing Ahmose's badge came around the curtain.

"Let this one be taken forth and questioned as is lawful."

Rahotep, remembering his own ordeal under the inquisitor's lash, could have felt pity had he not known that this man was truly guilty.

"Let the Hyksos be set aside and questioned by one of the scribes who can speak their tongue," the general continued. "But"—his attention moved to the captain—"here is another who has, I believe, something of importance to say—"

"This man is under the sentence of death as a traitor." Tothotep cut in. "Those with him are runaway slaves. He and they cannot testify in any court."

For the first time Kamose moved. He stood up and plucked from his brother's belt the officer's baton-flail.

"Let Rahotep of Nubia approach—" he said quietly, and something in his tone produced a silence throughout the hall.

The Scout captain moved forward and went down on his knees to "kiss earth" in the full royal salute. Kamose's sandaled foot slid forward, and Rahotep was startled as he realized the meaning of that gesture. Only a nomarch, or the heir of a nome, was allowed to touch the Son of Re's person in homage. As his lips brushed the gemmed strap of the sandal, he felt the soft flick of the baton thongs across his scarred shoulders and knew that in the sight of all from this hour forward his scars of infamy were erased, turned into the marks any warrior might bear from honorable battle.

"We greet the Hawk, the Friend-Who-Stands-on-the-Right-Hand-of-One, who commands Pharaoh's Scouts in war and is among the Shields of the Royal Person!"

Not only was his earlier sentence erased, but also he had been publicly welcomed into the ranks of those permitted to follow the Pharaoh closely on the field, with a grant of nobility equal to that of his vanished inheritance.

"Life! Prosperity! Health! May the Son of Re live forever!" His fervent thanks were echoed by the others, even the accused, for the pardon of the Pharaoh, given directly, was a great honor, even to those standing as witnesses.

"Now"—Amony brought them firmly back to the matter at hand—"let the Lord Rahotep give evidence of what he knows of this matter."

So the captian told all his tale, beginning with the tempestuous night on which he had been on guard in the palace, describing all that had followed—the attempt on Sekenenre's life, the meeting he had witnessed in the temple, and his own abortive attempt to save the doomed Pharaoh. He strove to avoid anything but the bare recital of facts for which he, himself, could vouch. And when he was done, it was the Voice of Amon who addressed him.

"And to this you will swear, knowing that now and on the day you journey to the horizon, your heart shall be weighed against the Feather of Maat and only the truth will prevail?"

"So do I swear, standing in the way of Amon-Re," he replied with equal solemnity.

General Amony nodded. "You have our leave to depart, Captain. Leave your prisoners in our care and wait where you may be summoned again, should it prove necessary."

Rahotep saluted and withdrew with the archers. He longed to know the outcome of the trial, if trial it could be termed. But there was no appeal against such a forthright dismissal.

Out in the corridor again Kheti sighed. "It seems that we are once more in favor, Lord. Let us enjoy the sun while we can. But what will they do with those traitors in there?"

"That we shall have to wait and see," Rahotep answered absently. He was more intent upon another problem. The news that the Hyksos king had appointed a general who was even now on his way to Thebes was startling. This must be a crucial moment for Kamose. Would the new Pharaoh surrender a token tribute to Avaris as his Vizier and those behind him demanded? Or would they now go forward with the plans of Sekenenre and advance to meet the future defiantly with ready spears and bows?

13

Up the Flail

"Of the three, he was the greatest danger." Rahotep turned away from the window in the guest room of Sa-Nekluft's house to face Nereb. "Zau believed in the rightness of his cause, Sheshang was ambitious, but Tothotep—" The captain discovered it difficult to find the right words to describe his mixed feelings concerning the priest of Anubis. "Yet the judges have seen fit to allow him to depart to his temple—"

Nereb sighed. "We are bound by law and custom. Even the Son of Re has each hour of his life hedged in by regulations as old as the uniting of North and South Egypt. Tothotep has claimed the right of judgment by Anubis. But do not think that that will mean his freedom. He goes to face the Jackal in his own way. Pharaoh has already been assured that he has departed to the horizon—Those of the inner shrine have so taken their oaths upon it. It was the privilege of his office to claim the Great One's punishment over the punishment of man."

"It remains to ask—how great was his power within the temple?"

Nereb stared down at the floor, and there was an odd note in his voice as he replied.

"It is Pharaoh's belief that those who serve the Jackal in His shrine must not for a space be interrupted in their petitions to the Great One, since they must beg His forgiveness for the evil His Voice has seen fit to do. Therefore, a guard has been stationed about that temple that none may enter or leave until the ceremonies of atonement and purification are completed, and for a space longer than that!"

"The Son of Re is wise; his justice covers the earth." Rahotep repeated the conventional answer to judgment with more emphasis than usual.

"Also that guard is drawn from the personal following of Pharaoh when he was yet but the Royal Heir," Nereb added in a carefully emotionless voice.

"There was some reason to believe that a guard selected with less forethought—?" Rahotep began daringly and the other officer caught him quickly.

"Those who are personally loyal to Pharaoh are bound to his interests by the warriors' code. That was revived in all its power in the regiments commanded by the two Royal Sons, though elsewhere it may be forgotten or practiced but in part."

"Zau was not alone among the nobles in believing that we do ill to provoke the wrath of the Hyksos. Which of the nomarchs have sent their hundreds behind their standards? Nebket—Elephantine—in part. But the rest?" Rahotep said.

"Pharaoh assembles his lords in council today," Nereb returned. "They have come to mourn the Pharaoh departed; they will listen to the Pharaoh who now reigns."

But Rahotep, as well as Nereb, knew the folly of hoping for much from that direction. The Nomarch of Nabket, the son of the Nomarch of Elephantine had come, true enough; their state barges were moored at the docks of Thebes. But the other major nobles were represented by lesser men. There were pleas of border unrest from the Nomarch of "The Land in Front," which faced Nubia, a plea that might well be true. The captain wondered if Unis were still alive—or had the rebel Prince Teti already rid himself of one who might be a rival?

Nereb might have been reading Rahotep's ranging thoughts at that moment. "This Teti, did your brother support him?"

The captain shrugged. "You saw how welcome the prince was in Semna when you were there. I had been away from the Viceroy's court more than five years. I have no knowledge of any pact that might have united Unis and Teti. But Unis is heir to the Lady Meri-Mut, and her family once held partial dominion over Egypt itself during the Years of Disturbance. However, if he thought to use Teti to climb to the high seat, I believe he has already had an unhappy awakening from some foolish dream. Teti is not such as will 'kiss earth' before any man. Nor was Unis one who could enforce his power upon Nubia. He is the eldest son of Ptahhotep, but he is not Ptahhotep!"

"Time!" Nereb sprang up from the stool where he had been sitting. "But give our lord time! We are between two snakes spitting poison—either or both must be slain for our safety, but we cannot kill them at the same instant!"

"I do think we have a measure of time in this," Rahotep said slowly. "Teti is not lacking in wits. He will wish to secure what he now holds beyond any question before he moves to gulp anything outside his present borders. To take the field against Thebes, and those who hold for Thebes, while Unis may still have some power in Semna is a folly he will not commit. And there has been no news that my brother has abruptly departed to the horizon. But I tell you, Lord, should we hear that Unis unfortunately trod upon some poisonous thing in the garden—then let us pound drums and mount archers upriver to await a storm. If Pharaoh will move at once against this Hyksos threat before Teti can make sure of his authority—"

That suspense seemed to be a part of the very air of Thebes. Under the ceremonial mourning for the Pharaoh departed was the unrest concerning the next moves of the Pharaoh present and future. Rahotep discovered that Zau was very far from being alone in his conservative fear of arousing the Hyksos and destroying the state of uneasy peace that had existed through the years of stalemate. Perhaps a goodly portion of the city was willing to pay tribute, willing even to welcome the alien general now on his way upriver, because they had no confidence in their ability to strike back. The battles that had crushed all their defiance generations earlier had grown worse in the telling, so that among the ignorant, the Hyksos were granted the powers and malice of evil gods, to whom men must resign themselves as they did to the searing winds from the desert.

The treason that had murdered Sekenenre remained a carefully guarded secret. Lest the Vizier and his fellow conspirators be considered martyrs to their cause, they were said to have died of the plague. But as yet no word had come as to how Thebes was to receive the Hyksos general or what was to happen to the army camped in the highlands.

It was given to Rahotep to be present as one of the royal guard when Kamose met with that small handful of nobles who had gathered at Thebes to greet their new ruler. Only two standards from the south—those signs of nomarchs or their heirs—were present. A second pair of standards of nomes near Thebes showed among a body of lesser courtiers—a handful of men standing in a hall where the passing of centuries had faded the paintings. Thebes was old, tired, worn—The court was shabby and shrunken. A prince of Thebes on the throne, daring to wear the double crown and defy the might of a widespread empire, was only a shadow Pharaoh as Rahotep was the shadow Hawk, Pharaoh and Nomarch in name more than fact.

The Prince Ahmose stood beside his brother's throne, the crooked sword of a royal commander across his arm, point upward, as the Crook and the Flail were balanced by Kamose. And in that tired company the younger prince, in spite of his statue-stillness, was doubly vibrant and alive.

"Life! Health! Prosperity! Blessed be the name of the Son of Re!" droned the chamberlain. "Let him sojourn in the Two Lands until the white bird turns black, and the black bird turns white, until the hills arise to depart from us, and until water flows upstream! Hail the One whom Re has set as a shepherd for His people!"

The company saluted, but it seemed to the captain that there was nothing spontaneous or enthusiastic in their greeting to their new lord. All were tired old men—for even those courtiers who were young in years had the selfsame air of weariness. There was no more vitality left here than there was in a sun-dried bone found in the sands of the outer wastes.

"Lord of the Two Lands—" After the ceremonious call of the chamberlain, Kamose's voice was the crack of a bow cord upon discharge of an arrow. He sat like a statue of his own divine royalty, but that flame that burned within his frail body licked out feverishly at the men before him.

"We have gathered to mourn him who has departed, aye, even Sekenenre, Son of Re, Lord of the White and the Red, Amon-on-Earth! Yet that is but a part of a greater whole—"

There was a faint stir in the lines of those men and women drawn up strictly according to their rank, standing each on the spot prescribed to his birth or office centuries before. No one spoke before the face of the Pharaoh without orders. But neither had the Son of Re ever addressed a court in the words Kamose now used. And that departure from rite and custom sent a decorous ripple across the hall, as a wind ripples a growing field of young grain.

"To what purpose is the power of Re—of Egypt—when our enemy sits safe in Avaris, a city built of stone torn from our hills, the blocks laid by slaves of our blood. One chieftain claims the two crowns in Avaris, while in Nubia another raises his hand to snatch the Crook and the Flail! We have lain in the years of darkness as did our fathers before us. Did not the divine Amenemhet generations ago set up his standard here in Thebes, tearing down the evil rule that was before him? And not easy then was the winning of his battle against Set.

"So I say to you now, the spider in the north grows fat upon its sucking of the Black Land. The shrines of our Great Ones have been thrown to earth or given over to the worship of their vile god. Upon our necks rests the yoke of oxen, for to the barbarians we are less than the beasts who break the fields for planting.

"The Son of Re cannot call upon the gods in sacred Memphis. Nor can he send grain from the fields, cloth from the warehouses to his people in their need. We are worn thin and old with servitude to a barbarian who knows not the Great Ones. And I say to you that the time has come to grapple with the aliens, to deliver Egypt from their defilement, bringing once more the ancient light to this land!"

The force of his words drew an odd hollow echo from the roof above them. He made a little sign to the chamberlain who produced a role of papyrus and stood ready to read.

"Listen now to the words of those who say they speak for you!"

There was a curtness in that, and once again a ripple of surprise passed over the court. Rahotep did not doubt that more than one courtier in that company already knew the text that the chamberlain was reading, perhaps had a voice in its writing. And what did such a man think now at hearing his own argument put so baldly?

"True it is that the aliens have advanced far into our land, and they have mocked us bitterly and laid upon us burdens of tribute and the force of their stern rule. But we of Thebes are secure in our possession of our lands here and to the southward, even right to the border of the Land of the Bow. Elephantine is a strong fortress to hold against Nubia, and its lord is with us, as are other lords. Do not the men of the south till for us the finest of their lands, and our cattle graze fat in the marshes? What is the north to us? Let the Asiatics hold the swamps of the north; ours is the heart of the Two Lands. If they bring out their strong men and war upon us, then shall we raise spear and bow in our defense. Then only will it be time for Pharaoh to lead us into battle."

"'We of Thebes are secure in our possession of our lands.'" Kamose repeated the words with searing bitterness. "Foolish men! While one of the Hyksos remains on the Black Earth, no man is secure! Even at this hour a general appointed by Avaris approaches Thebes, and he does not come alone—an army marches with him! I am the Shepherd of Egypt under Re. Remember"—Kamose stood up—"though I hold a Crook for the safekeeping of my people, also do I hold a Flail for the lashing of their enemies! Thus do I answer those who are 'secure in Thebes'!"

He raised the ceremonial Flail and brought its thongs singing down to rip the papyrus roll from the chamberlain's hands, sending it torn to the floor.

"Re has spoken!"

"Re has spoken!" the chamberlain echoed, his voice a startled whinny as he stared at the roll on the floor.

"Re has spoken!" A few of those assenting voices were firm, emphatic, but others trailed off as the Pharaoh turned and left the hall. There was a sigh of relaxation as the curtain fell across the doorway, the faintest trickle of whispering. Now the uncertainty of the city was gone. Thebes might not be happy, but her lord had made his decision. Sekenenre the warrior was dead, but Kamose the warrior was living.

And Kamose, the warrior, having made his decision, firmly and publicly, moved fast from that moment. Within the hour royal messengers flashed off in chariots, in fast-oared ships. The camp in the highlands was alerted; the naval vessels on the river gathered through the rising swell of the flood waters; the Hundreds of the neighboring nomes were summoned to join the standard of Pharaoh. Kamose broke with custom and decree. He might mourn his father in his heart, but he lingered to make no lengthy sacrifices at his tomb. Egypt, at last, was on the march!

The raid Ahmose had led upon the horse camp of the Hydsos had not prepared Rahotep for his second encounter with enemy forces. With one of the wild Bwedani from the desert as a guide, a small party of archers and Egyptian scouts struck deep into the territory surrounding Neferusi. The captain was familiar from childhood with the vast works of Semna, which had been almost a century in building. But now he viewed from a distance a city as well if not better defended by walls and buttresses.

"For a generation this had been the foremost Hyksos hold in the south." Nereb, lying belly-flat against the ground, shaded his eyes against the sun with his hands. "It is said to be a small copy of Avaris itself. To take it by open assault—"

His words dwindled. The other answer would be a siege. And that required time the Egyptians did not have. The scouting party had worked its way by night and day in a half circle about the city at a discreet distance. There was a single entrance, and the way from it led between walls in a sharp bend, so that those who came in or out needs must walk between two lines of fortifications to a second gate, under menacing bows and slings of the alert guards.

But Rahotep had seen something beside those walls and their sentries. There were men on the walls who were not armed, who labored under taskmasters' whips, either making repairs or adding new heights to already towering barriers. Several such parties were employed, had been employed in such toil during the two days they had been spying upon Neferusi. And how better could a man examine the fortifications then by using his eyes as he worked on them?

"In Nubia we have a saying," he said slowly. "'One may crack an egg from the inside.'"

Nereb, his eyes screwed against the sun, stared at him uncomprehendingly. Rahotep gestured to the distant walls and the men who worked there.

"What manner of men serve the Hyksos as slaves?"

"All manner of men. Their prisoner nets are cast far. They say that even the warriors of Minos are sometimes caught in them. But here they would be mostly men of Egypt."

"Suppose then we presented them with another slave.

Or do they keep so strict an accounting of their laborers that one more could not be added to a gang without their notice?"

As if in answer to that question, so apt an answer that Rahotep always believed it was sent by a Great One, Kheti slipped like a brown skinned shadow across the sands to stretch out beside them with a new report.

"Lords, a caravan—from the other side—approaching the city. Shall we capture them?" His eyes glistened with excitement.

"Not so!" Rahotep ordered. "Have I not said we must not be suspected here. Is it a company of warriors?"

Kheti spat. "Say rather a company of slaves, Lord. They march under the whip, and it is no officer's flail!"

"I would see this." Leaving Nereb in his chosen post, the captain followed Kheti out in a circle path, which brought them again to the north of the city. Though they had made some of that trip at a run—when they could find sufficient cover—yet the caravan was so close to the city gates that Rahotep had little time for a detailed study. That it was formed of slaves marching under guard, their arms strained painfully behind their backs, their elbows linked with cords, nooses about their necks beading them together, was plain. So—there were new slaves being brought into Neferusi. To work on the walls? A wild plan began to grow in the captain's mind. It was one with many, many weak spots, one in which action, and undoubtedly the life of the man who carried it out, would depend largely upon luck. Yet—it might give them a spy within the city and save them the costly siege that could doom their whole campaign.

"Is this the first such train to enter?" he asked Kheti.

"The first since we have watched, Lord."

"Knowing you, Kheti, I also know that you have marked out a place where such a train might be ambushed—"

"Aye." The Nubian was grinning. "Do we take the next one, Lord? Perhaps these dogs will give tongue—telling us all they know."

Another flicker of an idea, a small addition to his plan. "Not yet—but I would look upon one of these slave gangs closely."

Two hours later he had begun to think that the slave gang they had seen pass into Neferusi was the last, or else an extraordinary event instead of a usual one. Only two slow processions of oxcarts, heavily laden and well guarded by Hyksos warriors, had passed the reed thickets where Rahotep and Kheti crouched in vast discomfort, plagued by insects, the smell of rotting things thick about them, the slime of green mud covering their bodies.

But at the end of the midday rest a second slave convoy came along the road where the yearly flood was already sending fingers of wet across the baked clay. And Rahotep, studying that miserable party driven by his hiding place, saw that they were, indeed, mostly his countrymen. Marked with whip weals and the sores and bruises of constant ill-usage, they shuffled by, their eyes on the ground, lacking even the spirit of village asses set treading out the harvests. These were husks of men, and seeing them, a small portion of hope that nourished an offshoot of his plan died. None of these would turn upon their masters, even if their bonds were cut and daggers and spears put in their hands. Their guards treated them with the contempt some men feel toward animals. Instead of marching strung along the line, as they did when closer to the city and so under the eyes of their officers, the Hyksos—or rather in this case, the Bwedani mercenaries—strolled together, talking loudly and sharing from hand to hand a wine skin with the obvious intent of finishing off its contents before they reached Neferusi. Now and then one of them trotted along the line, flicking his whip over some stooped pair of shoulders, but the slaves did not exist to the guards as individuals—which solved part of the captain's problem.

When the caravan had passed, he withdrew to join Nereb.

"I would speak with the Royal Son—"

"You have a plan?" Nereb sounded almost accusing, as if he thought Rahotep should share his thoughts. But the captain was so intent upon the working out of his scheme that he paid little attention to his companion. He posted Kheti and Hori to watch the road, with orders to list the traffic there, with special attention to slave trains, and then he headed for the distant Egyptian campsite.

Accustomed to the smaller gatherings of border patrols, he looked upon that camp with amazement. It appeared to him that it had grown again a third in size since he had left it five days earlier. With its shield walls, its picket lines of burden animals, its horse and chariot lines, and its central gathering of tents, it now bore a close resemblance to a city of nomads.

But Rahotep's preoccupation with his own schemes was broken as he saw the identity of the scribe who attended Ahmose at the headquarters' tent. Surely Sebni had no place here! The fellow was of Zau's discredited party. So he kept his mouth shut, determined that unless he could speak in private to the prince, he would not speak at all.

"Provisions and slaves going in," Ahmose repeated a bit later. "They prepare then for a siege, as the added work upon the walls indicates also. But then we could not hope that they would do differently. They are a race that builds forts to hold—"

Rahotep noted that Nereb was watching him questioningly. He must wonder why the captain did not explain the reason for their sudden return to camp. But the prince clapped his hands and to the servant in the doorway he said, "Wine for the lords. They have had a hot journeying—"

When the servant returned, bearing a jar on his shoulder, he kept away from the corner of the tent nearest the entrance, and the prince chuckled.

"I have a new guard in training, kinsman," he said to Rahotep. "Since you have had notable success in that field, perhaps you can advise me. Come and see this mighty warrior newly added to our forces!"

He led the captain to the corner where the young lion they had taken on the hunt, muzzled, was confined by a leash. It growled as they approached, but the prince went down on one knee and fondled the unwilling head, looking deep into the topaz eyes until the growling died away.

"He looks apt to answer to your guidance, Royal Son—"

"As you do to mine?" The question came in a half whisper under the cover of louder words. "Aye, yesterday he took meat from my hand. Soon he will do without the muzzle." Then again in that low tone, "There is something you would tell me?"

"Aye!" Rahotep answered with the one word both question and observation.

"I would look upon your leopard, kinsman. Nay, Sebni," the prince added as the scribe arose and would have come to join them. "This is no affair of state whereof notes must be made for Pharaoh, but a matter of the taming of beasts. I need no attendance."

Once outside the tent, he spoke more quickly. "You are not lacking in wits, kinsman, to keep a hold on your tongue—"

"Lord, what does that one here?" Rahotep led the way back to his own tent, which Bis shared.

"It is better to have an untrustworthy overseer tallying in the storehouse where the master watches, than in a distant grainfield," Ahmose answered obliquely. "Also something can be learned from watching a spy who believes himself safe. But what have you to tell me?"

"I believe, Royal Son, I have found a way that one may enter into Neferusi and there learn something of the city and its defenses."

"Does this scout grow the wings of Horus or is he to be as invisible as a night demon?"

"He joins one of the slave trains now being brought into the city, and he labors on the walls—"

The prince stopped and faced the other squarely. "Always providing that he is not promptly speared by a guard who counts one too many on his man-tally—or is not uncovered within Neferusi to be fed to their god bit by bit."

"But what, Royal Son, if he is already provided with a

disguise such as will easily mark him as one of their captives?"

"That being, kinsman?"

Rahotep pivoted, showing the newly healed scars on his back.

"Being this, prince. I am amply fitted to play the part of a slave who has tasted the lash."

When the prince made no comment, Rahotep turned again, ready to argue his point. But the look in the other's eyes kept him silent for a moment.

"It was not in my power to spare you that, kinsman!"

"Do you think that I ever believed different, Royal Son? There was at that time a net about me that no man except those who wove it could loosen. But now I rejoice that this was so. Does it not give me the right to try this entry of Neferusi?"

"You throw sticks that are weighted against you. There is one chance in a thousand of your safe return."

"Not so, Royal Son. Believe me when I say that I shall lay my plans well and there shall be those outside Neferusi who shall stand by to bring me forth again."

"That there shall be!" promised the prince fervently.

Rahotep shook his head. "No men of these forces, prince. Let me depend upon my archers. This is a venture after their own hearts, and we have played like games before."

"Now you cannot tell me the truth! No man has entered into a city of the Hyksos in such a guise. I cannot allow you—"

"Royal Son, just now you said you regret what I received by mistake under Pharaoh's justice—can you not see that there was some design of a Great One in all this? Only a man so scarred would dare to try my plan. When you go into battle, you use the best weapon lying to your hand."

Ahmose sighed. "I see you will have it so, even if I set a contrary order upon you. But this is my will and yours also—you will lay your plan well and you will stay no more than a day and a night within that nest of stinging bees! If we win Neferusi through your efforts, claim what gold of valor you wish, even unto your father's office in Nubia, and Pharaoh shall confirm you in it!"

14

Icar, the Seafarer

"Pull that cord tighter, fool!" Rahotep ordered between set teeth and then was ashamed that he had allowed his tension to show so plainly, even to Kheti with whom he had shared almost every test and danger of his life since early childhood. Was it his warrior's pride now that kept him from calling off this wild venture? He did not know. Instead he shied away from investigating his uneasiness too closely.

The ceremony with which the Pharaoh had welcomed him back into the ranks of his "shields" might wipe out the shame of his conviction for treason, but some inward part of Rahotep still ached dully, as did his shoulders when he put too great a strain upon his scarred back—as they ached now, with Kheti efficiently tying his elbows together in the torturing bonds of a slave.

Mahu threaded through the dried reeds, which gave forth only the faintest of rustles to belie his skill as a scout.

"They come, Lord. And Dedun smiles on us! One of the guards must have been hurt—they carry him on a litter and

187

his fellows walk beside him. They seldom look upon the slaves."

The soft brush of fur against his leg brought Rahotep's attention to Bis. Now the cub's eyes met his, and to the captain it was as if he could read true understanding in them. They had trained vigorously during the past three days, using long hours, he and Bis. And now much of the success of his plan would depend upon how the cub would respond. Rahotep must enter Neferusi in the role of slave in the late afternoon. Bis would enter the city at nightfall on the next day. And with Bis's aid both of them might come safely out. But that word was only a shaky "might," with no certainty behind it.

"Stay!" Rahotep spoke the word distinctly. "Stay with Kheti!"

Since his arms were now in the slave halter, he nudged Bis toward the Nubian with his knee. Bis regarded the captain unblinkingly with that disconcerting gaze that is the gift of the feline clan, and then sat down, curling the tip of his nervous tail neatly over his front toes. Bis would stay.

There was a screen of reeds between them and the road. Behind Rahotep, and on either side of that highway, his men were in hiding. But now a whistling bird call from a fringe Scout heralded the coming of the caravan. A file of men, for the most part neck-noosed and arm-bound, wavered by, dull and broken-spirited. And then came a litter carried by four of their kind who had been pressed into the duty. On it one of the guards lay, his face flushed a dusky red as he breathed in tearing snores. Sun-touched, Rahotep thought.

Mahu had been right. The rest of the guards flanked the litter with an anxious attention that suggested that the stricken man was their commander. Only now and again did any run back to bring up the straggling line of slaves. Rahotep watched one guard make that tour and return to his post ahead. The slaves who had fallen into a shuffling trot under his cracking whip were closing up, and as the tail of that forlorn procession passed the screen before the captain, he drew a deep breath—such as he might have taken before plunging into the current of the Nile at flood—and stepped out into the trail to join them.

So much depended upon his luck at that second and during the few that would follow. To the outward eye he was filthy, as naked and ill-used as the rest. But would any of them show surprise and draw the attention of the guards? If that happened, he prayed it would be at once, while the archers hidden in the reeds could give him cover to escape. Let such a discovery be made beyond this thicket, closer to the city walls, and he would have to depend upon his own fleetness of foot. And once inside Neferusi, betrayal would mean only death, and not a clean or quick death.

His heart thumped heavily in his chest as he matched his pace to the slaves' shuffle and drew level with the last two men. One of them was half reeling, his face drawn into a skull's harsh angles under the thin coating of grimed skin, an unshaven beard straggling patchily from his jaw line. The slave's eyes were half closed, and he stared at the ground ahead as if he saw only it—or perhaps nothing at all.

Rahotep's other companion was of a different breed. He was no driven rack of bones close to the end of his miserable life, though he was as unkempt as the other. His head turned at the captain's coming.

It was then that Rahotep saw he was not an Egyptian. But neither was he of the same race as the Hyksos. His skin, under the grime and dust, was several shades lighter than the captain's own, and his matted hair was faded almost white under the strength of the sun. He was as tall as Kheti and, had he been well fed, might have matched the Nubian in strength of arm and limb.

Just as he was different in appearance from the other slave, so also was he far more alert to what lay about him. But though he studied Rahotep from head to foot in a series of sharp glances, he said nothing. And the captain began to hope that he would not, for now they were coming from the reed bed into the open territory about the city.

Or did this stranger expect to wait until Rahotep was entrapped within the walls and then give the alarm, so buying better treatment, perhaps even freedom, for himself? Though the hours the captain had lain in the dungeons of Anubis had seemed endless, longer yet was the space of time it took for the slave train to crawl to the gates of Neferusi and to enter the first of those gates and march between the encircling walls to the second.

Rahotep studied carefully the well-guarded entrance to the city. But more than half his mind waited for the eventual shout from the man marching next to him, the ultimate disclosure leading to his capture. But that betrayal did not come. The tall, fair-skinned unknown no longer watched him but marched with his eyes to the ground in front, and now his broad shoulders were a little bowed. He trudged along as if he had not only lost interest, but energy and spirit as well.

Even if his companion in the slave train did not call attention to him, Rahotep now faced another crisis. If the Hyksos administrator scribes were as meticulous in their duties as those of the Egyptian forces, there would be a roster of labor slaves and they would be checked off on that list. Discreet questioning in the royal camp had brought him no information about Hyksos affair. He had to trust to the Great Ones' favor in that respect as in many others.

It might have been the illness of the guard officer that caused the confusion as they entered the second and final gate of Neferusi. But in any event, no official produced any list and Rahotep, with his fellow bondsmen, was herded into a dark warehouse, already well tenanted by some of the city slaves. The stifling heat and horrible stench of the place struck them at the door, making Rahotep so dizzy for a moment or two that he lurched sidewise, stumbling against the light-haired stranger.

The man shoved him away roughly and, in the strongly accented Egyptian speech of the slave caste, grunted, "On your feet, stupid one. Do you think you are the captain to be litter-borne?"

That shove had sent the Scout captain against the wall, and he leaned there, very glad of its support, as he surveyed the hole into which they had been thrust. There were windows after all, but there were only four of them near the roof, and the air they admitted was negligible. The heat of the day was trapped below that roof so that most of the men prisoned there could only lie on the beaten earth floor, if they could find space enough to stretch out their cramped limbs, and pant like dying fish caught in a casting net.

Unless they were given some relief, Rahotep thought grimly, the labor gangs would be thinned by morning. Even men inured to labor beneath the sun and the fierce heat of the dry season could not long hold strength or health under this.

"You have chosen a bad lodging—"

The dark of the room had been intensified by the closing of the door, and Rahotep heard the locking bar rattle into place. But that sound was not loud enough to blank out the husky half-whisper. And the barbarous accent was that of the stranger.

"You also," he replied shortly.

The bark of sound that came from the stranger next might have been intended for a laugh, though there was little humor in it. "Not by my own will—" And in spite of the crudity of accent, the intonation of those few words hinted to Rahotep that the other was deeply interested in him and meant to press for an explanation.

"Not by my own will," the other repeated more sharply when the captain did not reply. "I am one Icar, a seafarer—or was a seafarer," he added with a bitterness easy to hear.

"You were wrecked?" the captain asked, not because he had any real wish to hear the other's story, but if he kept the fellow talking of his own affairs, he escaped awkward questions in return.

"Wrecked? Not so! Wrecking one can understand—such fortune is the will of the gods. But the seizure of the king's men—that is something else, not directed by any

191

god save a dark one!" There was hot passion in that protest. "Let one of these Hyksos claim a debt and swear to it before a judge of his own blood and a man's ship is seized, his body sold!"

"You are of the islanders who follow Minos?"

"Not so! I am of the northern lands beyond the Bull's kingdom. The gods gave me an ill gift at my birthing, an itch which tingles in my feet so that I must ever seek new places. But this is a new place I have no liking for—" He sighed, and slipped down to the floor, where in the dusky shadow his big frame was but a darker blot among the others already resting there.

"You term yourself seafarer," commented Rahotep without realizing where his idle words would lead, "yet I would have said that you know the feel of an ax haft in your hand. Or do you favor the swords of the northerners?"

"An ax *and* a sword, warrior! Aye, I know the swing of either—just as you do—"

Rahotep squirmed. This Icar was hitting too close to the truth. He replied to that hint swiftly.

"A battle captive needs must forget such skills when he is put on the slave block—"

"Aye. But never before have I seen a slave come out of hiding to join himself to his fellows by his own will. Rather is it that he takes to his heels in the opposite direction. Also, though you have rolled in the dust and allowed your beard to grow somewhat, you are too well fed and walk with too firm a step to have been long in bonds. Nay, I shall not ask you what you do here—what a man does not know he cannot be forced to tell. But it seems to me that you have walked into a lion's den for the purpose of thrusting your sandal hard against his nose. And what lion takes such impudence kindly?"

Rahotep chuckled. The wry humor of the barbarian seaman was contagious, and he began to wonder if he could not take the other a little into his confidence and include him in future plans. Icar plainly retained his spirit and, by the looks of him, much of his bodily strength. Certainly he would have little love for his Hyksos captors.

And the promise of freedom might bring him into partnership.

The bar at the door was lifted, and the portal opened to admit a set of Nubians bearing jars and baskets of hard bread. They might have been mobbed by the more agile of the penned slaves, but they were accompanied by overseers who used their whips freely to clear a space in which the food and drink was left. As the Nubians and the guards withdrew, there was a concentrated rush for the supplies. But Icar had already jumped in front of the jars and was using his fists furiously, shouting, "Sons of pigs! Eaters of dust! Take care—the water must not be spilled!"

His roar, trained to outblast sea gales, reached enough ears to stem that forward thrust, and Rahotep pushed up beside him as a ready lieutenant. A nucleus of the keener-witted and stronger slaves came to their aid, so that the jars remained safe, and Icar measured out a share of the precious liquid to each man, with the exactitude of one to whom water was often scarce.

Rahotep mouthed a portion of the dust-dry bread he did not wish but could not refuse, and then sipped a mouthful of water, glad of his training in arid living. But though he had withdrawn from the huddle about the supplies, he was not to escape Icar so easily. The seaman came to hunker down beside him, cradling his own share of the bread in his big hand.

"These Hyksos dogs do not know how to handle slaves," he remarked. "You get more labor out of man who is well fed and tended than you do from a rack of bones."

"It may be that they have so many necks under their yokes that they need not count the dead in their slave gangs," returned the captain bleakly.

"And Egyptians they need not fear—since they have been allowed to lie fat and untroubled in this land for many years—"

Rahotep curbed a sharp retort, suspicious that the other might be baiting him. He schooled all emotion out of his voice as he answered.

"How may a man revolt when all the weapons are in the hands of his enemies and his own are empty? Do you expect spirit-broken spectres to rise against their guards?"

"Yesterday I might have said 'Even so' to that. Tonight—tonight I am beginning to think that there is perhaps a spark of hope. And there may be those within this very room who might be inspired to active defiance were that hope made theirs also."

"Why do you believe that tonight?" asked Rahopep.

There was a lazy laugh out of the dark. "Maybe I have been favored with a revelation from the gods—or more likely I have seen a slave slink out of safe hiding to join a train of his fellows. As I have said, comrade in bonds, no man with wits in his skull would do that unless he had a strong purpose, and that purpose can mean no good to those who hold the power now in Neferusi! Tell me!" A hand closed about Rahotep's forearm, crushing the flesh painfully. "Tell me, what do you here? Is it some act of private vengeance or do you look to nose out secrets of Neferusi for another reason?"

"And why should I answer your questions, Icar?" Rahotep kept his voice steady, nor did he try to jerk his arm free from that vise.

"Because I am no born slave, man of the Two Lands—" He gave Rahotep the name Egyptians used for themselves. "And I have kept ready for the day when I might strike back at these oath-breakers and man-stealers! I love the Hyksos no better than you do. And I believe that you would not have entered Neferusi unless you not only had a plan in mind to put into action against these devil worshipers, but also a way to get out again. So I am willing to aid you in order that you may tell me of that way out—remembering always"—his light tone was gone and there was a harsh note in his voice—"that I can point you out to those who would be most eager to question you— with far less kindness!"

There was truth in every word of that. Rahotep accepted the sincerity of the man. And Icar would be an able comrade. His own plans were flexible enough to include the barbarian.

"You have guessed rightly. I am in Neferusi to see what

can be seen. And I plan to leave tomorrow night."

"And what must you see?" persisted Icar eagerly.

"The walls and the guards stationed on them, the forces within those walls—"

He had dropped his own voice to a half whisper, and now he felt Icar's grasp on his arm, which had loosened, grow tight again.

"Say no more, man of the Two Lands," he was ordered. "It is enough that you come here on such a mission. Let me contrive it when they call out the slaves in the morning that we shall both be in the same gang and put to the right work. I have lived among these Hyksos for a year. What I have learned of them is yours. Now, sleep if you can, for they rouse out the workers before dawn."

But Rahotep found sleep hard to pursue in the slave quarters of Neferusi. He regretted the hours that must lapse before he could be about the business that had brought him there. And when Icar's breathing close to his ear became an intermittent snoring, he half resented the other's ability to rest. Then he nodded into a broken dozing in which dream monsters lurked.

The seaman had been right. The guards came in with their rousing whips before the light was gray, and a second installment of food was brought to those penned in that stinking hole. Rahotep bit into a hot onion and cooled his mouth with the bread, which was half husks. But they were given only a limited time to eat. On order, Icar pulled at his shoulder, urging him to the door and whispering, "Those first out are deemed the strongest. They shall be used for the wall work—"

That suggestion was enough to make Rahotep press forward so eagerly that again his mentor had to caution him. "What slave runs to his toil, comrade? Be out early, aye, but do not clamor for labor."

They were lined up in squads of ten in the courtyard, and Rahotep kept to the side of the seaman. There were three Nubians also in his group, and he watched them speculatively. Like Icar, they appeared not to have suffered so severely from their hard life, though they were clearly underfed and overworked. But Nubians! If he could have the chance to sound them out, he might discover other lieutenants besides Icar among these chattels of the Hyksos. The rest of the group were a Bwedani—a small, wiry man with a vicious face, a criminal Rahotep thought, rather than a serf or war captive—and four Egyptians, dull, patient men with all the rebellion and intelligence starved and beaten out of them.

They were strung together in neck nooses, a minor torturous arrangement whereby any man not keeping pace with his fellows could well strangle his neighbors—so enlisting their vigilance to add to that of the guard. Thus they were marched to the walls, a destination Rahotep greeted eagerly.

He had thought that his life on the Kush frontier and the hardships of the past weeks had inured him to all discomfort. But he had not been before a burden slave, and he speedily discovered that neither the deserts of the south nor the dungeons of Anubis had prepared him for this. The Egyptians worked with dogged patience; the Bwedani shirked when he could, though their overseer was a conscientious man determined to get the best out of his squad, and the thongs of his lash found the back of the small man regularly until he was driven to pulling his weight with the rest. Icar and the Nubians had the greater strength, and they hoisted stones in a rhythm fitted to the Nubians' monotonous work song.

They were given rests measured by the sun's creeping up a notched stick, and during one such Rahotep, greatly daring, spoke to the Nubian who had thrown himself down between the captain and the pile of stones they were to set in place.

"By the horns of the Spotted Goat, this is work to roast a man in his own juices."

The eyes in that dark face opened, and the man stared at him.

"Who are you," he asked in the same low-pitched whisper, "who swears by the Spotted One of the bowmen?"

"One who has drawn bow cord in their company."

Rahotep bit down his excitement. By chance, or by some design beyond his comprehension, his password had been right. The man he had spoken to was, or had been, of a southern warrior clan.

"I am Huy who was tricked into taking service with these dogs of evil, only to discover that the service was not that of the bow but of the back." He spat. "And you who have also held the bow—what do you here?"

"If I say to make trouble for the sons of Set, will you believe it?"

Those white teeth showed in a leopard's grin. "Believe it? Rather will I say let me join in such trouble—"

"And there are others here of a like mind?"

Huy's head went back against the ground once more, and the captain was warned. His tender shoulders gritted against the rough stone, and he stared vacantly down at his hands as a detachment of Hyksos wall guards tramped by. But he had counted them and assessed their arms—slinger, spearmen, two bowmen.

"There are others—" That was the merest thread of speech from the seemingly sleeping Nubian.

The southerner had no time to enlarge on that, for a messenger was making the rounds of the work gangs. As he paused by each overseer, the resting slaves were shouted at and beaten to their feet and lined up ready to march away. From the exclamations of surprise about him, Rahotep gathered that such a move was contrary to ordinary routine, and for the first time since he successfully passed the guard the night before, the Egyptian captain felt uneasy concerning his own safety.

His gleanings that morning had been meager. A few hasty estimates of the types of soldiers within Neferusi from the bodies of troops he had seen from the wall, tag ends of rumor picked up from the slaves, most of whom were too brutalized to care or note the affairs of their masters, and a very healthy respect for the fortifications he labored to make even more impregnable were the sum total of his gatherings.

From the vast amounts of provisions being brought in by oxcart, he guessed that Neferusi was being prepared to stand siege. But he had overheard a comment from a gate guard going off duty that those heavily laden carts bore only a portion of supplies for the city, that the majority of their cargoes was the tribute collected from the surrounding districts, now to be sent north under the new general's orders to the Asiatic armies of the Hyksos.

Rahotep had set himself during the past hour to watch the arrival of such cart trains and their reception at the gates. While there was a guard about every three or four carts and the officer in charge had to present a tally to the gatemen, there was no search of the wagons themselves. A memory of the way they had transported their secret prisoners from the Valley of the Lizard to the royal city, together with what he had seen here, suggested a plan to him. But it seemed that he was going to have little chance to advance his investigations on the spot.

The messenger was now talking to the overseer of Rahotep's gang, but as he used the Hyksos tongue, the listening Egyptian was no wiser. It was Icar who warned him. Behind the overseer's back the seaman made a beckoning gesture, which the captain obeyed. He moved up to join the taller barbarian, so that when they were once more noosed neck to neck, he was between Icar and Huy of the Nubians. They then stood aside for the passing of a line of tribute carts and Icar spoke.

"They have heard that there is a spy in Neferusi, concealed among the slaves—"

Rahotep's hands had been at his throat to ease the pull of the noose, now they tightened on that chafing cord. How—who—?

"The word was brought to them from without the city," Icar added swiftly.

From without the city! Were there more traitors within the Egyptian camp? Yet he had thought his a well-guarded secret. Only the Prince, Nereb, and his own command had known what he attempted here. And Kheti would keep an eye on those of the archers who were noted as being loose tongued. Or had that hiding place in the reeds been discovered and were Kheti and the others prisoners now?

15

Nebet of Neferusi

The slave gangs that had been on the walls were herded back into the space fronting the inner barrier by the warehouse where they had spent the night. As they filed in, Rahotep saw what a mixture of races and nationalities they represented, for the empire of the Hyksos spread far beyond the boundaries of Egypt. There was more than just a sprinkling of Nubians, Asiatics from the Eastern lands, and some fair-skinned, fair-haired barbarians from the north, perhaps seamen who had fallen into captivity through the same trap as had closed upon Icar. But the majority were Egyptians, and Rahotep thought that with his scarred back he could well mix with these unfortunate countrymen of his without raising suspicion, unless he was personally known to the one who had betrayed his arrival in the city.

But whether he *was* known or not, this was the time he must be prepared to make his play for freedom. His right hand went to the cord that bound the slave's scanty apron cloth to his hips and then arose once more to the noose at his throat. Lying flat on his palm was the tiny bronze knife that had been Kheti's prized possession twenty-four hours earlier. He sawed at the neck rope under the pretext of easing its constriction, and then held the parted thongs together with his hand.

The knife was no weapon to aid him further. And now he could be generous with it. There were guards before them, but the Hyksos warriors paid them scant attention as long as they stood still. Rahotep's left hand brushed Icar's, pressing the small knife into the seafarer's grasp. The other showed no surprise as his fingers curled about it.

A party of Hyksos officers came along a side lane. Rahotep watched them narrowly, eager to see if they had a captured archer or an Egyptian in their midst—someone dragged here to point him out.

Icar's hand was at his throat noose. Then the knife was pressed back into the captain's hand again. Rahotep regarded his closed fist for a long moment before he transferred what lay within it to the other hand and so to Huy. Luckily the Nubian was quick-witted and mastered any sign of the astonishment he must have felt.

Rahotep was sure he could trust Icar. With Huy he might be taking a bigger chance, but his long service with Nubian warriors had given him a high opinion of their loyalty, courage, and resource in action, and he would prefer a Nubian as a fighting comrade to most of those he saw in Neferusi's slave pens.

He looked again to the Hyksos officers. They had come to the first gang of slaves, and the men were lining up before them for inspection. It was plain that they were searching for an Egyptian—those of other races in that gang were waved impatiently aside. But the natives were made to show their hands and their backs—inspected as if they were cattle put up to auction.

Rahotep glanced at his own fists. There were calluses there, old ones. A man could not use spear, bow, help to dig field fortifications, and not show hardened palms. But he wondered if the strip of lighter flesh on one finger, marking the place of his seal ring, could possibly show through the dirt he had rubbed in. And what about the same paler bands on his upper arms where his noble's bracelets had covered three-inch-wide circlets? Could they be detected? Even free of a neck noose, could he put up a fight with both guards and officers around him?

From the corner of his eye he saw Huy's hand touch that of his neighbor—another Nubian—and he guessed the knife was being passed along. But on the other side of that man was the wry-faced Bwedani in whom the captain did not rest any confidence and who might be moved to betray them all. He, Icar, Huy, the other Nubian—four of them against ten times that number of guards and the officers—unarmed, a hopeless fight—

Icar's fingers closed about his wrist in sudden cruel pressure. A warning—? But the Hyksos were not yet near. Then he was startled when the seaman shouted, "Up, eaters of dirt, fight for yourselves. They come to pick men to feed to their temple devils! They want meat for their snake-god!"

For an astounded second the slaves stared from the tall northerner to the officers. Then there came a murmur of protest, which rose in a wailing shriek, and the compound erupted in pure madness. The slaves before the Hyksos officers tried to shrink back, weaving here and there, knotted together by their neck nooses. And those farthest from that danger point faced their guards, screaming in an insane terror.

Rahotep was free, as were Icar and the Nubians. A small wedge of four, they plunged into the writhing mass of terrified slaves, swearing overseers, and guards. Rahotep saw two overseers pulled down by the sheer weight of desperate men, their whips torn from their hands, to be mauled to death. Huy grabbed one of those whips, reversed it, using its butt as a mace and so bowling out of their way a spearman.

The captain caught up the fallen guard's weapon. Icar stood over the moaning man long enough to snatch the dagger from his belt. Then they shoved shoulder to shoulder toward one of the lanes.

"Yaaaah! Waaaah!" Huy raised the savage war cry of his people and was answered by similar whoops from the twisting, whirling mass of slaves and guards. The first terror of the captives had risen to a frightening frenzy as those who had once been warriors remembered the past and determined to make one last stand against a common enemy. Twice Icar slashed a neck rope, put out a long arm to draw to them another freed fighter.

Once it was a squat, powerfully built man with a mat of red beard and a skin as fair as Icar's own, the other time a Kush with the filed teeth of a man-eater of the Rain Forests bared in the grin of a night demon. Why he chose those two, or if he did it deliberately, Rahotep did not know. But both fell in behind the seaman as if they knew him for a leader they could rely upon.

That insane tangle within the narrow space between wall and warehouse had sucked in most of the guards by now. And the officers who had been examining the Egyptian laborers shouted for help before they were overwhelmed, drawing more men away from the outer circle. Rahotep and Huy, using their weapons when necessary, made for a gap, and the others bunched behind them. Icar's bellow roared in their ears, rising at times above the war cries of the Nubians, both tending to drown out the shouted orders and calls of the guards.

"Waaah!" Drink blood!" screamed Huy, as he emerged a step or two in advance of Rahotep into a lane to face a squad of six warriors hastening toward the scene. Unfortunately for them, they were bowmen, and they were given neither time nor space to use their weapons to any advantage.

Huy reversed the whip again and brought the lash whistling across startled faces. Rahotep tripped one with the spear haft thrust between his legs and then fell on top of his quarry, banging his head back against one of the stones in the piles for wall building, so that the man went limp under him. He was able to arm himself with his victim's belt ax, coming up in the face of another guard with that blade swinging in the low and deadly arc he had been taught long ago.

Had the Hyksos been officered by one with his wits about him, perhaps they could have smothered Rahotep's small force, determined and deadly as the latter were. But Huy's first stroke of the lash had sent their commander crouching back against the wall, moaning, his hands over his eyes. And the men were totally disorganized by the attack they had not expected.

The Kush fought as a beast fights, with snapping teeth and rending nails, and Icar and the red-beard used their fists as well as the Nubians. When they were across that lane, they were all armed after a fashion, and those behind, if still living, had no interest in pursuit.

Icar slammed his shoulders back against a wall, and Huy followed his example. Together they formed a living ladder for their fellows, Rahotep being the first to be half-tossed to the top of the barrier. He scrambled across a flat roof of timbers coated with sun-dried mud, the typical covering of a poor district house, and hoped that the stuff would give them secure footing until they could leap the foot of space to the next. Running lightly along from one such roof to a second and a third, he flushed from his path two women and a child who screamed in fright.

The rest of the fugitives trailed him safely, and he dared to pause on the fourth roof to look about. But he had forgotten those towering walls about the town. Someone of the Hyksos officers had recovered from the first surprise and was going into efficient action. Slingers, stationed on the upper ramparts, were aiming into the melee below. And an overzealous marksman tried to reach the captain. Although that stone fell short, it sent them running on again.

But they were being headed away from the walls—to Rahotep's uneasiness. He dared not circle back for fear of capture. Had it been after nightfall he might have attempted a climb to the top and an attack upon some detachment of the guard. But in the full light of day there was no hope of that.

At length he swung by his hands from the edge of a roof and dropped into an alley from whence arose a cloud of buzzing flies and an awesome stench almost as bad as that of the slave warehouse. The others followed and clustered together for a moment, panting, looking about them for a new channel of escape.

Huy drew a heavy forearm across his forehead and grinned.

"Now that was a proper battle, Lord," he spoke to Rahotep, giving the Egyptian the title he would accord to any officer. "And you, outlander"—he surveyed Icar with open admiration—"have a pair of lungs in you! But how did you know they were coming to pick meat for their temple devil?"

Icar shrugged. "For all I know—they were not!"

Huy's grin split into open laughter, which his country-man echoed.

"So that was the way of it, white-skin? But I do not think these long-beards will relish your meddling—"

"Do any of you know Neferusi beyond the wall section and the slave warehouse?" Rahotep cut in crisply.

To his surprise the red-bearded stranger pushed forward the Kush. In a jargon of mixed languages, which was hardly intelligible to the Egyptian, he recommended the jungle savage as guide.

"This one—he live in temple—he tell—"

The Kush nodded violently and then clapped his hands together in pleasure as Rahotep demanded haltingly in the tongue of the border, "This place—you know? Where can we hide—until the big dark?"

The Kush spun around in the noisome alley, his nostrils expanding as if the horrible odor of the place masked another scent he would nose out. He quested so for a long moment and then pointed with an extended arm to the very heart of the city. Rahotep hesitated. Every step he took away from the outer walls added to his feeling of being cut off from escape. At the same time he knew that the city boundaries would be the first points covered by those striving to round up any escaped slaves. The fugitives could better go to ground somewhere in this maze of lanes and alleys where the soldiers would have to hunt them out house by house—until darkness gave them a small hope of cover.

The Kush stamped his foot with impatience and beckoned vigorously. It was apparent that he was entirely sure of himself, though why they should trust one of a race Rahotep had for years associated with every sly trick and wily treachery known he could not see. However, he had placed confidence in Huy and Icar, to his advantage, and the rest of them appeared willing to follow the jungle man, so he agreed.

Those festering, stinking lanes were populated well enough, but men and women dodged back into their filthy huts when they saw the fugitives coming. To the captain's surprise there was no outcry raised, no one strove to detain them or betray their passing. It was the red beard who provided a measure of explanation.

"Slaves!" He spat and swatted at the stinging carrion flies busy about them. "Masters no come here—without swords and whips open in hand and their back guarded—"

The Kush was boring deeper into the heart of this unsavory slum, which appeared to cover a large part of Neferusi's inner rottenness. He brought them at last to a door over which hung a tattered curtain, once splashed with dabs of raw, but now faded, color, in crude patterns that Rahotep recognized as being from the far south. With a second imperative wave of his hand, the file-toothed savage swung around the edge of this, and they pattered after him.

There was gloom within, almost as great as the gloom that had darkened the warehouse the night before. The fearful odors of unwashed skins, spoiled beer, and ill-cooked food made Rahotep's stomach churn uneasily. A woman, her face grotesquely overpainted in imitation of the elongated eyes and reddened lips of a court lady, sat on a pile of mats in the slit of light admitted by the single window close to the roof. She was very stout, the dull red sheath of her dress cutting under rolls of flesh at her armpits. A wig of frizzled false hair widened her already vast face to a monstrous expanse.

The Kush squatted down on his heels before her, chattering away in his own tongue, and Rahotep caught only a word or two that he could understand. But to his surprise the red beard swaggered forward and grinned familiarly at the mountain of woman.

"Nebet—" With his accent her name came out in an odd half-lisp. "So you still be alive, eh?"

She frowned, and on that wide face a frown approached the nature of a storm cloud and crackled several layers of paint. "Menon—thief—slave-dog— pig—" She recited the epithets as if they were all a part of his given name. "Two rings of copper!" Her cushion of a hand swept out, palm up in a demand for payment. "Nebet does not eat air, drink air—where is that you owe her?"

Red beard dared to chuck her lightly under her third chin and then dodged expertly the blow she aimed at him with a fist as large and heavy as Kheti's, laughing loudly at his near escape.

"Enough!" Icar took a hand, and red beard looked at the taller seaman as a simple warrior might look to his Commander of Fifty. Icar stirred the Kush with his foot, sending him silent. He spoke over his shoulder to Rahotep.

"What was this one telling her, comrade?"

The Egyptian captain was forced to shake his head. Bewildered, he had the feeling that the leadership in this venture was sliding out of his control to Icar—or perhaps to the woman. "He spoke too swiftly. I know a little of their speech, but not that well."

"Menon"—it was master addressing man—"who is this woman? And what is this place? You have been here before?"

But in turn Menon made his report in another tongue, one he must share with Icar, for the seaman listened closely. Then he translated for Rahotep.

"This is a place for those who have a greater liking for the night than the day, comrade—a place for thieves and such to take their ease. It is kept by one who does not welcome the Hyksos, and it would seem they do not come here often—or stay long—"

As he spoke, the woman had been glancing from face to face. Rahotep believed that her eyes were so accustomed

206

to the gloom of her surroundings that she was able to see as well as Bis in a half light. Now she was watching him intently, too intently—and with a shrewdness the captain did not relish. It was as if under that searching appraisal she was summoning out of the air to clothe him the uniform of a guard officer. And in that moment he would have sworn she had noted the telltale patch of lighter skin on his fingers, the marks left by his armlets between elbow and shoulder.

But when she lifted her huge hand, crooking a finger with absurd daintiness to beckon him forward, he advanced as if she were the Royal Mother herself.

"You seek shelter?" Oddly enough the harsh tone with which she had berated Menon was gone from her voice. Her speech was almost without the northern accent, close to the clipped tongue of Thebes, and he thought that she was of the pure Egyptian blood.

"We do, lady." He used the address he would have used to one of his own caste, unconsciously paying tribute to that voice.

"For how long?" She was businesslike, a lodging keeper.

"Perhaps until the middle night—" He hoped that was all. But with the city stirred up like a Kush border village after a raid, he dared not do more than hope.

"You must take your chances if they track you here," she told him tartly. "I shall say that you forced yourself upon a helpless woman—"

Menon snickered loudly and rudely, and she paused to glare at him, with a half-raised fist promising a future reckoning.

"Do they come here often?" Rahotep countered. There was no need to give other name to that "they"—both of them understood too well.

She laughed comfortably, richly. "Not too often, young sir. Oh, aye, they raid now and again—to recover slaves—or to get food for their god—" She moved uneasily and made an ancient secret sign with her fingers to ward off evil. "But when they come, it is in strength and poor old

Nebet has those who warn her. She also claims her just dues—" For the second time she glared at Menon. "And none of you carry any 'gold of valor' to pay for even a single jar of beer—" She surveyed their scanty slave rags disparagingly.

"True enough!" agreed Icar. "But have you not already said that we are desperate and evil men who have forced their way into the place of a weak and helpless woman?"

She turned her blackest frown upon the seaman, but she did not hold it. Her paint cracked again as she began to laugh, until her mountainous body shook helplessly.

"So you did!" she wheezed, "so you did! And also you have stirred them up as if you dropped an angry bees' nest into their midst—or else this one here tells lies bigger than he is—" She stretched forth one pudgy foot to point with its painted nails at the Kush. "Very well, warriors, take me prisoner and work your will here. I cannot withstand your rage and power!" With mock shyness she hid her face behind her hands and giggled—looking up quickly again to snap at Menon who had gone to a shelf and was coolly reaching down a jar of beer. "Go too far with your looting, pig-keeper, and you will feel the weight of my hand until your neck snaps in two! There is an end to Nebet's good nature and almsgiving!"

But she made no other move to stop him when he slopped the contents of the jar into a bowl and passed it with a kind of rough ceremony to Icar who in turn proffered it to Rahotep. The stuff was thin and sour, but it was liquid and it cooled his throat. The captain swallowed several mouthfuls and passed it back to the seaman who finished it off at one gulp, wiping his mouth on the back of his hand.

"A man fills his belly with more than just beer," Icar hinted. "We have teeth to exercise in something more solid."

For a second Rahotep thought that Nebet was about to flare into a rage once more. Then she clapped her hands, and a wrinkled hag of a Kush woman scuttled from an inner room, listened to an order delivered in her own click speech, and disappeared, to return with a tray on which there were rounds of poor cakes, some too-soft dates, and an evil-smelling cheese. They wolfed it down with avid appetites. Poor as the stuff was, it was infinitely better than slave fare. Huy belched and stroked his stomach caressingly when he had finished.

"It is not the sweet flesh of a young gazelle, nor yet the fat of a buck in good season—and there are no mealie-mealies. But it will do to fill a man between his front and his backbone," he remarked. "Only what does the old witch want from us in return?"

Nebet must have either possessed the magical powers with which he credited her or more than natural hearing, for she peered at the Nubian from her couch of mats and smiled chillingly.

"You name Nebet 'old witch' do you, black-skin? Mind your manners lest she show you how much of a witch she is!"

Huy attempted to stare her down. But he moved uneasily and then added placatingly, "A witch is a woman of power, great lady. Is that not so? And in this city I would say that you are a woman of power. But also I ask, what do you want from us in return?"

"Let us say that I toss sticks with the future—or that I am a teller of tales—" She spoke over Huy to Rahotep. "In this city the walls are hung with ears, and, as this toad from the south has acknowledged, Nebet has power of a sort—enough to summon to her what those ears have heard. Today there has been a queer story of a stranger who entered Neferusi to spy—coming as a slave when indeed he is that which hovers in the air and watches with the Great Eye—"

Rahotep froze. The archaic words of the Horus ritual struck at him with a breath of that dank cold he had known in the temple dungeons. Horus—the Hawk—the Great Eye!

"And this one comes as an arrow shot before a host, for it is whispered that the Flail is up and that Pharaoh marches again against ancient foes—" She was singsonging the words with the rhythm of one of the story-telling harpers, and on her massive knees her fingers moved as if plucking at the strings of an invisible instrument. "Only the Son of Re should look within his own host for enemies, since there they lie as worms within fruit! The Lord of the Two Lands has his warriors, his nobles to fight for him. But also there are others who shall remember on the proper day that they are of the old blood and that too long have the sons of Set sat here untroubled."

"And if arms were to be given to those of whom you speak?" questioned Rahotep softly. "Even within this city of Neferusi were such a thing to be done, what then?"

"We here have little to lose except life—"

"Yet," Icar cut in, "life is sweet enough for many men. Few face death laughing—"

"Death?" She brooded for a space. "Tell me, young lord, does not the warriors' oath say this?" Surprisingly she repeated the same words he had said long weeks ago to Methen in a Nubian fort.

"'Fight for his name, purify yourselves by his oath, and you shall be free from trouble. The beloved of the Pharaoh shall be blessed; but there is no tomb for one hostile to his majesty; and his body shall be thrown to the waters.'"

"You speak as a Leader of a Hundred, lady," he observed wonderingly.

"Within this part of Neferusi am I the Commander of a Thousand." She spoke with the complete certainty of undisputed authority. "A serpent spews its poison into Hyksos ears; beware lest it set its fangs within the flesh of Pharaoh! But if any lord who hates the Hyksos desires to put weapons in the hands of certain men within this city—let him haste to do so and then watch a red reaping! Remember that, Lord!"

"Be assured, lady, that I shall. But first it will be necessary to get out of Neferusi, for this time—"

To his disappointment she was shaking her head. "I am not so lacking in wit that I shall expose those who serve me without hope of their gaining something in return. You got into this city; you must have had some plan for getting out again. Follow it, Lord, by yourself. Remember, you are desperate men who forced yourselves upon the helpless Nebet—" She lengthened her vowels into a whine, but it was apparent that she meant what she had said. Outside this room Nebet would do nothing more to aid them.

16

Over the Walls

There was no moon, and as a consequence the Kush, for fear of those night demons well known to infest such a darkness, protested against issuing forth from Nebet's den—or rather from the very cramped storage room in which the fugitives had been hidden for the long hours of the afternoon and the first part of the night. Rahotep would have been content enough to leave him behind, but since he was admittedly the only one of the escaped slaves who knew the inner maze of the Neferusi slums well enough to act as a guide, he was pressed into service. Menon had a very limited knowledge of the city, confined to the immediate surroundings of the house of a Hyksos lord where he had been a burden slave until rebellion sent him to the heavier labor on the walls.

"Menon's an able lad in a tangle," Icar confided to the captain privately. "And well I can testify to that, for he was my steersman until these ape-noses of Hyksos sent us all to the market to be sold. He can be trusted to crack an arm or a neck in a good cause. I was sorry to have him sent south and be parted from him months ago. Aye, he can stand up in a fight, but he must have his orders. When he thinks for himself—then he gets into trouble. And that Kush is also a wild one—he was in my labor gang before, and even the overseer watched him from eye corners. They are not to be completely trusted—those black devils!"

Rahotep could agree to that. As a precaution, he assigned Huy to aid him in keeping a hand on the Kush so that he could not elude them in the puzzle of ill-smelling lanes and ways and leave them to blunder into trouble while he escaped. The Nubian, with an age-old distrust for his southern neighbor, put a noose about the Kush's thin neck and recited in a calm voice what would happen to the savage should he try to play them tricks.

The Kush led, still muttering protests under his breath intermingled with charms against night demons and petitions to gods older and darker than Set. Next, holding the rope, which leashed him as if he were a hunting hound to be loosed on some field, came Huy and Rahotep abreast. And so narrow were some of the ways that their outer shoulders brushed house walls as they skidded and tramped through noisome muck. Menon kept in touch with one hand linked into Rahotep's waist cord, and in turn, Icar had a similar hold upon him, while the other Nubian, Nesamun, brought up the rear.

For arms they had four daggers, three taken in the riot and a fourth wheedled out of Nebet, who had parted with it very reluctantly indeed, having flatly refused to provide them with a guide in the place of the Kush, or with any other aid. In addition, Nesamun dangled a length of cord in one hand. He swore that he was adept in an old trick used along the border for the disposing of awkwardly placed sentries, and this night Rahotep was desperate enough to put aside his squeamish dislike of it.

Scout training had taught the captain the art of quiet passage, and the Nubians and the Kush were silent shapes who glided rather than walked. But Menon was not their match, and twice he blundered into bad footing, which led him to swear in a strange tongue until a warning buffet from Icar cut him short. The seaman himself came up against the advance party with full force as they paused where the lane they had followed gave upon that wider way that paralleled the city walls.

Though the district in which Nebet had her hole was largely dark and they would have been totally lost in it lacking the Kush's leadership it was different in this quarter. Torches blazed at intervals along the walls, and Rahotep could see the movement of men both above and below. He knew the point he must reach. But now he was afraid that it would be of little use to follow his plan. The riot must have alerted the Hyksos.

He had tracked behind the Kush blindly. Now he saw they were too near the gate. The point he and Kheti had chosen earlier lay to the north, a quarter of the way around the wall. At that section the repairs and rebuilding that were engrossing the city's governor had made necessary the erection of a short ramp, so that capping stones of some weight could be brought up from the outside. The ramp was a rough thing and was in the process of being dismantled. A man could not have climbed it, even at night, without an immediate challenge. A man could not, but—

Rahotep drew level with the Kush and held his lips close to the man's ear. In the click speech of the border, he gave an order he hoped would bring them to the right place. The Kush chattered a protest, little of which the captain could understand, which ended in a choked gasp as Huy jerked his leading noose. Then the Nubian's head was at the savage's other ear, and he snapped an addition to the Egyptian's order that set the Kush shivering.

With a little whimper the man turned to the left, and their small party strung out in the half light, progressing by quick rushes and long pauses from one safe area of darkness to the next. Rahotep, expecting any moment to be hailed from the top of the wall, watched those heights with such concentration that he was hardly aware of what passed on his own level, though Huy warned him twice in urgent whispers.

At length they stood beneath the point he judged the right one. It was between two of the torchlit spaces, and there could not be more than one or two sentries above, for the surface of the wall narrowed there, the sides sloping toward the top. Rahotep leaped across the open and pressed against the surface of the barrier, making his body as flat as possible. He listened, alert to the slightest sound in the night.

A call from one sentry to the next was passed along, and the captain spread himself even tighter against the stone when it was echoed from overhead. Then came the faint scrape of a sandal on stone, the thud, thud of a marching man, tapping a spear butt as a device to keep himself awake—as Rahotep had seen and heard countless other midnight sentinels do in the boredom of the long, quiet hours.

Twice the captain heard the man pass over his station, timing him by the beating of his own heart, which seemed to him now to be throbbing almost in his throat. This was not a fixed post; the man had a beat that took him for some yards back and forth across the crucial spot. And Rahotep hoped that Icar and the rest were watching the sentry from the other side of the street.

The guard had reached midpoint; now he was heading away, as far as the Egyptian could judge. The captain shaped his lips, and from his throat came the cry he had practiced so carefully time after time in the wastes beyond Neferusi. Twice he voiced that yowl, one not out of place in any Egyptian city and one that the sentries must have heard so many times in a night that it would not awaken interest, for the house cats of Egypt were apt to voice such songs. Only—would the right cat answer him now?

Tense, his fingers rigid against the wall in concentration of body and brain, Rahotep waited. Then came what he had hoped for, had hardly dared to believe he would hear, an eerie feline wail with a quaver that was doubly realistic and of which Kheti was extremely proud.

He visualized every move that must be made outside the wall. Kheti would free Bis of his leash. Already he

216

would have wound upon the cub's body the rope, leaving its end in his own hands. Bis would be given the proper order, and the leopard's soundless pads would mount the rubble of the ramp, passing noiselessly where a man's weight would bring the guard's attention. Bis would climb with the fluid feline grace of his kind, he would crouch on the wall, he would—

Against the torchlight something moved, shot through the air. There was the thud of a landing body, not close to the wall, but across the open space. Rahotep hissed urgently, hoping that the leopard cub with his uncertain tolerance for strangers would not set upon the men hidden there.

A blot of black flitted across the street; behind it something trailed in the dust. Then a furry body hurled itself upon the captain with a throaty purr of pleased recognition. Rahotep caressed the round head, whispered lovingly into a pricked ear as he went down on his knees, so that the familiar head butted against his chest. He found the rope end made fast to the cub's collar and twisted about the body for safer keeping. The knots gave under his fingers, and his single quick tug was answered from outside. Their risky ladder out of Neferusi was in his hands!

Bis growled as a figure made the crossing of the street in two leaps and joined them. Icar spoke, his voice reduced to a half squeak in his effort to whisper.

"Do we move now, Egyptian? There is a smell of trouble here. We had better be on our way."

"There remains the sentry—" Rahotep looked up to the top of the wall.

But Icar had turned and beckoned. The others joined them, the Kush coming only at the jerk of the rope Huy still held upon him. Rahotep brought them to the climbing cord, keeping Bis under control when the leopard cub would have actively protested the strangers. Nesamun chuckled.

"The next task is mine, Lord!" He popped the coil of cord he had carried into his mouth and reached for the rope. Then he was climbing as the others crouched below.

The Nubian had chosen his time well. Now the sentry was heading away from him and the Hyksos' voice rang out in the periodical call that went from guard to guard about the walls of Neferusi. But the sentry never made a return trip. A dark figure suddenly loomed behind him and there was a quick movement. Arms flailed, and a spear fell to the stone as those arms beat the air and then went limp. A moment later a man marched once more along the wall top, but from this new guard Rahotep knew they had nothing to fear. He slapped Icar on the back in signal, and the seaman went up the rope with the agility of one who was familiar with uncertain footing and heights above water-borne decks.

Then the captain turned his attention to Bis. With the slack of the rope he made a sling for the front quarters of the cub and gave a jerk to the cord. Spitting and growling, Bis was swung aloft. There was a sharp exclamation from above as if the two there were having some difficulty in freeing the cub from his lashings. Then the rope dangled loose once more. Huy pulled the noose from the Kush and chattered at the man in his own click speech. The savage bounded away into the darkness. It was plain he did not want to join in their venture outside the city.

Menon and the Nubian followed swiftly on Rahotep's heels as the Egyptian captain climbed. Icar met them at the top while Nesamun still walked the sentry's beat.

"Your cat went over the wall," he informed Rahotep, "after using its claws on us. Do we follow it now?"

"We do. But I had better go first. Those who wait below expect one man only, not five."

"Good enough."

Rahotep slid down the other side of the line. He dropped into a pool of dark so thick that it was as if he were being swallowed up in the nether world where Set ruled. Hands closed upon him, easing him down for the last foot or two, and he heard Kheti's soft chuckle.

"So we have you safely out of the lion's den, brother! I do not believe that any of those Egyptians in the camp believed it could be done."

"Aye, you have me—and others! Stand by to aid them—"

He tugged a signal, and one after another the fugitive slaves joined them. Then with an archer beside each as a guide, they progressed—by way of irrigation ditch and dried-up garden, by house walls of villas and every other piece of cover the Nubians had scouted through the waiting hours—into the borders of the wasteland and so on the trail back to camp.

"Pharaoh has come." Kheti supplied news as they trotted ahead, hid for a space, and then went on again. "Paugh—those Hyksos patrol like the elephant—one can hear them a league away!" He lay beside Rahotep in a muddy ditch into which Nile water was seeping, as they heard a body of men moving warily, but with far too much noise, half a field from them. "Pharaoh has come and there is talk of a battle. But the river rises fast, and soon it will cover the fields. Can a man fight up to his waist in water, Lord? That we have not tried as yet."

"Let us petition the Great Ones that we shall not have to! They are far enough away now—let us go!" Rahotep was consumed with eagerness to give his report. If the Pharaoh was in camp, then indeed the time had grown very short and the army must be preparing to move.

Kamose must welcome field service for more than one reason, Rahotep thought some hours later when, close to exhaustion, he was brought to the royal tent. Hedged about with stiff ceremonial as the ruler was in the royal city and on his necessary progresses through the land, only in a war camp did he have a measure of freedom from the tight hold of custom and the past. It was no dread half-divine ruler that Rahotep faced now, but the keen-faced officer he had first seen on the quays of Thebes.

"Thus it was—" He finished his report of the period within Neferusi and added his own suggestion as to how this first outpost city of the Hyksos might be cracked open for Egyptian taking.

The final decision, any decision, would be Pharaoh's alone. But Kamose had gathered a backing of military and naval advisers who represented the best native might of his sadly shrunken and invaded land. Besides General Amony there was a second "Leader of Standards"—Thesh—who had dealt with the Bwedanii of the western deserts to some purpose and whose reputation as a fighter under stark circumstances had penetrated into Nubia, so that the men of the border patrol held him in high respect—though he was seldom to be found in any formal gathering of his peers.

He was a sun-dried stick of a man, his beaked nose jutting from under the wrapped headdress of a roving tribesman so that he resembled the very foe he had spent a lifetime in warring upon for the protection of upper Egypt. And he fidgeted now, his dark eyes never still, as if the light walls of the tent confined him in some way and he would be out and gone.

Amony, Thesh, Meniptah—a naval officer under whose placid but firm control lay the transportation of supplies and men up the Nile, the fleet of small war vessels intended to harry the Hyksos' shipping and river towns. Meniptah was a sleepy mountain of a man whose mind appeared occupied with distant matters until he shot out some penetrating question, which was apt to startle the unwary—as he did now.

"So it is tribute carts, is it? But this is not the season for the paying of tribute, Captain. Those in the fields will shortly sow, not reap."

"It was said within Neferusi, Lord," Rahotep returned respectfully but holding to his point, "that the invaders are sweeping all but a bare minimum from the storehouses because they are about to launch an attack to the east where mountaineers threaten their Asiatic holdings."

"And you saw these wagons enter into Neferusi?" persisted the naval commander.

"It is so, Lord. In my time of labor on the wall I counted twenty—in three different trains—all guarded by small parties of Bwedanii under a Hyksos officer."

"Bwedanii—" Kamose looked to Thesh.

"They hire their warriors to the Hyksos when they need food for their bellies, Son of Re." The border officer

220

answered that half question. "If it is a matter of sending a force under the outer guise of Bwedanii—then we have no problem."

Rahotep fought down all sign of elation at this promise of backing from such a general as Thesh. Now he began to fear that the project might be taken out of his hands entirely and that he would be allowed no part in it. And that fear almost became a certainty when the Prince Ahmose broke in.

"It is a way to pass those walls. And armed slaves within might cause such confusion that the enemy would be divided and hampered until too late. One cart could be halted halfway through the inner gate so that it could not close—"

Amony laughed. "Young blood, young blood! But this I say also, Son of Re." He turned to Kamose. "The big battles must come later; we cannot hope to take Avaris in a day. And we have no men to waste in siege or open assault upon a well-defended city. So must we use the secret fangs of a serpent, rather than the open claws of a lion—until we have such a force at our backs that Apophis himself will see the dust cloud of our marching from leagues away!"

"Then you advise this plan?" the Pharaoh asked.

"I advise any and all plans which have the thinnest chance of success. Son of Re, we need a victory against odds! Let us take Neferusi and those nomarchs who have shaken their heads against our folly will muster their hundreds under standards for the march. Aye, they are close to traitors now—since they will not rise at the bidding of the great seal. But they will have no excuse after a victory! And this plan does not call for the risking of more than a company. A cautious man does not win wars—one needs to have that caution edged with audacity when the need arises!"

"Thesh?" Pharaoh appealed to his second general.

"I have seen wilder action succeed, Son of Re. Thanks to your captain here, we do not venture in wholly blind. To risk a company is not too much."

"Meniptah?"

The stout naval officer shrugged. "Were it to be done with water under the keel, then I would wag my jaws aye or nay. But this is not my kind of war. Only I say this: we must have Neferusi in our hands before we dare to advance downriver. It is the rallying point of the Hyksos in the south, and to leave it untaken is to plant a burr under the tail of a wild horse—we dare not do it!"

Amony laughed for the second time. "And when, Meniptah, worthy driver of ships, have you also taken over the schooling of wild horses? Nevertheless, you speak with the tongue of Maat in this matter. The Nile rises; soon we shall not be able to attack—lest we sink to our necks in field muck. Therefore, if we capture Neferusi, we must do it at once. And this plan of tribute wagons has some points of worth in it."

The Prince Ahmose tapped the sheet of papyrus they had unrolled and pinned down upon the floor. The generals sat cross-legged on mats about its edge with the prince while the Pharaoh had a stool, his greater height causing him to lean forward at an angle to follow the route his brother was tracing with the end of a writhing brush as a pointer.

"Five columns to come in—with the city for a core. Lord Meniptah has transport enough to take men up to here and here—" He jabbed the map in two places along the curve that was the river. "They will ride on reed rafts, towed by oared barges of light draft. And upon signal they will cut loose and head for the shore. Any who spy upon them will believe until the last moment that they hope to pass Neferusi.

"To Lord Thesh the desert approach from the east—one column—and he also must provide us with Bwedanii robes—"

"Us—?" Kamose asked softly.

For a moment his energetic younger brother was plainly disconcerted and looked his few years. Then he answered with a firmness with which Amony might have questioned an order.

"Son of Re, I claim the rights of a Royal Son. The first

attack must be led by the eldest prince of our line as is the custom!"

He did not speak defiantly, but with the certainty of one stating his position, and Rahotep knew that the ancient custom was in his favor. Though there were only two males of the royal house alive now in Thebes, it was not only Ahmose's right, but his duty, to lead the first assault upon Neferusi—under the prince's standard.

"And I, Royal Son"—Amony consciously or unconsciously acknowledged that right in his address—"am to bring up from the south—?"

"Pharaoh advances from the south," Kamose replied with the same quiet sureness his brother had used a moment earlier. "Lords, it is in our mind that our cause shall flourish or die here at Neferusi, though this is but a small city, the farthest and least of Apophis's outposts to the south. If the Great Ones look upon us with favor, then shall we take Neferusi and cleanse it of the foreign evil. It shall be a symbol of a land freed from darkness. And if we fail at Neferusi, then we are broken men, for our army shall melt away and not again in this lifetime shall we be able to challenge Apophis and his hundreds in any field. The plan seems to us to be good. No man can foresee all sequences of action; much depends upon the ability of separate commanders. Let us start to move by sundown— the Nile waters wait upon no man's convenience."

Rahotep drew near to Ahmose as the meeting broke up. He was still uncertain as to his part in the attack. Greatly daring he spoke first.

"Royal Son, by your favor I claim the right to be one to enter Neferusi with the carts," he blurted out.

The prince's broad lips drew back from his prominent teeth, giving him some resemblance to a happy Kush. "How else, kinsman? Do I not need eyes which have been there before to seek out weak points? Pick your men quickly—your Scouts—perhaps those slaves you brought out of the city, if you can trust them. Twenty determined men can cause much disaster when they strike in surprise. See your men are well fed and have their best weapons.

Let the former slaves draw such arms as they favor from the smiths. We assemble beyond the horse lines at the tenth hour, and then we shall see what else we need in the way of equipment."

But the tenth hour was none too far away as Rahotep discovered when he plunged into the preparation of his command. He found time to shed his own slave guise and put on the dress of a captain. And when he joined his chosen party, he was astounded at the change in the men who had come with him out of Neferusi.

Though Menon's bush of red beard, startling enough in the crowd of closely shaven Egyptians, still decorated his square chin, he had a clean kilt belted about him and carried across his shoulder the heaviest mace he had been able to find. The Nubians were examining bows with some dissatisfaction, finding the lighter Egyptian weapons far below their standards. But the biggest alteration lay in the seaman Icar. Bathed, his face clean of beard, his fair hair drawn back by a bronze circlet, he looked like a sea prince of Minos. And he moved and spoke with the authority of a man who had captained his own ship. In shedding his beard and his rags, he had also shed years, so that now he appeared little older than Rahotep. Icar had selected from the supplies of the weaponsmiths a sword of unusual length, foreign war spoil, the Egyptian captain thought, and he was swinging it as he joined their party, as if to learn its balance against future use.

Rahotep's party were the first at the assembly point. Ten Scouts were drawn up behind Kheti, the other two Nubians from the city hesitatingly joining that group a pace to the rear, not yet accepted by their countrymen as equals, but eager to be with their own kind. Icar and his late steersman lingered to one side. They were hot enough for the promised action, but they had never been part of an army before.

Rahotep swung his sistrum, and his archers stood to attention as he inspected their arms and equipment with close attention. They had already passed Kheti's hawk eyes, but no officer would forego a second inspection in this case.

The captain heard the creak of cart wheels and turned around. Two of the clumsy carts, each with a team of six oxen instead of the usual four, were turning to join them. And he had just time to signal the salute to his men as Ahmose tramped up.

17

A Matter of Tribute

For the second time Rahotep drew close to the gates of
Neferusi. But now before him rolled one of the oxcarts,
and behind his shuffling feet was the other. They were
heavily laden carts, and as such should be welcomed by
the unsuspecting Hyksos officers at the gate. But those
bulging bags on the top held only dried marsh grass, and
under them, in sultry confinement, lay the Scouts and
some picked men from Nereb's command.

The driver who pricked the lead oxen of the first team
into their best pace wore the loose cloak of a Bwedani with
its hood drawn well over its head. Rahotep and the man
matching step with him at the second cart were similarly
disguised, as were the six men playing the role of
guards—straggling now in the slight disorder of bone-
weary men. Under those cloaks, supplied by Thesh, were
two veterans chosen from the desert general's small force,
Icar, Huy, Kheti, Nereb, and Nereb's principal Leader of
Fifty, while the driver of the foremost cart, swinging his
goad pole with all the concentration he brought to any
necessary action, was the Royal Son Ahmose.

They had rested an hour before dawn and were fresh enough, though they put on the semblance of weariness to deceive the gate guard. Rahotep rounded the cart ahead to be near the prince as they approached the city walls. He had told all he knew about that gate in the exhausive questioning to which Ahmose and the Pharaoh had subjected him hours before. It was his turn now to put that knowledge to the test.

At least there was no sign of suspicion along the walls—they could not have sighted those other lines of men who were using all the natural cover afforded by irrigation ditches and reeds to ring in Neferusi. There were Egyptian scouts avidly watching the carts, and when the last of those entered, Kamose would signal the general attack.

Would the Pharaoh also be able to cover against the treachery that had murdered his father and betrayed Rahotep within Neferusi before his mission was accomplished? But Kamose and his brother had been warned—they must take the precautions. Rahotep's part in the coming battle was centered upon these two carts and the necessity of their gaining entry to the city.

One of Thesh's veterans slogged up without being summoned. Since he spoke the desert speech perfectly, he was to answer the gate challenge, having been coached by Rahotep on what he had heard during the day on wall labor. They came to a stop before the outer gates, and the desert scout hailed the guards.

His shout bore fruit. The massive leaves came slowly open and Ahmose used his goad. The oxen put their shoulders to the yokes and the cart moved ponderously onward. Nereb allowed the short space between the two wagons to widen before he set his own beasts to moving, though the Hyksos guard yelled at him angrily to close up.

They made the sharp turn to the left to follow that inner way to the second portal, the carts moving clumsily and slowly—so clumsily that Nereb's wagon fouled the gate leaf and it could not be closed. The Hyksos officer shouted again from his post on the heights. And when Nereb's cunning efforts only jammed the gate yet more, the man came down, thoroughly exasperated, to use his whip freely on both the supposed Bwedani driver and the bewildered oxen, with the result that the latter stopped short and stood blowing in slow anger and bewilderment.

Meanwhile, Ahmose's party had reached the second gate and were almost through it before the commotion behind them attracted the attention of the guards there. One underofficer strove to clear the second gate, ordering his men to put their shoulders to the clumsy vehicle and manhandle it through.

"Re above us! Re favor us!" Ahmose leaped to the top of the cart ahead and with a marksman's eye began hurling the upper layer of the stuffed bags at the milling and bewildered guards. Those missiles were not heavy enough to injure, but they provided the necessary confusion until the men hidden below burst out, scarlet-faced and gasping, but with daggers and spears ready.

Rahotep saw Icar throw off his hindering cloak and cut his way with that whirling long sword to a corner where a gang of amazed labor slaves crouched against the wall. With an ear-punishing whoop, the seaman swung that sword, slicing through neck nooses, while Menon roared something in the speech of the labor lines and tossed daggers in their direction.

Then the fighting closed in with a swirl as the Hyksos struck back. It was a mad matter of thrust, strike, and away. Rahotep sent a screaming Bwedani mercenary to the ground and then caught sight of a stair to the top of the wall. He looked about him for Kheti and saw Huy instead, using a limp Hyksos officer as an overseer might use a flail to scatter a pocket of resistance.

"Wahhhhh—waaaah—!" The captain gave the full power of his lungs to the Nubian war cry. He was up three, four of the steps now, and he saw heads turn in his direction. With a beckoning sweep of his arm, he summoned the archers and waited only to see that four of them, including Kheti, were fighting their way to join him—before he turned to take the stairs at a runner's pace.

He met a Hyksos guard within three steps of the top, and he might have met death at that same instant, for a shortened spear was aimed at the base of his throat. But another death, a black one, had streaked behind him and now slashed with fangs and claws at the spearman. Totally unprepared for such an attack at his legs, the man swerved, lost his footing, and, with a scream of terror, fell out, to strike upon the cart.

Rahotep, shaken, scrambled on to the top. But he had his bow ready and now he reached for an arrow. Bis crawled belly-flat before him along the wall crest, his eyes slits of green anger, his ears flat against his skull. Less than half-grown though he was, the menace in that silent advance slowed the next guardsman who had run forward to meet the captain. And that slight pause gave the Egyptian a chance to get to steady footing. A whistle in the air ended in a grunt of pain, and the Hyksos went down, an arrow protruding from between his ribs.

"Waaah—" The roar of the Nubians rang out above the clamor below. Kheti, Huy, Kakaw, Mahu—they were taking the stair on the double. Rahotep was already intent upon clearing the stretch of wall above the gates. As his first arrow bit skyward and the loosened bow cord drummed against his grandfather's silver braces, he reached for a second shaft.

"This is as easy as shooting meat for the pot, brother," shouted Kheti. "Let us pluck strings while Dedun so smiles!"

However it was only for a short space that they had the advantage. Hyksos slingers and Bwedanii bowmen were not napping. Already they had conquered the shock of their first surprise—shields went up against arrows and the battle swayed back to the gates.

Mahu staggered back, his face a gory hole spouting red as some slinger loosed a well-aimed stone. The Nubian clutched at the air with an agonized cry and then was gone.

"Spread out!" Rahotep shouted. But he commanded no green boys. The archers were already skimming along the space their arrows had cleared, pausing to shoot and then run again. They did not provide targets easy to mark down.

It was then that Rahotep saw Huy deliberately leap from the wall to the cart. Someone had killed the oxen, immobilizing the heavy wagon at the inner gate as the other had been left to block the outer. A chariot headed full tilt down the blocked road, but the driver was expert enough to pull up in time when he sighted that obstruction. He was not expecitng, however, to meet Huy who jumped up beside him.

There was not even a struggle. The gaudily dressed officer was tossed from his vehicle as Icar appeared out of nowhere to grab at the reins of the rearing horse. By main strength the seaman got it down on four feet again, then forced the snorting nervous animal back while Huy slashed with his dagger at its harness. When the horse was free, Icar did what Rahotep thought could not be done—he mounted on the surprised animal's back astride, knotting one hand in the coarse mane that was braided with ribbons, while with the other he swept his sword in a curve over his head and shouted something to those slaves who had joined in the fight.

With a party of them racing behind him, the northerner headed the horse back into the town, a small wedge of determined men bursting into those crooked lanes where Nebet ruled.

Then those on the wall had only their own segment of the fight to follow, for the slingers were well within range and Nesamun dangled a broken arm, forced to drop his despised Egyptian bow for an ax. Wedging his injured arm into one of his chest belts, he made the same jump. Huy had taken earlier, landing in the cart and so reaching the ground where his ax would be more effective.

"—ten!" Kheti's voice was growing hoarse. "Ten sent to face Dedun's crocodiles this day! Ho, this is hunting, brothers! Let us claw these dogs as they have never been ear-clipped before!"

"'This army hacks the land of the horsemen,
    It fires the houses of a host,
    It slays their tens of tens, their tens of hundreds.
    Rejoice, ye sons of the bow, this army treads upon
        kings!'"

That was Kakaw, and the regular whistling of the arrows, the drum of released bow cords, kept time to barbaric thunder of his war chant.

"'It slays their tens of tens, their tens of hundreds!'" Rahotep took up the words. Kheti added his bull roar as if the very howling of those boasts would blow away all opposition.

"'This army hacks the land of the horsemen,
    Mighty is the elephant as he goes out upon his foes!
    Rejoice, ye sons of the bow, for you tread upon the
        faces of kings.'"

"Lord!" Mereruka called, barely audible in the din, "Pharaoh comes!"

Rahotep released an arrow and dared to glance out across the plain beyond the wall. A line of chariots was sweeping in toward Neferusi in a wide arc, which seemed to cover half the land, and beside them ran footmen. The standard in the center chariot was no brighter than the blue helmet of him who guided it so skillfully.

"Ho, more than the Pharaoh comes!" warned Kheti, and Rahotep's attention snapped back to the action at hand.

Which was very well, for exposed as they were upon the wall, they were now the target of not only the guards along its expanse, but also of small groups who had climbed to nearby housetops. They lost Hori before they fought their way into a breathing space. Rahotep was determined to dispute every foot of retreat. But at the same time he ordered his men to take what cover they could until they could see the direction for a most telling thrust.

"Waaaaah—" That war cry did not come from the small party on the gate wall, but from the city itself. Rahotep inched his way to a point from which he could look down into Neferusi, and he was just in time to see the rottenness of the poor quarter break wide open. Men—and women too—with starved, maimed bodies, faces carved by hatred into the masks of Kush night demons, poured out. That first wave was led by Icar, still miraculously astride his mount, using his voice and the flat of his sword to urge on his cohorts. He was heading them to the stalled wagon at the gate where the Hyksos had been driven back. And now this fetid wave from the dens, such as Nebet's, went to that wagon. Men pulled, scrambled, tore for the weapons that had been brought them, even fought among themselves for possession of a spear or dagger.

Those who had been aiming at the archer party on the wall now turned a measure of attention to the boiling mass in the streets below. And Rahotep and Kheti sent their men on to the top of one of the square towers above the gate, giving them better protection as well as height for good bow work.

The first wave of the Egyptian advance without hit the wall of Neferusi now. Men seeped over and around the first cart, cutting into the passage before the second gate. There were Hyksos bowmen and slingers on the roofs to thin their numbers. But those same defenders had to face in return the fire of the archers on the tower. And though men fell below with pierced bodies and smashed bones and heads, the entering stream swelled and steadied.

"Re for us!" The rallying cry of the regulars grew stronger. A human battering ram had formed, the point of which was the troops chosen by Ahmose and Nereb—those that were still alive and on their feet. They had fought their way to the foot of the wall stair and now they came up, while Rahotep's men covered them as well as they could.

"Clear the wall!" The prince stood now at the top of the

233

stair, motioning men past him. And every second one of those newcomers wore a coil of rope about his waist, prepared to drop that line to the companies without.

A rope bearer died with a dart in his throat, coughing out his life across the prince's feet. Ahmose tore loose the cord he bore, trailing one end of it behind him as he ran on. Archers and slingers cleared the way, pouring a rain of missiles ahead while the others dropped their ropes down the outer side of the walls.

"Re with us!" That became a thunderous petition rising to the sky. Men crawled up the ropes to gain the crest of the walls. Some fell, but others moved on to help in the sweep that cleared more surface, gave space to sling over other ropes.

In the city itself there was dire trouble. The ill-armed slaves and criminals from the slums were fighting after a vicious fashion of their own. It was a fighting that skulked and ran and could not be organized to any purpose except to afford confusion generally.

Worse still, they were looting the dead and beginning to knife the wounded of both sides. Rahotep shot a rogue in the space below who was about to slit the throat of a feebly resisting Egyptian archer.

"Brother!" Kheti sputtered in his ear. "Why can we not take to the roofs over there? Then we can watch this scum as well as help clear the streets."

"And how do we get over to them?" Rahotep demanded. By the design of those who had fortified Neferusi there was a wide street girdling the buildings of the city, leaving a gap between them and the wall top. And below was the muddle of battle through which it might be possible to fight one's way, true enough, but to descend into it and then try to reach the heights again would be wasteful of both time and manpower.

"By that bridge, Lord—"

The captain, his eyes following the other's pointing finger, could not at first see the possibilities of the wreckage Kheti had marked down. One of the inner leaves of the second gate had been forced askew by the oxcart as the fighting swirled back and forth across it. Now it was more than three quarters of the way across the street, wedged so by bodies and two wrecked chariots the Hyksos had driven in to disaster.

Perhaps a man *could* edge along the top of that frail support, but Rahotep was inclined to doubt it. However, Kheti must have taken his silence for consent, for, slinging his bow over his shoulder, the Nubian officer dropped to the gate and ran along it, his outstretched arms balancing him—as he had run along log bridges in the Kush country. And with the same unconcern, Kakaw, Mereruka, and the others one by one followed his example. From the end of the gate the Scout jumped to the roof of the gatehouse and then climbed from that to the roof of a taller building behind it. Bis crouched on the ledge from which the archers had jumped to the gate. With his head cocked a little to one side, the leopard cub watched the swift passage of the men and then went after them in his turn. Rahotep laughed wryly. Though he was not too certain of his own power of balance and footing, he had to bring up the rear of that strange procession—and a triumphant shout and beckoning from Kheti who had reached his goal across the street acted as a spur.

The captain kicked off his sandals for a better grip on that narrow path and took off, the portal seeming to him to sway dangerously under his weight. But at last dark hands stretched down to him and he was drawn up as he had been out of the dungeon of Anubis.

Breathing hard, he stood on the new attack point looking about him. It was now possible for one to make a way from roof to roof into the heart of the city. And he was not alone in that idea. Small parties of warriors, both Egyptian and Hyksos were appearing aloft now, moving back and forth, disputing advances in small fierce melees, which were only samples of the conflict in the streets.

Now the Egyptians held more than half of the wall surface. More and more men were climbing up the ropes and sliding down into Neferusi. The Hyksos, prevented from using their chariots to any advantage in the streets, harassed by the looters and freed slaves, rolled down in determined, enraged companies upon the section about the gates and the walls, hoping to trap their enemies against those barriers and to grind them to defeat. Again and again groups of well-trained foot soldiers charged. But the bowmen on the walls, which the Egyptians now held, and the small parties on the house roofs opposite, cut them down from above until some of the narrow lanes were so choked with dead and wounded that they were walled off to both defenders and invaders.

These fortifications had been built to withstand sieges, against the possibilities of assaults from without. But Neferusi was an ancient Egyptian town to which the foreigner's walls had been added as an afterthought. And the Hyksos found themselves now being forced back, away from the few open spaces where they could have used their more telling weapons, into places where no man could sling a spear or draw a bow cord without ramming his arm ineffectively against his neighbor.

But there was a second place for them to rally, and it was there they prepared to make their stand—the old hall of judgment, where the nomarch of this nome in the old days had once held court, and the temple of their god had been knitted together into an inner fortress where again there were strong walls—with a wide space about them.

Slowly, as the long minutes passed and the royal forces bored in from all sides, the Hyksos, in spite of their skill at arms, their confidence and training, fell back to that fortification for their last stand.

Rahotep gulped water out of an earthenware bowl, his eyes upon that second wall and the bristle of spears and bows along it, which told that it would be no nut easy for the cracking. A squadron of chariots was drawn up before its gate, facing toward the encircling city through which the boil of battle was advancing, slowly but relentlessly. There was no hope of using those vehicles in any but a few streets leading to this center, but here in the open they might prove of some value.

Kheti crossed to the roof where Rahotep stood, and the

captain offered him a drink from the jar of water Kakaw had found while prowling the deserted house under them. The Nubian underofficer drank as if savoring every drop, making his report between gulps.

"They have left us no other way in, Lord, save to batter through those gates yonder. And that will be like facing a lioness with cubs when one has but a broken spear. We cannot play that cart trick on them a second time—"

Rahotep, granted this short breathing space to examine their gains, knew a growing wonder over their success so far. He had been used to the short punitive expeditions and attacks along the border, and had a healthy respect for such chieftains as Haptke. Warfare there was something of a grim game between usually evenly matched opponents. But since his birth his ears had been filled with tales of the unconquerable Hyksos and their skill in battle, their superior strength of arms, their unbeatable regiments. Was it now true that their long years of consuming the fat of a supine Egypt had set up an inner rot in their organization? Or had they never been the super warriors legend had painted them?

Now he could understand why this first victory was so important to the royal army. It would destroy that legend of the enemies' invincibility, provide a cushion for any future defeat. And so—he faced that smaller fortress before them—this, for the sake of their whole cause, must be cracked open and utterly destroyed! Though how it was to be done, a captain of Desert Scouts could not see.

What he *could* do, he would. So, he dispatched Ikui to bring up a supply of arrows, gathering them where he could along their back trail. Kakaw, having once proven he could provide water, was sent to nose out food. And Rahotep made preparations for fortifying the roof on which they had taken their stand.

"Aim at the officers—and the drivers of those chariots." He gave what he knew to be unnecessary orders, but he added one other, which was a stern warning. "Be sure of your mark. We cannot present these sons of Set with the contents of our quivers unless they pay well in return!"

Kheti was measuring the distance from their roof to the wall of the inner fortress with a wishful eye. With the right wind and a great deal of luck, he might be able to nick some unwary defender. But it looked as if there were none of those, for no man showed more than a portion of helmet or shield, unless he were well out of range.

"So, Hawk, you have found a vantage point from which to strike?"

Rahotep spun about to face the Prince Ahmose. The Royal Son's broad face was banded with a crust of blood and dust, and he had a strip of stained linen, torn from some kilt, bound about his upper right arm, while only the ragged end of his prince's tassel bobbed from his headdress. But he crossed the flat surface of the room with the tread of an unwearied lion, coming to survey that space where the chariots shifted and waited to charge, with an eye that marked every advantage and disadvantage of their own position.

Stationed at every good point the Nubian archers nursed their dwindling supply of arrows, waiting for the return of Ikui. Now and again one would loose a shaft. And three out of five of such found their mark. But it was far from enough to turn the scales of battle in Egypt's favor.

"Your will, Royal Son?" Rahotep took his stand behind the prince.

He had done the best he could in locating this station. But he and his men, he knew, were only a small fraction of the forces Ahmose had to move about, and the prince might see fit to order them elsewhere.

"You cannot reach the walls from here?"

"With a lucky shot—perhaps. But many arrows would be wasted, Royal Son."

Men were coming into the square below, the first of the Hyksos forces pressed back by the Egyptian invaders. They were pushed, against their will, back into the circle of the chariots. A few had won behind the horses to the fortress gates. But those portals remained closed. For a moment or two they milled about as if puzzled and then turned to face outward again.

"They have sealed the gates," Ahmose stated. "Those below are to be left without—either to conquer or be our meat!"

But it appeared that not only those huddled below were to harass the advancing Egyptians, for Ikui, a bundle of arrows of all lengths and kinds under his arm, came across the roofs at a messenger's pace, shouting a warning that turned them all around to look at the city at their back.

"Fire!"

18

Beautiful in Victory

Smoke streamed up into the brazen sky—a dirty-yellow stuff that reminded Rahotep vaguely of another time and place. Looters? Or had the Hyksos set it going to cut off the invading force? Most of the city buildings were of sun-dried brick. But their inner walls, their roofs were well cured wood and would be eaten out speedily by fire.

Ahmose made a decision. He waved one hand toward the filling square.

"Shoot the horses!"

Though the captain was no charioteer, he had been long enough with Pharaoh's army to know what a bleak choice that was for the prince. If the Egyptians were able to capture only half of the well-trained animals below, they would double their own striking power. To kill a horse was like cutting off part of their own future. But now they must be sacrificed.

The archers snatched shafts from those Ikui had salvaged. Some they discarded as useless for their bows. But within seconds they were facing back into the square ready for a volley.

"Loose!" Rahotep gave the order and the bow cords thrummed. Hands reached for other shafts, and animals went down kicking, or, maddened with pain, charged out of control into the lines of Hyksos footmen.

"Loose!" A second—third—fourth volley blasted the chariot lines in the square. And they could not retreat out of range since the doors of the citadel were barred at their backs. It was a nasty business, sheer slaughter of the helpless horses, and the prince watched it with his hands gripping the slight parapet of the roof until the knuckles stood out.

More and more the Hyksos were being driven back into the open space. These men did not come running, some weaponless, as had the first wave. They backed in, their faces still to the enemy, contesting grimly for every foot of space they had to concede. The smoke was thicker also. As a tendril of it set Rahotep coughing, he at last captured the fugitive memory of a few moments earlier. Just so had the fire eaten out Haptke's raider's nest on the Kush border. Kush—He did not give the signal for the next volley; instead he caught at Kheti's arm to deter him from shooting.

"Kheti—fire arrows!"

The Nubian lowered his bow and then raised it again at another angle so that his shaft was now aimed into the sky, rather than at that tangle below. He drew cord to the fullest extent and loosed, while all of them stood watching that arrow spiral up into the air. Up and up as if Kheti's target had been the sun disc of Re! Up and now down—spinning—But could it reach? Was the angle right?

Down—behind the fortress walls! Only chance could make it a lethal weapon there without better aim. But fire arrows need not be aimed for killing, only for a safe landing. And if the roofs of the buildings within that circle of wall were like those in the rest of Neferusi, fire arrows would find tinder to eat upon!

Rahotep knew that such a feat of strength was beyond his own powers. But Kheti could do it, had just proved it could be done. And Mereruka, while he had not the exact eye for expert aim at such a distance, had in his wrestler's arms and shoulders the ability to send a shaft the right distance. Kheti, Mereruka—perhaps Kakaw and Intef—

"Oil—" He turned to Kakaw. "Search out if any lies in the house below. And rags—or we can tear our kilts if need be—and live coals—"

The prince needed no more explanation, since he had seen that arrow land true behind the fortification walls. He was squatting on the roof, selecting from the pile of arrows those best suited to the new purpose, choosing with a critical eye. "To stampede game," he observed, "it is sometimes necessary to fire the reed beds. Perhaps these reeds will also give up their lurkers. Do you as you can here. It shall be done the same elsewhere." He got to his feet and went to the edge of the roof, jumping to the next without any word of farewell, making his way so to a small Egyptian detachment who had taken to the heights two houses away—though Rahotep doubted whether any Egyptian archer, no matter how skilled, could hope to put arrows over that wall.

Kakaw came back driving before him a wrinkled house slave. The latter was burdened with lengths of linen to supply half the army with either bandages or fire tow, and he was close to gibbering with fright as the Nubian, his own hands occupied with an oil jar and a basin containing coals, barked at him to start tearing the material smaller.

They worked together at fashioning the arrows until Mereruka and Kheti each had a supply at his feet—though their concentration was not so great that they did not keep a wary eye on their surroundings. The portion of the city that had been fired was sending up smoke trails, and the distant din of battle was swollen now and gain by rumbles that might have signalized falling walls—perhaps destroyed deliberately to choke out flames with their enveloping rubble. Had a portion of the army been forced to fight the fire to escape?

It was not until later that Rahotep learned that the mob from the stews had finally been better organized under Icar, Huy, and Nebet and flogged back to fight against the fire. Their fear for their own forfeited lives turned them not only against the Hyksos they routed and harried, but against the flames as well.

Now removed from the inferno of fighting and fire, the Nubians made their arrows, to introduce the same foe they were fighting elsewhere into the enemy stronghold. Kheti sent the first arrow up and out. His effort was echoed from other points facing the fortress. The Nubian's shot went in; the majority of the others fell short. One set a chariot ablaze and the driver lost his head, leaping free, while his horse, terrorized, tried to flee from the danger behind and only dragged the fire with it through the ranks of a spear company forming up after having been routed from a street. The Egyptians pursuing them were scattered in turn, opening lines to let the flaming vehicle through.

With the care of men shooting at a mark, those on Rahotep's rooftop sent their arrows one by one over the walls. Rahotep's hopes sank as there was no sign of any answering conflagration. At the best, it had been a slender chance, but it might have made all the difference in the world for his own side. Even a fire that did not flush the Hyksos out of hiding but that drew men from the walls to fight it would have had a small advantage.

"Waaaah—" Kheti raised the shout, holding his bow at arm's length above his head and shaking it in triumph at the sky while his feet shuffled in the warrior's dance. "Dedun, smile upon your elephants! This army moves in victory! Aye, we fire the walls of the enemy!" He added to the song they had earlier voiced.

A pillar of smoke was rising. No, not a pillar, a veritable curtain! The captain could only guess that one or more of the fire arrows had made a lucky hit upon some depot of supplies, a guess that was very right he was later to discover. Bales of fodder brought for the horse lines and not yet properly stored were tinder to that flame. And the fire was fed in turn by supplies of oil as the heat cracked the earthen jars. The Hyksos' assembling of supplies added to their own defeat.

The archers marveled at the swift spread of that smoke,

its thickness testifying to the area that must be enveloped. And other fire arrows flashed through the now murky air—to stampede the horses in the open space or to land on the walls.

"It would seem that their god is annoyed with them," Kheti remarked. "Do their shaven heads beat on the floor and call upon him now?"

Trumpets sounded along the walls of the fort, and Rahotep noted, not for the first time, the advantage of that form of military summons. It could blare forth across the din in which his own and other officers' call sistrums were completely drowned. But beneath those brazen throated horns he could catch that other sound Kheti must have heard, the clang of a gong sounding from a temple enclosure.

"Amon-Re with us!" His fingers made the sacred sign, averting any power of evil now doubtless being summoned to aid loyal followers.

"The Great Ones favor those who raise strong arms in their own behalf," observed Kheti. "Let the Hyksos' shaven heads howl for their snake one to come. Doubtless he will—to eat them up! In the meantime, we tickle ribs here and there—to hasten that arrival."

Bis, who had expressed his dislike of the whole situation by sitting at the far end of the roof, his tail switching now and then in feline anger, padded toward Rahotep as if he sensed the coming of some crisis. His head up, the cub squalled in furious rage at the inner fortress. The Nubians watched, their surprise deepening to awe.

"The Gift of Horus sings his battle cry, brother!" Kheti gave the cub wide room. "I think that we must be close to the end of this."

Apparently the Hyksos crowded into the square below had that same feeling, and in their case it was colored by something close to desperation. Trumpets screamed defiance and attack, and their forces surged out, away from those gates behind which arose that growing cloud of smoke. But they had waited too long to make that last sally. From the roof tops, from the mouth of every street and lane, came a ready rain of arrows, sling-shot stones, well-flung spears. Those moments of confusion and doubt, the toll the archers had taken of the chariot horses, had given the Egyptians time to consolidate their stands and bring up reserves and ammunition.

As it had in those few frenzied minutes when they had fought to keep the gates open, so now did the battle come to be, for Rahotep, not a matter of strategy and pattern but a personal involvement in which he was only aware of what lay in an immediate circle about him. He knew—dimly—that Mereruka and Kheti continued to use the fire arrows. But the rest of his company drew bow at the embroilment below.

Three times the Hyksos charged outward from their stand about the fort walls, and three times that attack ebbed back, thinned and battered, leaving tide marks of dead and wounded behind. The smoke at their backs was shot now and again by leaping torches of flame, and the breath of that furnace, which must be expanding in there, licked out at the men on the walls—even to the roofs where their enemies stood.

Rahotep's own command was forced to retreat a roof's width, and Kheti stood watching the fortress with concentration. The captain spoke first.

"That is an oven. They will have to issue forth—"

"Or be baked as are loaves of bread. Just so, brother. But perhaps they will choose baking in an oven in preference to meeting those whom they have sent to the slave yokes or tried to feed to that dark god of theirs. By the Spotted Goat, Lord, this is a proper war! Did I not once say that here in the north we might find us a master by whom we could rise—"

"Neither this fight nor this day is yet ended—" Rahotep warned.

"But both are close to ending. Ha—they do not like the oven. The loaves now issue out—"

He was right. Those who had huddled against the gate of the inner fortress were being swept aside. The portals were opening, and their trumpets set up such a clamor that

Rahotep believed an attack in force was being signaled.

The breathing space had been of the shortest. Hyksos, with the grime of fire fighting tarnishing their shields and body armor, came out to challenge the Egyptians ringing them about. And to Rahotep the rest was wild confusion of which he could not make any connected tale to tell in the after years.

There were small vivid pictures to hold in memory—some of which troubled his sleep at night, most of which he did not care to dwell upon. Kheti was right, as he was so often. The unleashed fury of the Egyptians was a flail laid upon the Hyksos with crushing force. Men with old wrongs eating at them are not kind in the vengeance they take.

When he came wholly to himself again, the captain was leaning against a wall gagging at the stench of things burning and at something he had just seen in the temple where the Hyksos had worshiped. How Rahotep had come there, or why, he could not have answered coherently, but he regained a measure of sanity when he saw a familiar figure stride up to the altar.

Ahmose, with Nereb as his shield bearer, a party of limping, tattered guards at their back, gave one glance at the scene before him and barked orders. Those who had been busy there slunk away, as if they too had been suddenly awakened out of some nightmare, not able to understand why their hands were red or what they had been doing to those things whimpering away their lives at the feet of an unanswering god.

There was one body on the altar itself that had been left there by the priests of Set. Ahmose surveyed the poor, mutilated thing dispassionately, though Rahotep saw a small muscle along the prince's jaw jerk once.

"So, Sebni—when we found you gone in the dawn, we suspected you had fled to those you deemed the better men. An ill choice for you. Pharaoh has been at last fully avenged—but it would not have been to his liking to have the punishment this."

But the traitor on the stone of sacrifice was long past

answering to any judgment save that of Osiris behind the Gate of the Horizon. The prince spoke over his shoulder as if giving orders to some scribe of the records. "Let this matter be marked." He caught sight of Rahotep and beckoned the Scout captain forward.

"So you survive, kinsman. And your men?"

Half bewildered still, Rahotep looked around. If he had led his whittled command here, he was not aware of it. But it appeared that he had. At least that was Mereruka's stout form at the side wall, and the archer was supporting Kheti who came up limping, a sodden rag about his thigh, though he was still able to grin and raise his ax in salute to the prince. Kheti and Mereruka—there, too, were Ikui and Kakaw, smoke grimed so that their brown skins were charcoal black—four. They had lost Mahu and Hori on the city wall. Sahare—Intef—Anhor—Baku—no, there was no Baku, no Heti, to answer his unspoken roll call. Ten archers and two officers had jogged out of Kah-hi. Six archers and two officers, wearied and wounded, stood here in Neferusi. And Bis—for the leopard cub crouched at his feet licking a gash in his shoulder, but still alert for battle.

"You see us, Royal Son—" He spoke the formal words of reporting for duty with an effort.

Ahmose raised the ax he had won from the Hyksos commander at the storehouse fight in the salute he would return to a leader of a thousand. "I see you, Captain, I see you, archers. This day you have done well—for into Pharaoh's hands have you helped to deliver a city!"

Indeed Neferusi—or what was left of that battered city—was delivered into the hands of the royal army. And battle weary as they were, there was much to be done before any man could rest. Through the hours of the night, as he stumbled about posting guards, seeing to the fighting of fires, generally making himself useful, Rahotep was to come upon Egyptian warriors so sunk in fatigue that they were curled up among the dead in exhausted slumber.

He was relieved of duty sometime later, and then he was in a room where lamplight, limited as it was, picked out such luxury as he had seen only in the royal apartments of Thebes. Blinking at the surroundings stupidly, he let Intef steer him to a couch and strip off his grimed rags. He fell asleep while the archer was still rubbing him down with the oil, which relaxed muscles and eased all hurts.

"Lord!"

Rahotep climbed a slope out of a soft, dark pit, dimly aware that someone was shaking him gently. He opened his eyes foggily and then shut them against the brightness of sunlight.

"Lord!" The summons was imperative and that hand on his shoulder relentless. Reluctantly, very reluctantly, he turned over and looked up blearily at a brown face, which was upside down over him. Then he recognized Ikui.

"Lord—" For the third time the other called. "Pharaoh has sent for you. Rise! Anhor"—the archer turned to call to someone still beyond eye range—"the captain wakes— make ready for him."

Rahotep sat up. There were improvised pallets about the floor of the chamber. One one Kheti lay snoring, his bandaged leg bound to a spear shaft to keep it straight. On another sat Nesamun nursing his broken arm across his chest. It, too, had been expertly tended. And the other Nubians, lounging at ease or fast asleep, had the outward appearance of well-satisfied men.

When the captain stood in the washing place with Anhor ladling the water over him, he came fully awake and fired a volley of questions at his attendants, which they answered to the best of their ability.

Aye, Neferusi was completely under Egyptian control. The remaining Hyksos were now imprisoned in the slave warehouses.

"But there are few of them," Ikui supplied, "for, Lord, these men are mighty fighters, and it was to their mind to go and greet their god with the blood of many enemies hot on their hands. So only a few threw down their arms before us. Rather did they choose to fight to the death. And in the inner courts there is still a tower where their lords hold the door and will not come forth, so that

Pharaoh has ordered that there be no more useless killing of our men, but that a guard shall sit down there and watch until lack of food and water brings them out. And the people of this town who were slaves unto the Hyksos have come forth to 'kiss earth' before Pharaoh, rejoicing. Now they labor with us to hunt down those who hide from capture, for they hold a high hate against these horse lovers! And if the tales they tell all comers be true, then rightfully do they nurse that anger."

"Lord"—Anhor came back into the small bathing place, clean clothing across his arm—"they have not yet brought up our baggage from the camp. But the women of this house, who had no cause to love their master, have fashioned this for your wearing before the Pharaoh. And the hours grows late—"

The captain found his new kilt to be of the finest linen, and the belt that held it was set with garnets and gold in the form of a bull's head with gemmed eyes. There had been no striped cloth to fashion the proper headdress, so the one he wore was of a dull red. The silver bracer must serve in place of his noble's bracelets and gold-of-valor armlet for formal adornment. Somehow he had clung to his baton throughout the melee—they had found it on him when they rolled him into bed hours before.

As he returned to the improvised barracks room, Rahotep found the archers alert and smartened up, with Kheti criticizing and scolding from his pallet, in high dudgeon because he was forbidden by the healer priest to set foot to the floor without permission.

"You—Kakaw—" he was saying as the captain came in, "must serve as the Lord Rahotep's shield man in my place. Pull that belt tighter, goat with a sheep's wits! Let me see a line of warriors worthy to wear valor gold and not a gathering of boys not yet bearing their man scars! Intef—you stand like a shy maiden about to see her chosen lord at the paying of the marriage price. Put those shoulders back, stupid one, and that chin up. Aaah— doubtless you will march before the Son of Re as oxen ambling into the threshing floor. Lord"—he appealed to

Rahotep—"speak you to that shaven skull who says that I must be bound by one leg like a gander in the field and have me cut loose so that this rabble will not altogether shame Nubia before all eyes!"

Rahotep, with some difficulty, swallowed a smile as he inspected the line standing at attention under the tongue lashing of their invalided leader. As his own, their uniforms were improvised, but with method so that all wore kilts of the same red as his own headdress. Their headbands were proudly set with the feathers accorded a victorious warrior; even if those feathers had plainly been looted from different sources and did not match in kind or color. But each man's ax was polished and gleaming at his belt, his bow pointed skyward behind his shoulder, and he carried a filled quiver. The captain turned to Kheti.

"This guard does you credit, Leader of Ten. They will stand proud in the presence of the Son of Re, as is their right, since they have won their plumes! Even as you, Kheti, son of Ahati, the Strong Lion, son of Forge, the Warrior of Many Shields, the son of Khorfu of the Stone Ax"—he had lapsed into the Nubian tongue of the border army, and those names and titles rolled sonorously through the room—"even as you, Kheti, who shall henceforth be known as Kheti of the Great Bow!" He raised his baton flail in salute, and behind him the archers' fists went up in the homage of their own race.

Kheti's hands were balled in fists upon his knees as he stared back at the captain.

"It is well, brother?" asked Rahotep softly.

Kheti appeared to have some difficulty in answering, and when he did, it was in a small voice.

"It is very well! Stand for the pride of the Land of the Bow before the Son of Re, that he may know we breed *men* in the south!"

Kamose was holding court in what must have once been the justice hall of Neferusi. The walls were blackened with smoke, the roof had been burned away so that they stood under the open sky, and there was the smell of burning and death warring with the incense given off from the line of braziers someone had assembled between the rows of pillars that now supported nothing.

The Pharaoh still wore the blue helmet, thus signifying that he gave audience as the leader of the army and not as the Son of Re, so his officers did not "kiss earth," but saluted as they approached upon summons. Rahotep, at the head of his small force, waited for orders.

"The Lord Rahotep, Captain of Desert Scouts, together with his command."

He heard Prince Ahmose's call and marched forward, though by custom he did not raise his eyes to the man on the improvised throne.

"The Lord Rahotep, Commander of a Thousand!" That correction came in the usual hurried speech of the Pharaoh. He spoke as if he were harried by the passing of time, that there was so much to be done that he grudged each moment's delay.

Rahotep went down on his knees. "Life! Health! Prosperity! May the Son of Re live forever! I am one unworthy of his notice! Let the Son of Re know that this one is less than the dust on his sandals, unused to the leading of a Thousand—"

"The Thousand shall be of your own raising and training, Commander! Six bowmen stand behind you now. We would see a full regiment of their like. We are told that countrymen of theirs have been enslaved within this city, men who threw off their bonds and fought with our army. Do you seek them out and make of them a weapon for our hand. This duty do we lay upon you here and now. Giving also this 'gold of valor' that all men shall know how well you have served Egypt this day—"

Someone had come up beside the captain, and he realized that he was to have the great honor of being handed his award by the Royal Son. He dared to glance up as the Prince Ahmose slid from his own upper arm a broad gold band supporting a dagger after the new fashion. At the same time one of the officers at the foot of the throne tossed an ornament to each of the archers.

The silver bracer clicked against the dagger as Rahotep

advanced to put his lips to the Pharaoh's sandal strap. To be whirled from a simple Scout captain to Commander of a Thousand was a dizzying experience—even if it still lay before him to bring those thousand men into line before he had a regiment.

He came out of the hall to face the city eagerly. Had Huy, Icar, and Menon survived the battle? Perhaps they would aid him in seeking out the men he must have.

An officer saluted him—Methen!

"Lord—" the older man began, but Rahotep shook his head.

"Not 'lord,' Methan!" He dropped his hands on the other's shoulders in a kinsman's greeting. "Praise be to Re you, too, have seen the end of this fighting unmarked!" Then he stood back, planting his fists on his hips as he surveyed the city. "I do not know if I shall make a commander worthy of Pharoah's notice, but he has set me a task and I must be about it. I need archers for bows and bows for archers! Shall we go questing for them both?"

He went on into the murk of the city, Methen walking beside him, the Nubians at their parade tread trailing him as they had out of Kah-hi months earlier. Bis trotted soft-footed and unleashed to his right. Shadow Hawk he might be, he thought with some secret pride, but a shadow warrior he was not!

Issac Asimov

Phyllis A. Whitney

Beautifully written stories of love, intrigue and mystery put together as only Phyllis Whitney can.

☐ BLACK AMBER	23943-8	$1.95
☐ BLUE FIRE	24083-5	$1.95
☐ COLUMBELLA	22919-X	$1.75
☐ EVER AFTER	24128-9	$1.95
☐ THE GOLDEN UNICORN	23104-6	$1.95
☐ HUNTER'S GREEN	23523-8	$1.95
☐ LISTEN FOR THE WHISPERER	23156-9	$1.95
☐ LOST ISLAND	23886-5	$1.95
☐ THE MOONFLOWER	23626-9	$1.75
☐ THE QUICKSILVER POOL	23983-7	$1.95
☐ SEA JADE	23978-0	$1.95
☐ SEVEN TEARS FOR APOLLO	23428-2	$1.75
☐ SILVERHILL	24094-0	$1.95
☐ SKYE CAMERON	24100-9	$1.95
☐ SNOWFIRE	24246-3	$1.95
☐ SPINDRIFT	22746-4	$1.95
☐ THUNDER HEIGHTS	24143-2	$1.95
☐ THE TREMBLING HILLS	23539-4	$1.95
☐ THE TURQUOISE MASK	23470-3	$1.95
☐ WINDOW ON THE SQUARE	23627-7	$1.75
☐ THE WINTER PEOPLE	23681-1	$1.75

Buy them at your local bookstores or use this handy coupon for ordering:

FAWCETT BOOKS GROUP
P.O. Box C730, 524 Myrtle Ave., Pratt Station, Brooklyn, N.Y. 11205

Please send me the books I have checked above. Orders for less than 5 books must include 75¢ for the first book and 25¢ for each additional book to cover mailing and handling. I enclose $_____ in check or money order.

Name _____

Address _____

City _____ State/Zip _____

Please allow 4 to 5 weeks for delivery.

FREE
Fawcett Books Listing

There is Romance, Mystery, Suspense, and Adventure waiting for you inside the Fawcett Books Order Form. And it's yours to browse through and use to get all the books you've been wanting . . . but possibly couldn't find in your bookstore.

This easy-to-use order form is divided into categories and contains over 1500 titles by your favorite authors.

So don't delay—take advantage of this special opportunity to increase your reading pleasure.

Just send us your name and address and 35¢ (to help defray postage and handling costs).